PRAISE FOR PATIENCE GRIFFIN'S BOOKS

———————ကလ———————

"Griffin has quilted together a wonderful, heartwarming story that will convince you of the power of love."
-*New York Times* bestselling author Janet Chapman

"Griffin's lyrical and moving debut marks her as a most talented newcomer to the romance genre."
-*Publishers Weekly* starred review

"A fun hop to scenic Scotland for the price of a paperback."
-*Kirkus Reviews*

"Start this heartwarming, romance series!"
-Woman's World magazine

"With the backdrop of a beautiful town in Scotland, Griffin's story is charming and heartwarming. The characters are quirky and wonderful and easy to feel an instant attachment and affection for. Be forewarned: You're likely to shed happy tears."
-RT Reviews

"Ahhh, this series is my own little vacation to a land I love, even if the land in this series is a fictional Scottish fishing village where the men are braw, kilt-wearing, and have full respect for women."
-Gourmonde Girl

"The best thing about this series is the way that it touches you as a reader. The characters are deeply written, with flawed characteristics that make them seem familiar – like real people that you know and see every day."
-Ever After Book Reviews

"I dearly loved this romance, and I dearly love this series."
-Book Chill

"Patience Griffin gets love, loss, and laughter like no other writer of contemporary romance."
        -Grace Burrowes, New York Times bestselling author of the Lonely Lords series and the Windham series

"Patience Griffin, through her writing, draws the reader into life in small town Scotland. Her use of language and descriptive setting had me feel like I was part of the cast."
        -Open Book Society

"Griffin has a knack for creating characters that I find engaging from the opening page. I love the Kilts and Quilts series."
        -The Romance Dish

"I love Patience Griffin!! These Kilts and Quilts books are among my favorites EVER!!!"
        -Margie's Must Reads

"Ms. Griffin paints a vivid picture of Gandiegow with the ever meddling members of the Kilts and Quilts. Fans of LuAnn McLane and Fiona Lowe will enjoy The Accidental Scot."
        -Harlequin Junkie

(About *The Laird and I*) "I have read it. I'm reading it again. *laughing* It is like putting on your softest nightgown and slippers."
        -Becky, a reader

"This author has a way of choking me up in parts and that does not happen a lot to me. If you are looking for a great series to fall in love with then I suggest you give this one a try."
        -www.AHollandReads.com

"Patience Griffin seamlessly pieces compelling characters, a spectacular setting, and a poignant romance into a story as warm and beautiful as an heirloom quilt."
        -Diane Kelly, author of the Tara Holloway series

——————— ଚୈଷ ———————

BOOKS by PATIENCE GRIFFIN

Kilts and Quilts series:
Romantic Women's Fiction

#1   *To Scotland with Love*

#2   *Meet Me in Scotland*

#3   *Some Like It Scottish*

#4   *The Accidental Scot*

#5   *The Trouble with Scotland*

#6   *It Happened in Scotland*

#7   *The Laird and I*

#8   *Blame It on Scotland*

#9   *Kilt in Scotland*

#10 *Hitched in Scotland*

Sweet Home, Alaska series:
Romantic Women's Fiction

#1   *One Snowy Night*

#2   *Once Upon A Cabin*

#3   *Happily Ever Alaska*

The Wishing Quilt

From the author of To Scotland with Love

Hitched in Scotland

Patience Griffin

Copyright © 2025 by Patience Griffin
First Printing June 2025

All Rights Reserved

———————

This book and parts thereof may not be reproduced in any form, stored in a retrieval system, or transmitted in any form by any means—electronic, mechanical, photocopying, or otherwise without prior written permission of the author and copyright holder, except as provided by the United States of America copyright law. The only exception is for a reviewer who may quote short excerpts in a review.

Cover design by Kathleen Baldwin

ISBN 978-1-7320684-7-6

This is a work of fiction. Names, character, places, and incidents are either the product of the author's imagination or are used fictitiously, and any resemblance to actual person, living or dead, business establishments, events, or locale is entirely coincidental.

Published by Kilts & Quilts® Publishing

Dedication

For PhD, Kathleen Baldwin (my bestie!), and my readers.
I couldn't have written this without all your love and support.

Pronunciation Guide

Bethia (BEE-thee-a)
Buchanan (byoo-KAN-uhn)
Cait (KATE)
Deydie (DI-dee)
Moira (MOY-ra)

Definitions

Bairn—offspring; a child 14 years and under
Boot—the trunk or back of a vehicle
Céilidh (KAY-lee)—a party/dance
Coach—bus
Eegit—a foolish, insensitive person
Fash—(fash) worry or to be upset
Gandiegow—means squall (in Scottish)
Heilan' coos—Highland cows
Hob—the top part of a stove where food is cooked in pans.
Hogmanay—the Scottish celebration of the New Year
Ken—understanding
Kibosh ('kī͵bäSH)—though many people think it's Yiddish, kibosh's earliest use was probably in an Irish neighborhood in London in the early 1800s.
Reiver—someone who steals
Shite (shite)—expletive
Tatties—potatoes
Torch—flashlight

Chapter 1

CONOR MASTERSON ignored the people putting decorations up that were supposed to bring holiday cheer to the Edinburgh Airport terminal. He didn't want to think about Christmas on November 12th ... if ever. He was more of a bah humbug guy than the Father Christmas type. He didn't mind giving presents; it was all the merrymaking that went along with it that really got to him. Besides, he was in too much of a hurry to give it any thought. His mobile phone rang.

He didn't plan to answer but then he saw it was his Uncle Magnus calling. Conor had no choice but to pick up now. "Hullo." The word barely left his mouth before his uncle spoke over him.

"Lad, when will ye be home? We need ye back in Whussendale to tweak the loom. The ole girl ain't working properly and she needs yere attention."

Conor wasn't a lad. At twenty-nine, he'd been around the block a time or two. He'd even been married ... and divorced.

Most days, he felt like he'd aged into an old man, as if his best days were behind him. Though he had to admit that what few best days he'd had, hadn't been so good.

At least his second career was going better than his first; this time around he was a weaver. He'd learned a lot from his uncle by spending his school holidays and summers at the wool mill. But when he married, he'd become a butcher at his father-in-law's shop. Not because he loved it, but because it was expected. When the marriage ended, so had the job.

"What's going on with the loom, uncle?" Conor asked patiently, though the shuttle to take him home was scheduled to leave soon. "I'll be back to Whussendale before evening meal. I can take a look at it then."

"Good, good. Ye seem to be the only one these days who's able to make the ole girl purr."

Conor smiled into his cellphone. At times, Magnus acted like he was in a serious relationship with the equipment at the Victorian era wool mill—Whussendale Woollens. The wool mill was the main industry—nearly the only industry!—in the small village. "I'll see ye this evening. I'm anxious to tell ye about all I learned at the weavers' conference." Immediately, Conor regretted mentioning the progressive conference, which displayed all the new techniques in wool making and weaving. He wanted to take back the words.

"Och, lad, ye'll not be speaking again to me about making changes to our equipment in the weaving building, now will ye?" Magnus's tone was firm. In this one area, he and his uncle didn't see eye to eye.

Conor shook his head before answering. "The ancient equipment can't keep up with the orders. You know that. We're way behind." Not only behind on orders, but on updating the equipment to this century. "Improvements need to be made.

It's the reason the laird sent me to the wool conference in the first place." At least that was Conor's assumption. He needed to speak with the laird to make sure they were both on the same page before he discussed this further with his uncle.

"Whussendale Woollens needs no improvements," Magnus growled, a sound that made Conor think that his uncle had swallowed gravel and then was spitting it back at him. "She's been a working wool mill for more than two hundred years without changing. What makes ye think some conference people know what's best for her and what's best for us now?"

It was like arguing with a stone wall. Wasted breath is what it is. His uncle was the stubbornest man alive. Though Conor might be the next stubbornest. He tried again to talk sense into the old man. "At a panel of wool mill owners, who—"

Magnus cut him off, this time with a diversion. "Oh, aye … before I forget, Sophie wants to see ye immediately on yere return. She's got another lass for ye to consider. And Hugh said to tell ye that he also has a line on a new woman for ye to date." His uncle played dirty; there were no two ways about it.

Conor clenched his teeth. For some reason, unbeknownst to Conor, the laird and his wife had decided it was time for him to get back into the dating game. But his divorce had only been finalized a year ago! Right before the holidays. Conor wished he could pretend that Christmas didn't exist. He also wished women didn't exist, but Hugh and Sophie were constantly bombarding him with this woman and that. He wanted to tell those two to mind their own damned business. But no one spoke like that to the laird and his missus. "Please tell Sophie and Hugh that I'm tired of being fixed up with every female within a hundred-mile radius." Och, he shouldn't have said it so plainly. He should've filtered his reply, but Conor was known for not mincing words. "Never mind," he amended to his uncle.

"I'll speak with them when I get back." He glanced at his watch. "Listen, I gotta run. I don't want to be late for the shuttle. I'll see ye when I get home." He hung up.

Home. It was a funny word, and Conor was surprised how easily it had rolled off his tongue. Fourteen months ago, Conor couldn't claim to have a home at all. But Uncle Magnus had changed all that. Regardless of Conor's spats with Magnus over bringing Whussendale Woollens into the twenty-first century, Conor would forever be grateful to his uncle for coming to Glasgow after his marriage fell apart to gather him up and bring him back to the wool mill community he'd known as a kid. It was as if history was repeating itself. It was exactly what his uncle had done when Conor was a boy and his parents were separating. As then, as now, his uncle had breathed new life into Conor, and made him a weaver.

Though he loved his uncle, Conor considered Magnus a stubborn old fool—unmovable, especially when it came to change. Progress was a filthy word in Magnus's book, and in the book of the other old-timers at the wool mill. Staying the course was the name of the game for them. If it ain't broke, don't fix it, was another saying of the elders in Whussendale. Now orders were down, costs were up, and there were constant delays in deliveries. The loom—the old girl, as Magnus called her— couldn't help but break down often. She needed a lot of TLC. Well, Conor could be stubborn, too. He'd just have to make them listen. The wool mill would run so much better, more efficiently and more profitably, if only they would embrace the improvements he could bring to the small wool mill in the Highlands. They had to look beyond their archaic thinking and ancient ways of doing things. If only ...

Conor pocketed his phone, slung the strap of his duffel bag over his shoulder, and hurried through the terminal. He wished

Uncle Magnus hadn't called, when he had because Conor had been having a good day. But not so much now. He wasn't looking forward to continuing the argument when he got home. More and more, Conor was considering leaving Whussendale for one of the more progressive mills. But that notion sat like spoiled meat in the pit of his stomach, because he owed Magnus more than he could ever repay.

Conor checked his watch. He hated keeping the shuttle van waiting. He blindly turned the corner and—bam!—ran into a woman. And not just any woman. A verra attractive woman! Automatically, he reached out to keep her from toppling over. She looked to be about his age, late twenties, but he wasn't always the best person to guess someone's age, especially when it came to the opposite sex. Her beautiful brown eyes were wide with surprise, and the sprinkle of freckles across her nose complemented her golden complexion. He was mesmerized. While he knew he should probably let go of her, he couldn't; he wasn't done cataloguing her features. Her long, dark brown hair had a slight wave and was lying haphazardly across her shoulders. He stopped himself from repositioning her locks so he could take a closer look at her face. What he could glimpse, he liked. She was neatly dressed in a sophisticated gray pantsuit and wearing a tight pink sweater, which showed off her curvy assets nicely. He wondered what it might feel like to pull her close and hold her.

He shouldn't have let his mind go there. Actually, he'd done well these past fourteen months to not think on women at all, especially attractive women. He just hadn't been interested after what he'd been through. Right now, he purposefully pulled himself together and let go of her. He wasn't looking for a date. Far from it. Being dragged through the muck and mire by Morag, his ex-wife, and her extra-curriculars had given

Conor enough reason to never date again. With that thought, he stepped back. "Madam, are ye okay?"

"Um, fine. Yeah, sure." Her accent wasn't Scottish but American. Raspy and sultry, or maybe that was just his imagination playing tricks on him.

He retrieved her fallen spinner bag from the floor and thrust the handle at her. "Here."

She took it but didn't meet his eyes. "Thanks."

"Are ye sure ye're all right then?"

"Yes. Don't worry about it."

He didn't want to leave her if he'd caused any damage—either to her person or to her property. He was, after all, nearly a foot taller than her and five or six stones more in weight. "If ye're sure, I have a ride to catch."

"So do I. Go."

He nodded, then hurried toward the exit. He looked back to make sure she wasn't still standing there. But he saw she was hurrying in the same direction as him. But so were a lot of other people.

He scanned the vehicles outside and easily spotted the blue plaid van with Shuttle Up Scotland plastered on the side. He raised his hand to Paden, who was standing next to the vehicle. Conor hurried over, got in the back seat, and shut the door. "Thanks for waiting."

"No problem. I'm picking up one other passenger as well," Paden said as he slid behind the wheel.

A second later, the door opened beside Conor. He automatically scooted over to make room, but stopped suddenly when he saw it was her. Again!

The driver picked up the clipboard. "Ye must be Abby

Potter."

"Yes," she said.

"Both going to Whussendale, I see. Are you two together?" Paden asked.

"No," the woman—Abby—said.

Conor frowned. Paden should know better than to ask such an asinine question of him. The man knew his history. Hell, everyone in Whussendale had been privy to his tale of woe. Conor wanted to tap Paden on the shoulder and remind the man that only last week, while Conor was giving his vehicle a tune-up, Paden had ferreted out every last detail of what had happened with Morag. How she had irrevocably changed Conor's views toward women and marriage from favorable to unfavorable ... forever.

"Miss Potter, me name is Paden Smith. Buckle up and I'll get ye to Whussendale safely." The fifty-something man loved to charm the females. Probably hoping to enhance his tip.

"Nice to meet you, Paden," Abby said.

"Och, ye're from America then. What part?"

"St. Louis, Missouri. Born and raised in the Midwest," she said. Conor noticed she had a nice smile. She seemed like a kind and friendly lass, too—not stuck up—since she was willing to engage in conversation with Paden. He also couldn't help noticing she wore very little make-up. A natural beauty.

"Are ye here on holiday, then?" Paden asked, looking in the rearview mirror at Abby, then over at Conor. Conor thought it was none of Paden's business ... and that the man should concentrate on the road instead of the attractive American.

"No, not on holiday," Abby answered.

Conor was curious what not on holiday meant but respected her for not divulging her life's story to a couple of complete strangers.

Maybe at one time, he might've chatted up a lass like the one next to him, but he wasn't interested in getting tangled up with another woman and her drama again. Though the divorce was some time ago, he remembered like it was yesterday how beaten up he felt about his best mate running off with his wife. Especially since Steven had been the one to advise him to let Morag stew in her own unhappiness. Steven owned the pub across the street from his ex-father-in-law's butcher shop. When Conor was first married, right after his da died, he and Steven had become fast friends. Steven had been that close confidante that Conor needed during that tough time. So when things got rocky in his marriage, Conor listened when Steven insisted that Conor leave Morag to her own devices, telling him that Conor couldn't fix whatever was going on with her anyway. Conor wondered when and how Steven had become such a good actor, because later, Conor had felt like a fool when his wife and best friend had run off to Spain and married days after their divorce was final.

He had to admit that life with Morag had never been easy. She would probably say the same about him. They were only eighteen when they started up. Then his dad died suddenly two months later, and Morag suggested they get married. She laid out the reasons as if they were cards on the table, logical and in order: they could live in the house that she'd inherited from her grandmother; Conor could work in her father's butcher shop; he'd have her family to embrace him now that he was alone. At the time, Conor had been unmoored and Morag's plan felt like a life preserver. It would steady him, make him secure. But as it turned out, it was all a mirage. He should've let Morag cancel their wedding when her father told him she was having second thoughts. Instead of talking her into walking down the aisle,

Conor should've let her go.

Things certainly didn't get better after they tied the knot. By the time he figured out what he'd gotten himself into, it was too late. Morag was never happy, though he had tried his best. He believed that when ye get married, ye stay married. In the end, she hadn't felt the same way.

He shook his head, shoved the past to the back of his mind and returned his thoughts to the present. But it was hard for him to keep facing forward; he couldn't help but glance over, every wee bit, at the lass next to him. What was it about her that drew him in? He hoped Paden would drop her off first as Conor longed for some peace of mind. But then he remembered the fight that lay ahead of him in Whussendale. Damn it, he needed his work to mean something. It was the only purpose he had left in this world. He had failed at being a husband. He was determined not to fail at being a weaver, too. He knew he was right about the needed improvements.

From nowhere, an explanation about why this Abby was going to Whussendale crept into his mind. Maybe she was going to attend one of the quilt retreats that were held there sometimes. However, he didn't remember there being one scheduled. Or maybe she was related to someone in Whussendale, like when Ryn McBride came to Scotland to meet her cousin Maggie Armstrong. Paden was keeping up an annoying stream of chatter as he spoke about himself, his family, and his three dogs—Tic, Tac, and Toe. Conor probably would've paid more attention if the American lass was the one who was talking about herself. But he decided it would serve him better to keep his thoughts contained, instead of noticing every little expression on her face.

He shifted his gaze to the scenery out the window so he could mull over his own situation. When he first arrived at

Whussendale Woollens, he felt as if he'd been pulled from the North Sea—half-dead, and close to drowning. But things had changed since then. Now he wondered if he would be satisfied with Whussendale in the long run, especially if the business never grew or kept up with the times. He'd promised himself that he would never settle for the status quo again. That, if need be, he'd rock the boat, make waves to get the life that he wanted. But his uncles and the other village elders had become roadblocks. Conor would hate to go to another wool mill especially since Whussendale was part of his heritage. But wouldn't it be nice if the innovations he'd discovered while doing research in his time off, the same innovations spoken of at the conference, could become a reality at Whussendale Woollens? Wouldn't everyone be happy if the wool mill was more efficient? More environmentally friendly? Certainly, Laird Hugh McGillivray would think so. Conor resigned himself to the fact that he'd just have to go over Magnus's head and speak directly to the laird about the changes that would be better for them all. The workers, the environment, and the bottom line.

Once again, Conor glanced at the person in the seat beside him and wondered what was up with her. Why Whussendale? And why was he so transfixed by her? For reasons beyond his ken, he wanted to know more about her, but he especially wanted to know what she was doing here in rural Scotland.

Chapter 2

THE SCOTTISH VILLAGE of Whussendale was the size of a dime and wasn't close to what Abby Potter had expected, not in the least. The village consisted of a row of houses, a few businesses, and a church. The shuttle was through the town in the time it took to blink. Within a couple of minutes, they were pulling into the wool mill, which seemed to be the crowning glory of the area. The wool mill wasn't a single structure but a compound of stone and wood-sided buildings, with quaint stone cottages behind the mill and the whole compound in the shape of a crescent. Actually, it reminded her of a horseshoe. Whether the horseshoe was facing up or down—*good luck pouring into the village, or good luck pouring out*—she didn't know. What she did know was that the reality of what she'd done was starting to sink in.

But there was no time to dwell on it as the shuttle driver brought the van to a stop at the edge of the first building. "We're here," he said cheerfully as he parked the van, but his tone didn't stop the trepidation that rose up inside her. She glanced over at her shuttle-mate. The large Scot, who'd kept his gaze toward the window for most of the trip, was still frowning, the same frown he'd had from the time they'd left the airport in Edinburgh. He was the silent type. Restless, maybe. Good-looking, absolutely. But not the kind of man that she could be interested in again. She was still reeling from what she'd done to Aaron on their wedding day. Besides, she wasn't looking for a new man. Romance was the furthest thing from her mind. She'd come to Scotland for a change of scenery and to escape her problems at home—the disappointment she'd cause her friends and family, her frosty-as-ice mother, and her now dead job in St. Louis.

She glanced at the Scot again and didn't reproach herself too much for itemizing his features. Scowling Scot had a nice physique, a gorgeous full beard framing a beautiful face, and hard muscles accentuated by his tight black tee shirt. He wore a kilt made of mostly red, green and black plaid, which accentuated his athletic-looking legs. Mostly, though, she noticed his broad shoulders that seemed to be carrying the weight of the world.

They were kindred spirits in that regard, but she doubted they shared any other common ground. She liked to think of herself as a silver-lining type of person. Without a doubt, she was a *pleaser*, though that particular trait had brought her nothing but heartache.

Paden ran to the back of the van and started removing their bags. The chatty driver had kept her engaged the whole trip, almost to the point that she could ignore Mr. Scowling Scot, who never offered his name. When Paden had spoken to him, his only answer had been a grunt, which she assumed meant, "Leave me alone." Abby didn't know Scowling Scot's story, and right now, she had enough problems on her own plate without worrying over him. At least his kilt and Paden's acknowledgement said he belonged here, whereas she was certainly a fish out of water. *Big city girl lands in rural nightmare.* She'd given up everything that was familiar for a chance to make a go of it on her own—both professionally and personally.

But perhaps she'd been too impulsive. When she'd seen the ad:

WEDDING PLANNER NEEDED
Experienced only
Whussendale, Scotland

she didn't think twice. She immediately sent in her resume and application. Whussendale, according to the advertisement, was establishing itself as a premier wedding destination, and the job would be to make that happen in a timely manner. Hugh McGillivray responded by email, asking her predictable questions like "What is your experience managing destination weddings?" and "Are you willing to travel internationally to bridal shows to get the word out about Whussendale?" as well as strange questions like "Do you have any experience with sewing and quilting?" She answered yes to all, and before she knew it, the job was hers, without a single face-to-face interview, which she'd thought odd. She'd expected there would be at least a Zoom meeting with the owner, Mr. McGillivray. Perhaps her references had been enough or Mr. McGillivray had been hard-up for someone to pass the test of his unusual questions. Now, after seeing where she'd landed, she understood why he'd chosen her so quickly. The candidate pool must've been minute ... because the town was microscopic. The place also seemed deserted. And it was located in the middle of nowhere! Why hadn't she accessed Google Earth to get an idea of where Whussendale was and the size of it? She certainly would've thought twice about accepting the position. It might be impossible to have a successful wedding business without the infrastructure to support it.

She tightened the belt on her coat. There was a chill in the air here. St. Louis had been enjoying a bit of warm weather which can sometimes happen in late fall. As she stepped from the van a different kind of chill ran through her. *What have I gotten myself in to?* They were hours away from a major city, and surprisingly, the open spaces made her feel claustrophobic. Which was weird, considering where she'd grown up. She loved the bustle of the big city—something always going on, always something to do. Even the traffic was no big deal to her. St. Louis felt cozy; Whussendale didn't.

Paden set her bags at her feet and scurried into the front seat of the van. "Bye, now." He shut his door without waiting for a response and sped away.

She turned to Scowling Scot to ask if he could point her toward where she might find Mr. McGillivray, but she was too late. Her shuttle-mate was halfway across the compound with his duffel bag in hand, making her feel as insignificant as the dirt thrown up from the wheels of the shuttle as it left.

The pit of her stomach confirmed her every fear.

Why am I always so rash? Always rushing into decisions. Always going out on a limb without a safety net. "Now what am I to do?"

She scanned the area, but saw no one except the Scowling Scot as he disappeared into one of the far buildings. Gone was the sense of adventure and the hope of starting over. Doubt, dread, and regret were her only companions now. Those three emotions had been lurking since landing in Scotland, but now it felt as if they'd settled in for the long haul. She was also beginning to feel like a fool. Maybe she'd gotten it all wrong and the job had only been a hoax. Hugh McGillivray had promised to reimburse her airline and shuttle fare when she arrived. But maybe that too had been part of the ruse. A shaky breath escaped her. It wasn't the first time her impulsiveness had gotten her in trouble. She'd been catfished before by thinking she'd made a new friend online who invited her to a quilting gathering, only to find out it wasn't a girl, but a group of guys pledging for a fraternity. She'd felt stupid for showing up at their frat party with her sewing machine and a stack of fabric. Would she ever learn?

If Hugh McGillivray did exist, wouldn't he have been here to greet her? She'd texted him when the shuttle driver said they were nearly to Whussendale.

Disheartened, Abby exhaled. She'd given up an apartment she loved. She'd burned bridges with Belle Weddings, her employer of eleven years, the last four as Belle's lead wedding planner. All because of a man! Belle's son, Aaron. Now Abby felt deserted as a blast of frigid air flash-froze her bones. She had to do something. She couldn't stand here all day—it was getting dark. She frowned, pulled up her hood, grabbed the handles of her suitcases, and decided to start knocking on doors. Surely there was someone in this village who might know Hugh McGillivray, as small as the place was. If not, she could always ask someone to call her a shuttle to take her back to the airport. While she waited, maybe *that someone* might be kind enough to give her foolish self something hot to drink, which would not only warm her up but comfort her, too.

Resignedly, she started walking, and at the same time, she saw a man emerge from the building at the top of the crescent. He stopped, waved, and smiled, acting as if he knew her. Relief spread through her. He had to be Hugh McGillivray! The cold air didn't feel so ominous now, as he hurried in her direction.

"You must be our Ms. Potter," he exclaimed when he was a few yards away.

"Mr. McGillivray?" she asked, though they had to be close in age.

"Laird McGillivray," he corrected—not with any snobbery or

conceit, only stating a fact.

Laird? How had she not known that piece of information? Just another tidbit she would've found out if she'd only done a deep dive on Whussendale. But she'd been too busy tying up the loose ends of her life so she could leave St. Louis behind.

"Ye can all me Hugh," he said kindly. "I'm so sorry I wasn't waiting for you when the shuttle arrived. I was trapped on a phone call with a distributor." He offered her his hand and they shook. "My wife Sophie wanted to be here to greet you, too, but she's been called away to the kiltmaker's shop. Apparently, there is some emergency having to do with kilt buckles. Here, let me get those." Hugh pointed to the building straight ahead before taking over her cases. "Let's head inside the receiving building. There are people waiting to meet ye."

"People?" Abby was happy to meet him—ecstatic, actually— but she wasn't up to encountering a bunch of new faces, not right now. She was jetlagged, stressed out from worrying over the unknown, and just wanted to crawl into bed for a few hours to recharge.

"Don't worry, lass. You're going to love living in Whussendale." His proclamation didn't convince her. She trudged after him anyway.

He took her to the third building in the crescent and opened the door. She was shocked that the place was packed. A random selection of men and women registered in her mind—a woman knitting, men lined up at the back with their arms folded across their chests either in boredom or impatience, a woman holding a rope that was tied to a lamb with a blue bow around its neck, and a large contingent of women who were sorting quilt blocks at three tables grouped together.

"Quiet down, everyone," Hugh said above the noise of the room. "I want to introduce Ms. Potter." He motioned for her to step forward. "She has come from St. Louis to help us."

"To help us do what?" said an elderly lady.

"She's a wedding planner." But Hugh hadn't actually answered the woman's question. He turned to Abby. "That there is Gunna. She works in the carding machine area of the mill." He then focused his attention back on the group. "Some of you might have noticed that I've been working at changing the direction of Whussendale and I believe I've come up with a stellar plan. As you all know, cheaper fabrics from other countries have become available causing the demand for quality woollens to drop along with the population of the village. Whussendale is going to pivot from being a *wool only* community to one that showcases artisans, such as potters, glassworkers, painters—"

"Quilters!" said a woman holding up a stack of quilt blocks.

"Yes, Coira, quilters. I think the quilt retreats, like the ones in Gandiegow that you and the other ladies have been holding, have made a nice difference to our village. But we need more. I believe Whussendale can become quite a tourist attraction, if we *all* embrace the changes that will be coming."

Grumbles went up around the room, making Abby feel awkward and on the wrong side of things. She wondered if she should take a seat, or better yet, sneak out, while the laird spoke to his people. But there was no real way to slip past him without drawing attention to herself. She was stuck.

"I believe the best way to start that change is to offer up Whussendale as a destination wedding venue. Hence, the reason Ms. Potter is here," Hugh said, glancing over at her and smiling.

But Abby thought there was a major hole in his plan. She held her hand up. "Excuse me, Laird McGillivray?"

"Yes. Do you have a question?"

"I do." She'd have to tread lightly and not be direct, but she needed to point out that the village was too small for what he wanted to accomplish. "I'm concerned about where we might house the wedding party and the guests here in Whussendale. I didn't see any accommodations when we drove through town." There hadn't been one hotel along the highway and byways since they'd left Edinburgh!

"Aye, good point," Hugh said. "Until we get that portion squared away, the guests will stay in my home."

Some in the crowd were nodding their heads. But Abby didn't believe his house could be big enough, judging by the size of the cottages within the village and the cottages sitting behind the wool mill buildings.

Hugh smiled at her, chuckling. "My home is Kilheath Castle, which has many bedchambers, all fixed up and ready for guests. Plus, I have plans to build a hotel of sorts—a boutique hotel—on the property to host larger parties in the future. We're going to get Rachel from Gandiegow to help us lay it out as she has a lot of experience in running hotels."

A loud male harrumph echoed across the room as an ancient man struggled to his feet. His chair scraped the floor, which was as irritating as fingernails on a chalkboard. Abby was shocked to see the Scowling Scot from earlier sitting next to the old man. And the Scowling Scot no longer scowled but had become a smiling Scot instead—a much improved version of himself. Actually, quite appealing, if someone asked her. Why was he smiling now? He must've liked what the laird said.

"Yes, Magnus, what is it?"

"Laird, no disrespect, but ye sound like a numpty. Why would we want to bring in a bunch of outsiders to ruin our idyllic village?" The old man, known to her now as Magnus, dropped his rheumy eyes on her as if she were the snake brought to a wedding.

Scowling Scot was frowning again and shaking his head. Clearly, the old man and him were on opposite sides of the argument. "Sit down, uncle," he hissed as he reached for the old man's arm, but the old man pulled away from his grasp.

"I agree with Magnus," Gunna said as she waved a hand. "The old laird, *yere father*, never would've approved of such changes."

"Aye, me, too," said an old codger from the back wall. "Gunna there has the right of it." At that, grumbles erupted from others around the room.

A woman rapped her cane hard against the floor before standing and then made her way to the front. "I have something to say to ye all—" she spoke over her shoulder "—and to my nephew, too."

"What is it, Aunt Davinia?" Hugh said, clearly subdued.

Aunt Davinia spoke to the laird. "We have to be careful with change around here, nephew. Do you hear me?"

Hugh's frown increased as Abby's skepticism over Scotland grew. She never should've left the U.S. She should've faced the embarrassment over her canceled wedding instead of high tailing it to Scotland. And she never should've left Belle Weddings, though she hadn't had much choice. If she had made better decisions, she wouldn't be in the middle of a village fight … in the middle of Nowhere, Scotland!

"But Auntie—" Hugh said firmly.

"Where's your wife?" Aunt Davinia asked. "I'm sure she would agree that Whussendale is perfect as it is."

"She's with Willoughby in the kiltmaker's shop." Hugh turned to Abby. "Willoughby is the master kiltmaker and his brother Magnus, over there, is the master weaver. The villagers have dubbed them *the Wool Brothers*, an accurate title." He turned back to his aunt.

"We should table this discussion until everyone can be here," Aunt Davinia said decisively. "Don't you think?"

"No, we should put it up for a vote now, laird," Magnus said.

"Oh, aye," Gunna said, bobbing her head.

Hugh wasn't swayed. "No, it's not a good idea to put it up for a vote." Abby guessed the laird usually had the last word in making the decisions for the village. Hugh continued on. "But we will talk more about this at a later time." He pointed in the direction of Magnus. "Conor, can you show Ms. Potter to the cottage you readied for her?" Abby was puzzled, but at least she now knew Scowling Scot's name. But why him? There were other men in the room, ones who didn't look at her as if she'd caused their bad mood. Why couldn't Hugh have chosen a more agreeable man to show her to her cottage?

"Aye, I'll take her." Resolutely, Conor stood and leveled his frown in her direction as he made his way to the door. "Come."

"Ms. Potter, I'll see you tonight at the evening meal," Hugh said. "We have much to discuss."

"That sounds good." But she wasn't feeling confident that things would be better by then.

As she walked up to Conor, she considered asking him what she'd done to offend him but stopped herself ... for now. She needed to break the old habit of thinking *she* was the problem. This was something one of her early therapists had pointed out. She would often feel responsible for other peoples' attitudes and emotions. She'd perfected this trait in childhood because her mother was always in one foul mood or another. That was the last time Abby had seen the therapist because her mother decided the woman was a charlatan.

Abby looked at her surroundings, feeling like she could really use a *booster shot* of therapy, right about now. But she'd bet good money there wasn't a therapist within two hundred miles of Whussendale.

Conor lifted his hand. For a moment, she thought he might take her bag from her, but instead, he was only passing her and leading the way. By the speed at which he was hoofing it across the compound, she wondered if he wasn't trying to put distance between them. It would've been nice if he'd let her walk beside him, converse with her a little, maybe say something—*anything*—encouraging to put her at ease. But he didn't. With her luggage clunking behind her over the cobblestones, she hurried after him, grateful for knowing how to walk like a city girl.

He stopped at a stone cottage with a yellow door. "Here."

So apparently, he was still capable of speaking.

The yellow door was a happy accident. She loved yellow. Loved daisies. Surprisingly, a thought came into her head—if she stayed long enough in Whussendale—that she'd plant daisies outside her door. And buttercups. Maybe some yellow forsythia, too. If these flowers could even grow in Scotland. She made a mental note to do a Google search later.

Conor pulled out an old-fashioned key and unlocked the door. She was pleasantly surprised when he held it open for her. "Go on in. I need to show you a few things."

"Okay," she said tentatively and walked past him. He stepped in behind her and closed the door.

The cottage's walls had been painted white. She suspected that in summer, the room would look bright and cheery with the sun shining through the windows covered by the yellow-checked curtains. A few feet away, there was a small kitchenette, a loveseat and chair in front of the fireplace, and a small table with silk flowers in a vase in the middle. Artificial flowers made sense as winter had certainly arrived in the Highlands.

Conor gestured at the radiator against the wall. "We mostly use the hearth to warm the cottages but Sophie, the laird's wife, insisted I point out the radiator. Do keep in mind that heat is expensive in Scotland. If you want, I can make a fire for you right now. Hugh told me to keep the wood stack at the side of your cottage continuously replenished." He motioned to the two doors on the far wall. "One leads to your bathroom. The other is yere bedroom. You should feel lucky that you got one of the big cottages."

"*Big* cottage?" She glanced around. The place was a fraction of the size of her condo in St. Louis.

He shot her a look. "Aye, big. My place next door *doesna* have the separate bedroom as you have. Just a comfy twin bed at the far wall."

She scanned him from head to toe, unable to imagine his big frame fitting on a small bed. She put her hands up in defeat. "I'm not complaining. You have to remember that where I come from the houses are a bit bigger than they are here. It's just a shock, is all." She walked over and opened the first door, which happened to be the bedroom. There was a blue colorway quilt on top. Abby wondered where she could get the pattern.

"Now that ye're here, you'll have to adjust yere perspective and possibly yere expectations. I don't know if you noticed ... Whussendale isn't fond of change." Conor's scowl was back in full force. "Here. Let me show you the rest." He went to the fireplace and picked up a box from the mantel. "Matches. Newspaper is in the basket."

He was a man of few words, but she wasn't going to judge him. He was, after all, giving her the complete tour of her new, perhaps temporary home. She'd have to get used to the on/off switches that controlled the appliances in the kitchenette area, the clothes washer under the kitchen counter, and how to control the hot water temperature from a flattish tank that hung above the kitchen counter as if it were one of the three small kitchen cabinets on the wall.

"That should give you a good start," he said as if concluding his obligation.

She thought he might offer his phone number, in case she

needed anything else, but he didn't. "Thanks for your help." But as she said it, an uncontrollable yawn overtook her, making her eyes water. "Sorry about that."

"You should rest before the big dinner tonight with the laird and his wife."

"Excellent idea." She yawned again. "I guess I'll see you around?"

"Aye. I work at the wool mill, journeyman to the master weaver, my Uncle Magnus. He spoke up at your welcoming."

Some welcome! she thought wryly.

Conor opened the door, ducked his head so he wouldn't hit the header, and left without saying goodbye.

But two minutes later, Abby had questions. She ran to the door and looked outside but Conor was nowhere in sight. Hugh said she was having dinner tonight at the castle, but she had no idea where the castle was located. She thought about booting up her laptop to send Hugh a note to ask for details, but suddenly, she was too exhausted to pull out her computer. She was more tired than she'd ever been in her life. It felt as if she'd hit a brick wall and couldn't push through, not even for the littlest of things. The bed in the bedroom seemed to be calling to her. It couldn't hurt to take a quick cat nap. Maybe after she rested, she'd be able to face whatever Scotland threw at her next. She went into the bedroom, slipped off her shoes, pulled back the quilt, and crawled into bed. A moment later, she was sound asleep.

Chapter 3

WHEN HUGH WALKED OUT of the weaver's building, Aunt Davinia was waiting for him outside.

"I need to have a word with you, nephew." She stood ramrod straight and pointed to where Conor was leading the American lass into her cottage. "From where I stand, that lass would make a great match for Conor. Don't ye think?" She didn't give Hugh a chance to answer. "It's a brilliant idea to make those two into a couple. You and I both know that I have the gift when it comes to knowing who is right for whom."

Hugh had to hand it to her. His aunt had matched him to Sophie, the love of his life.

Aunt Davinia nodded, as if she'd been listening to his thoughts. "I did a fine job of finding ye a wife. Sophie is the sweetest lass from Gandiegow and has been quite the asset for Whussendale." She nodded again as if adding an exclamation point to her statement. "Everyone knows that Conor needs a woman to calm him."

"Aye." He and Sophie were discussing it just last night.

"That lad is always going against the grain, which makes for trouble with Magnus and the wool mill, and any others within earshot of them going at it. *Aye*, Abby Potter will be the solution for Conor."

"Perhaps." He'd found it was best not to play too much into her schemes.

She looped her arm in his and led him away from the others filing out of the building. "There's something else I need to tell ye. I support the changes you plan to make."

"But earlier, you said—"

Davinia cut him off. "Och, ye know how it is. The older folks in town need to think that I'm on their side so I can help you accomplish the changes you want to make. You must realize that it will have to be done delicately. Ye should've started laying the seeds long ago."

But he had been laying seeds quietly, so as not to upset the balance of the village.

Aunt Davinia glanced over at him. "But that's water under the waterwheel now. If I'm not being clear enough, here is what you should do. Do not make a bunch of changes all at once. I beg you to take it slowly. For your own sake and the sake of the village."

"I hear what ye are saying." Sometimes it was just easier to placate his aunt.

Davinia patted his arm. "Good lad. But I do have concerns of my own. I'm afraid the village will not welcome the newcomers, like Ms. Potter. There wasn't one smile in the whole place for her today. Perhaps ye should have *welcoming classes* for those that need it."

Hugh nodded. "That's actually a good idea."

"I believe Sophie might be the perfect one to lead such a

class," Davinia said. "Yere lass won over Willoughby and that in itself is quite a feat, don't ye think?"

Hugh chuckled. "I agree. Sophie has a magical quality about her. She had my heart from the get-go." He held the door open to the building that housed his office.

"Then that's settled then," Davinia said. "But now let's talk about Abby and what we can do for her."

Conor walked beside Magnus down the long driveway to the castle without speaking to his uncle because his irritation with the old weaver hadn't subsided. When Conor tried to speak with him again about improvements to the mill, Magnus had shut him down. Conor was beginning to think this was an argument that he wasn't going to win, and it was the first time he'd been truly upset with his uncle since he'd come back to Whussendale. Aye, they argued most days, but it was never over something this important.

A few minutes later, they reached Kilheath Castle. Magnus seemed to struggle a bit with the steps leading up to the door, which made Conor realize, once again, that his uncle wasn't nearly as spry as he had been when Conor was a lad. He took the lead, knocked, and waited. From the other side of the door, it sounded as if the Wallace and the Bruce—Hugh's two deerhounds—had reached the door first; the sounds of scratching and whining and a few barks of welcome reverberated through the oak door.

A moment later, Sophie opened the door with the tall dogs pushing past her to get to Conor. Everyone loved the laird's dogs, but Conor had a special place for them in his heart, caring for them more than most. When he first returned to

Whussendale, they had distracted him from his misery over his divorce. The dogs butted their heads against Conor, vying for his attention, nearly knocking him over. Surprisingly, though, the dogs left Magnus alone. They must've sensed that his uncle was too elderly and a bit frail to withstand the onslaught of two huge, rambunctious beasts. Instead of ushering the humans in immediately, Sophie looked beyond Conor's shoulder. "Is Abby not with ye? I assumed you would fetch her and bring her to the castle." Sophie reached for her coat and slipped it on. "I'll go get her."

"Nay, I'll go." Conor should've thought about bringing Abby. She was right next door to him, for heaven's sake. Sophie had on her apron, which meant she'd been helping Mrs. McNabb in the kitchen. Of course he should be the one to fetch the American lass, but he wasn't happy about it. Abby felt like a disturbance he didn't want or need right now.

"Thank you, Conor. I need to be in the kitchen to mash the tatties and to check on the meat pies."

Conor stepped to the side, holding the door for his uncle to pass through.

"I'm not feeble," Magnus groused. "I can hold the door open for meself, ye know."

"I know," Conor said, feeling a bit ashamed for being so upset with his uncle. "I'll be back shortly."

Magnus grunted and went inside.

Conor made an about-face and hurried back down the long driveway. He told himself that he would be more tolerant of his uncle. But ... what if the wool mill didn't make the changes to upgrade their processes? Surely others could see that the wool mill would be left behind. Eventually the mill would have to shut down. He shuddered just thinking about such a bleak scenario. He only hoped the laird would set Magnus straight at dinner, help the old man to see reason so their feud could end.

Conor expected to see Abby walking toward the castle, but he didn't catch sight of her all the way back to her cottage door. When he knocked, no one answered, which was strange. He knocked again, and when she still didn't answer, he twisted the knob and glanced inside. "Hullo? Abby, are ye here, lass?" No answer and no one was bustling about the living area. Where could she be? He stepped in and headed to the bedroom. And it was there that he found her sleeping as if in a fairytale. He wasn't sure what to do. The old story, if he was remembering it correctly, would have him kissing her awake. But that was ridiculous. Instead, he moved forward, bent over, and gently shook her shoulder. "Abby, time to wake up."

She rolled away from him, still asleep.

He tried again. "Time to wake up, luv. The laird is waiting dinner on ye." He sat on the bed and brushed her hair off her face, unable to stop himself from noticing how soft her hair and skin were. "Lass? Do I need to rummage through the bathroom cabinet for some smelling salts?"

She rolled into him this time, wrapping her arm around his body. Once he was over the shock of it, he couldn't stop the automatic pleasure of feeling her clinging to him.

"Wake up now," he said hoarsely as if his vocal cords had been replaced with sandpaper.

Her eyes popped open and she looked at him in shock. She scooted away as if she were a sand crab propelling itself backward. "What are you doing in my room?" she squawked.

He went to his feet and took a couple steps back. "Sophie, the laird's wife, asked me to fetch ye for dinner."

"You should've knocked first."

He grinned, cocked an eyebrow at her for a long moment, and then rubbed his knuckles. "Me hands are bruised from pounding so hard and so long on yere door, lass. I decided I better come in and check on ye, lest Sophie and the laird string me up for not doing my due diligence. When I saw ye lying there"—he pointed at the bed—"I wasn't sure if ye were still breathing." He chuckled then. "But yere loud snoring let me know ye were still alive."

"I do not snore," she said defensively.

"Sure. Sure. It must have been the wind outside making all that racket." He raked his eyes over her. "Do ye need to freshen up before we go?"

"Give me a minute, please. Shut the door behind you."

He left, closed the door as directed, and went to stand by the fireplace. He didn't know why he'd been flirting with her, something he hadn't done in ages. He needed to remember that his worries were too numerous to add a female to the list. But a little diversion might be what he needed to calm his ire over Uncle Magnus's stubbornness.

The bedroom door opened and a more put together Abby appeared, wearing a dress, heels, and her long locks perfectly tamed. He couldn't help but admire what he saw.

"You do dress for dinner here, right? At least they do on *Monarch of the Glen* and other TV shows and movies set in Scotland. Plus, I saw that you changed into a dress shirt with your kilt."

He nodded. "Aye, the laird likes us to observe the old ways." But then Conor frowned, thinking he might be wrong about Hugh and his progressiveness for the wool mill. What if he wasn't on Conor's side about bringing the wool mill into the twenty-first century? Hugh seemed proud that Whussendale was one of the few continuously working Victorian wool mills in the world.

"I'm ready to go if you are," Abby said, which brought Conor out of his contemplation.

"Aye, ready." He went to the door and held it open for her.

"After you."

As Abby passed by him, he caught a whiff of perfume—something familiar. Flowery. Had Morag worn that same scent? He shook it off and followed her.

They walked along in silence for a few moments. Conor had the feeling that something was bothering the American lass; she was chewing her lip. He didn't know her well enough to ask what was worrying her. Besides, he had his own problems to mull over. But he had only gone two steps more when his curiosity got the best of him. "What's wrong, lass?"

She glanced at him but immediately returned her gaze straight ahead.

"Nothing's wrong."

"You should tell that to your expression."

She glared at him for a moment. "Since you're feeling so chummy now, tell me why you were frowning all the way from Edinburgh to Whussendale."

"No reason. I was fine," he lied.

"You certainly didn't look fine." She looked away and whispered, "Except you do."

He wasn't sure what she meant. Was she trying to say that she thought he looked *fine*? If that was the case, he thought about giving himself a celebratory high-five. Because, well, he thought she looked *fine*, too.

She glanced over at him again. "I might have been rash," she confessed. "I assumed I would be welcomed by all, especially since Whussendale is the size of a peanut and could use the economic opportunity. But it seemed earlier that the crowd doesn't want a wedding planner in your corner of Scotland. Or do they just not like me personally?"

"Being a wedding planner is not the problem." He paused for effect. "It's what you represent."

"And what's that?" she asked.

"Progress. Change. The *status quo not remaining the status quo.*" The same issue that Conor was having with Whussendale, too. "The laird says he has a vision and he'll get his way in the end, I suspect." At least Conor hoped so. "Folks here are loyal to the laird, regardless of what they think of change." Conor might have projected more bravado on the subject than what was due. Hugh knew better than to rock the boat, while Conor was known to ruffle more than a few feathers.

The castle came into view then. "Kilheath Castle," he announced.

Abby stopped and gaped. "Wow! It's so picturesque. The turrets, the ivy growing up the walls … everything!"

"Aye. Let's keep going." As he walked, he glanced over several times to watch her taking in the castle and the loch beside it. It was strange that he was delighting in her delight. It wasn't something he was known to do.

When they got to the steps, Conor reached out to put a hand to the small of her back but stopped himself. She was more than capable of making it up the stairs without his guidance. At the top of the stairs, he raised his hand to knock, but the door opened before he could. Hugh was on the other side, holding the collars of the Wallace and the Bruce, barely keeping them from rushing Abby. The dogs whined and wagged their tails profusely, unable to contain their enthusiasm.

"Come on in, Abby. Don't mind the Wallace and the Bruce," Hugh said. "They just want to make friends. We've been holding dinner for ye both."

Abby stepped in. "Sorry we're late." She held out her hand for the dogs to sniff. "Jetlag must've gotten the best of me." She glanced up at Hugh. "Sweet dogs."

Sophie reappeared. "Are ye hungry?"

"Oh, yes. It smells delicious," Abby said.

Hugh pointed the way. "Mrs. McNabb is the best cook in all the Highlands. And Sophie is no slouch when it comes to the kitchen. I'm a lucky man."

Abby followed the laird but she looked back at Conor as if she were making sure that he was coming, too.

"Did Conor get you settled okay?" Hugh asked congenially.

She glanced one more time at Conor. She looked a little off-balance and didn't answer right away so he spoke for her. "I showed her around her cottage." He'd done his duty to his laird.

"What I mean, is there anything more ye need for your cottage?" Hugh offered. "Just name it and Sophie and I will take care of it."

"Oh, everything's fine. Perfect, in fact." But she didn't look like everything was perfect. She seemed uncomfortable, making Conor wonder what he could do to calm her.

They stepped into the dining room with the long table. The room seemed too big for such a small dinner party. However, only the far end of the table had been set, making things a bit cozier.

"Go sit by yere uncle," Hugh said. "Abby, sit across from Conor. We've come up with a plan for ye."

Conor felt relieved. "So ye've decided to make the improvements that I told Magnus about?"

Magnus harrumphed unpleasantly.

Hugh shook his head. "Nay, the plan is for both you and Abby, not the improvements. We'll talk about those at a later date. We want to talk to ye about the wedding shawls. You and Ms. Potter will work together to come up with something unique, special for the brides and grooms who have their weddings here in Whussendale."

"What?" both Conor and Abby said simultaneously. Conor

noticed his uncle was smiling.

"It seems only fitting since we're a Sheep-to-Shawl operation. Abby, I expect you'll want to get started putting together a plan to speak with brides and grooms at the bridal shows in both the U.S. and the U.K. The first one will be in Inverness and it's coming up fast." He turned to Conor. "Ye'll be the one to show Abby around, give her an in-depth tour of our facilities from the sheep in the fields to the dye shack to our wool store."

"But, laird, what about my duties as weaver?" Conor said in frustration. "I'd really like to talk to you about what I learned while I was gone. There are loads of things we can do to improve our processes."

"I appreciate that, Conor. But later. Right now, helping Ms. Potter set up the wedding venue is our number one priority." Hugh pointed to the table. "Everyone else get seated. Sophie will be in directly with the fresh bread she's been baking. Also, Mrs. McNabb made meat pies and haggis stovies for tonight's feast, my favorite."

Conor looked at Abby—maybe to blame her—but she looked as shocked as he felt.

Sophie came in carrying two bread baskets and set one in front of Hugh and one in front of Abby. Conor should've felt honored to be eating at the laird's table, but he was too put out to feel anything beyond annoyed.

Hugh put his hands out. "Let's say grace."

Conor automatically took his uncle's hand. He had to reach across the table to take Abby's. He didn't look at her but bowed his head.

Hugh thanked the Almighty for the food, the shelter, and the wool mill before ending the prayer with an *Amen.*

Conor looked up, but Abby was looking at Hugh at the head of the table.

"Laird McGillivray?" Abby said. "I have a few questions."

"Call me Hugh," he said.

"Will do." She nodded. "My first question is why did you ask me in my emails if I could sew?"

Sophie laughed and looked at her husband. "Hugh should've explained." She turned to Abby. "Whussendale has recently started hosting quilting retreats. We were just curious if ye would be joining us while we sewed. It's a community activity."

Abby smiled. "Now it makes sense."

"Aye. Sorry about that, Ms. Potter," Hugh said.

"Please call me Abby."

"Aye. Abby." Hugh continued. "Also, Sophie and I were brainstorming about how to make Whussendale's wedding venue stand out."

Sophie took over for her husband. "It was my idea to ask if our wedding planner could sew and quilt. Gandiegow, our sister city, started the quilt retreats and we've been learning from them and having our own. Our other idea is to gift a wedding quilt to each couple who gets married here."

Magnus jumped into the conversation. "But didn't the laird just say that we're to give the couples a special wedding shawl?"

"Yes, isn't that overkill?" Abby chimed in.

Conor wondered the same thing, but he'd have to point out to Abby later, when they were alone, that she should be careful about questioning the laird's decisions outright. Though, Conor did admire her moxie. His uncle, on the other hand, seemed to get away with more breaches in protocol due to his age, as other elders in the village did, too.

Abby smiled broadly. "What if the wedding shawl was part of the basic wedding package here in Whussendale, and if the couple wants a wedding quilt—let's say for guests to sign during the reception we could provide that as an add-on. A little something extra to boost revenue."

"Brilliant," Hugh said, turning to his wife. "What do you think?"

"I agree," Sophie said. "Oh, I almost forgot." She turned to Abby. "I asked Oliver Middleton from Gandiegow to work on a website for you. He'll be here in a couple of days to show you what he has so far. In the meantime, I need you to come up with the official name of the venture."

Abby dug around in her bag. "I brought a list for you to look at." She handed it to Hugh, who handed it to his wife. "I certainly don't want to make that decision on my own. The name will need to fit Whussendale's brand."

"I'm fond of Whussendale Weddings," Hugh said.

Abby leaned her head to the side as if she wasn't completely on board. "Whussendale Weddings is catchy, but the problem is that it doesn't tell the whole story. You mentioned in your email that you wanted to grab some of the international market. How about something more descriptive, like Tying the Knot in Scotland." But then she frowned. "Though, now that I'm saying it out loud, I believe it's a bit too long."

Hugh and Sophie nodded as if they agreed.

"Let's see," Abby said. "We need to capitalize on the popularity of Scotland. Maybe something like *Weddings in Scotland*. Not that exactly, but something more captivating. We should talk about who your target audience is first."

Sophie glanced over at Hugh. "We don't want Whussendale to only host luxurious weddings, but informal weddings here as well, so anyone can afford to get married here." She scanned Abby's list. "Oh, this one is perfect! Hugh, what do you think of 'Hitched in Scotland'?"

"I like it." He turned to Abby. "It's descriptive. It's catchy. Just like you suggested. With that name, we could attract all kinds of couples. What do you say, Abby?"

"I guess it's the winner. But do you worry that Hitched in Scotland sounds less professional, too casual?"

Conor cleared his throat. "Maybe having a less starchy name would actually fit nicely and at the same time, set Whussendale apart from all the other destination weddings here in Scotland."

Magnus put his fork down, hard. "Tourists will ruin this place."

"I hear what ye're saying, but we need to boost our local economy if Whussendale is going to be viable in the long term," Hugh said. "Surely, ye've noticed our young people leaving for jobs in the big city?"

"Aye," Magnus grumbled.

"It's settled then. Hitched in Scotland. It's descriptive and the name will help boost the SEO." He looked over at Sophie.

"Hitched in Scotland might really speak to the younger crowd and also the older-young-at-heart couples as well," Sophie said.

Magnus picked up his fork, holding it over his plate. "I reckon using the word *hitched* let's people know that this wedding destination thing isn't acting like it's too big for its britches."

Everyone at the table laughed.

Hugh smiled. "Thanks for getting on board, Magnus."

"Hitched in Scotland it is." He pivoted the conversation. "For the website, we're going to defer to your expertise. You'll have final say, Abby."

"I'm anxious to get started." When she glanced over at Conor, he noticed that her cheeks had turned pink.

He better make it clear to the lass from the get-go that he wasn't going to start something up with her. A new relationship was a bad idea. It didn't matter who it was. Aye, he was attracted to her; who wouldn't be? But Morag had crushed any good feelings he had toward ever getting seriously involved with a woman again. He'd married young—too young. Barely out of short pants. He knew now what a mistake it had been. He'd been rash. Emotional. *Eighteen!* And perhaps immature—though, he hated to admit it. He'd let Morag call all the shots. Conor should've been his own man and not gone along with it. If he'd taken the time and truly looked at who he was, he would've known that Morag wasn't right for him. Or at least, he would've seen sooner that Morag was never content with him, no matter how hard he tried to make a go of it.

"There's one final thing," Sophie said, bringing Conor back to the here and now. "Conor, ye'll be going with Abby to vend at the Bridal Shows, both here and abroad. Hugh and I've discussed it at length and think it's best."

"What? Why?" Conor said louder than he should've, especially since he was questioning the laird's wife. Abby looked shocked by Sophie's declaration, too.

Hugh cleared his throat as a way of reprimanding and then spoke. "We've done a lot of research on how to get the word out about weddings here in Whussendale. The number one thing is to get in front of people. The bridal shows are a great way to do that. We've booked booths and lodgings for you and Abby. One in Inverness and one in Edinburgh to start. In the future, we'll send you two to the States as the U.S. is a much larger market to tap into for Whussendale Weddings—no, Hitched in Scotland."

"But why me?" Conor did his best to filter his words and hide his feelings, working hard to keep his face neutral. It would do him no good—or the weaver's shop, for that matter—if he lost his temper with the laird and got ousted from Whussendale.

"Actually, it was Sophie's idea."

Sophie picked it up from there. "I say give the people what

they want. The vast majority of attendees at the bridal shows are women. I believe we'll get double the bookings if the brides and their mothers have the chance to speak with and take a gander at a brawny man wearing a McGillivray kilt. Abby, what do you say?"

Magnus let out a little chuckle but didn't expound more on his feelings.

"Well, I-I ..." Abby was tongue-tied and her cheeks were turning even a brighter pink now.

"It's an excellent idea," Hugh interjected. "You'll both go. The Inverness bridal show is the weekend before St. Andrews Day."

"But what about the weaver's shop?" Conor asked. "Who's going to take my place while I'm gone?"

"Who do you think?" Magnus harrumphed. "I'll have things in hand. I've been working at the weaver's shop for fifty-seven years. I'm not too feeble to keep on running it, am I?" His uncle lifted his hairy eyebrows at Conor.

"Of course not," Hugh and Conor said together. His uncle was old but he was still in control of his faculties.

Sophie lifted the platter of meat pies. "Anyone want more pie?"

Conor glanced at Abby and was surprised to see her staring back at him. Immediately, she averted her eyes.

She straightened her shoulders. "Laird McGillivray, is it possible to giveaway one of the wedding shawls you were talking about at the bridal show? It could be a special drawing for the attendees, and it would be a way for us to collect their information for the newsletter I plan on sending out on a regular basis."

"That's a brilliant idea. Sophie and I couldn't come up with a good giveaway, but ye've nailed it." Hugh turned to Conor. "Do you think there's time to make a wedding shawl to take to Inverness?"

"Nay," Magnus said, while sliding another meat pie onto his plate, "but we have several in stock."

Conor frowned. Roping him into the Hitched in Scotland venture was an asinine idea. He considered leaving the table in a huff. He could've used the excuse that he needed to get weaving on the wedding shawl, if only Magnus hadn't put in his two pence worth about having shawls in stock!

Conor hated this whole idea. Not the weaving part, but being the prime beef for women to ogle at the bridal shows. On top of that, he just couldn't imagine spending so much time with Abby. He was a strong man, but he was concerned that the American lass would notice his weakness for her.

Apparently, he must've made some kind of movement because Hugh laughed good-naturedly. "Conor, relax. Enjoy yere dinner. Ye can worry about the wedding venture in the morn."

But Hugh had pretty much ruined Conor's appetite. In the next moment, though, a rebellious idea took hold of him. "Laird, can I make a deal with ye? I'll willingly go along with this bridal show idea if we can discuss improvements to the wool mill."

Magnus choked on his meat pie and Conor pounded his back. When Magnus quieted, Conor glanced over at Hugh, who was giving him a deliberating stare. Aye, Conor might have crossed a line, but everyone knew the laird was a fair man.

"I'm making no promises now as to what improvements might be done. But I do promise that I will hear ye out. But at a later time."

Abby yawned and everyone shifted their attention to her.

Sophie stood. "We've talked enough business tonight, don't

ye think?"

Hugh nodded in agreement.

But Conor didn't think so. He opened his mouth to try again, but Sophie cut him off.

"Let's finish up so our American guest—"

"Not a guest," Hugh said. "Abby is one of us now. This is her home."

"Right," Sophie agreed. "Conor, when we're done here, ye'll walk Abby back to her cottage."

Chapter 4

ABBY SAID GOODBYE to Conor's uncle, the laird, his wife, and then left the dining room. She could feel Conor's displeasure. Not because he was so near—he was right behind her—but because she'd felt his disapproval of her from nearly the start. Maybe not when they'd bumped into each other at the airport, but certainly when she took the seat beside him in the shuttle. As soon as the heavy front door of the castle closed behind them, she turned to Conor. "Now that we're alone, could you stop glaring at me?"

"What?" He sounded both shocked and incensed. Not too many people could've pulled that off.

Abby continued her mini-tirade. "It's not my fault that Laird McGillivray has assigned you to help me with the wedding venture."

"You certainly didn't speak up and tell him ye didn't need any help. I'm a weaver. Not some wedding planner's assistant."

"I know that," she volleyed back. "The reason I didn't say

anything is because I don't know them. The way I see it is that it falls on you to talk to Hugh and Sophie."

Conor shook his head. "It'll do no good. Once the laird has an idea in his head, it's hard to get him to change course."

She put her hands on her hips. "Then do me a favor." She didn't wait for him to give his permission. "Lay off with the glowering. Especially at me."

He nodded. "Fair enough. It's not your fault."

She was surprised he'd acquiesced. She stared at him a second longer before spinning back around and flouncing off down the long driveway. Moments later, she slowed her pace, realizing she couldn't quite remember how to get back to the cottage. Should she turn left or right when she got to the end of the lane? She had been half-asleep when she'd walked with Conor to the castle. Or had she just been distracted by having the handsome Scot beside her? She was in a sad state if she couldn't locate her cottage in this small community. It went beyond being a fish out of water. Besides not knowing the way of things around here, she was beating herself up for rushing into the agreement to come to Whussendale. And it really bothered her that she needed Conor for the littlest thing … like finding her way home.

She stopped suddenly and let him come up beside her.

"What's wrong now?" he asked, this time with a concerned look on his face.

She wouldn't own up to being directionally challenged. But she could give him a smidgen of truth. "I feel bad that they're making you tag along with me."

"I'm not sure why they want me to babysit you." He didn't say it sarcastically or with anger, which was a nice change. He seemed more puzzled than anything. Hugh and Sophie had put them both in this awkward situation.

"Well, Sophie said you'd draw people into the booth." Which was obvious. *Look at you!* Actually, Abby had a hard time *not* glancing at him every other second. But she suspected there was some other reason they'd assigned Conor to help her. It was nothing specific, just a feeling.

The old her might have spoken up and asked straight out why Hugh and Sophie wanted Conor to help her. That outspokenness of hers tended to drive her mother crazy, and Abby had decided to turn over a new leaf—to wear life as if it were a loose shirt, as her therapist had told her. Besides, Abby was too jetlagged to question her new bosses. Maybe after she was well rested and settled, she would ask what they were trying to do. Abby had assumed she would be doing most of the setup on her own. She was used to doing things by herself. Her mother had made sure of that, like when she told her to stand on her own two feet and shipped her off to boarding school.

Abby glanced over again at her handsome escort and felt bad for him. She understood why he was displeased and she was going to work on not taking it personally. Meeting Conor had been unexpected. But the truth was that nothing so far here in Scotland had been as she'd anticipated.

Her cellphone gave a *blip*. A text from her mother, Joann: LET'S MEET UP FOR BRUNCH ON SUNDAY.

Abby exhaled. "Oh, brother." Not what she needed right now.

"What's wrong? Why are ye frowning at your phone?" Conor shook his head then. "Never mind. It's none of my business."

"It's okay." She could've ignored his question. But she was also trying to be more transparent with people and more honest with herself. "It's my mother."

"Is everything all right?"

"Not really." She looked up at Conor and saw something akin to empathy. "Don't judge me but I kind of didn't tell her about Scotland." Or about quitting Belle Weddings, though it was the obvious next move after Abby dumped Belle's son Aaron at the altar. Surely Aaron had filled her mother in as the two of them chatted often on the phone. Or maybe Aaron had broken off contact with her mother, which Abby seriously doubted. Either way, Mother would not approve of Abby quitting her job and coming to Scotland—essentially running away.

"Where does she think you are?"

"I guess back in St. Louis?"

Conor's expression was disapproving. "You should let her know you are here." His frown deepened. "I don't mean to pry but where does yere mum live?"

"In St. Louis also." Two blocks away from Abby's apartment. Yes, it was a strange setup. Especially since her mother was the one who'd arranged it. It made no sense that Mother would want her close by. Abby had spent her formative years three states away at Foxhill Hall, school for girls. She always felt as though her mother was dissatisfied with the test tube baby she'd acquired at the fertility clinic she managed. Her mother was exact, efficient, and an expert at withholding affection if Abby didn't bend to her every wish. Perhaps her mother wanted to live near Abby so she could control her.

Conor gave her a look that felt hard and sharp. "Let her know that ye're alive and well in Scotland."

"Well, um." Abby didn't know what to say. Not to him and definitely not to her mother. "I'll let her know." Yeah, when she felt up to it. But just then, the chime went off again, reminding Abby that she hadn't opened the text. "Excuse me." She turned so her phone's screen couldn't be seen by Conor, then typed out a quick reply. Sorry. I CAN'T MAKE IT. I'M OUT OF TOWN ON BUSINESS. All true...with a few omissions. Tomorrow, when Abby wasn't feeling so weary, and so displaced, she'd take the time to write her mother a long note about where she was. If asked, Abby wasn't sure what to say about why she'd left, and if she were being honest with herself, there were other things that she wasn't ready to examine either. She glanced over at the gorgeous Scot. Yup, her attraction to him was one of many things she wasn't ready to analyze yet.

"What about *your* mother?" Abby asked, hoping to guide the conversation in a different direction. "Haven't you ever told your mother a little white lie before? Or omitted some important details?"

"Nay. My mother was a lovely woman—firm but fair. My da, too." His look was grave, and she'd picked up on more than the past tense when referring to his parents.

"I'm sorry for your loss. For both of your parents."

Shocked, he regarded her for a long moment. "How do ye know my mum and da passed? Can ye read peoples' minds?" His quizzical gaze made her wonder if he thought she were a witch or something.

It wasn't the first time that someone had questioned her intuitiveness. "Listen, sorry for assuming. There was sadness in your voice. I just guessed."

He huffed, then growled. Apparently, he needed to prove he was beyond such syrupy emotions. Maybe he wanted her to see that he was as sentimental as a riled badger.

They didn't speak the rest of the way. She spent that time trying to figure out what she could say that would put them back on an even keel. But it was futile. Instead, she decided it was more important to pay attention to which way they were going. She catalogued the landmarks so she wouldn't feel lost the next time she made the trip this way: A loch on one side of the castle, a humongous tree with intertwining exposed roots with a ton of personality, a small reflection pond, and a stone wall.

But the realization hit her that no matter how much attention she paid, she felt sure it would take a long time before she didn't feel so lost here. *If ever.* For the past four years and five months, she had been one half of a couple. Now, she was single, ungrounded, and totally unsure about her future.

Before she knew it, they were standing outside her cottage. She didn't want to go inside just yet. Maybe Conor would offer to take her for a stroll, give her the Scottish tour of the place. Perhaps he'd ask her into his cottage for a nightcap. Or she could be the one to ask him, right? But she wasn't sure if there was any alcohol in the cupboards. She hadn't checked. She opened her mouth to say something to extend the evening, but she had waited too long.

"Goodnight," Conor said. Unceremoniously, he turned and walked away, flipping his collar up, as if he needed added protection against the weather. Or maybe it was against her.

Abby watched him go and tried to come up with some reason to call him back. She felt so alone she'd take anyone's company right now. He didn't go into any of the cottages. Instead, he kept walking, until he went inside one of the stone buildings. It was probably the weaver's shop.

Finally she took two more steps, crossed the threshold, and closed the door. She could call her mother just for someone to talk to. But Abby was sure that she couldn't withstand her mother's criticisms right now. Because of her rash actions, she would have to get used to being lonely.

But wouldn't it be nice if she didn't have to.

With a dry dishtowel in hand, Hugh took the rinsed plate that Sophie held out to him. They'd gotten into the routine of letting Mrs. McNabb leave right after dinner, which gave the two of them an opportunity to speak freely while they cleaned up.

Sophie frowned at him. "Conor seems unhappy. Do you think ye should let him out of it?"

Hugh chuckled. "It was yere idea to attach him to the wedding venture in hopes of distracting him from his misery. I believe Abby will do, don't ye?"

Sophie sighed, rinsed the sauté pan, and then handed it off to Hugh. "But Conor, it seems, will be fighting battles on two fronts. First Magnus and the improvements that Conor wants to make to the weaving building, and now the task of immersing himself in setting up Hitched in Scotland. You agree that's what we're calling it?"

"Aye. I like Hitched in Scotland. It's the perfect name. But on the other subject, don't you get the feeling that there's something about—"

"*Abby*?" Sophie finished for him. "I have a feeling that she'll settle Conor by changing his perspective."

"Aye. If nothing else, she'll be a distraction for him. He's so stuck in his misery over Morag. That ex-wife of his better not come around here looking for Conor. If she does, I'll make sure that the lot of us run her out of the village."

Sophie smiled. "Husband, ye know ye're something special. I'm a lucky lass to have landed ye." She dried her hands on her apron, pulled the kitchen towel from his hands, and tossed it on the counter before stepping into Hugh's arms. "I love you, laird."

"I love ye, too, Mrs. McGillivray." He kissed the top of her head.

"One of the things I love about you is that ye want to help all the people of Whussendale."

"It's my duty to do so." Hugh's parents raised him to be an upstanding laird. "More than that, it's my honor. And I think that setting up Conor and Abby will be good for him ... and possibly good for all of Whussendale."

Sophie laughed. "I just had a thought and I know ye won't agree, but I believe you have a bit of Aunt Davinia in ye. That matchmaking streak."

"I do not," Hugh argued. "She meddles too much for my liking."

"Aunt Davinia is the one who put the two of us together," Sophie reminded him.

"Yes, well. This is totally different." Hugh needed to defend himself. "Aunt Davinia enjoys conniving. Do ye not remember how she went about matching you and me? Very backhanded, she was. As far as Conor is concerned ... I was straightforward and told him what the plan was."

"Not exactly." Sophie laughed as she went up on tiptoe to kiss his chin. "You didn't spell it out completely."

"I figure he's smart enough to get the gist. Did ye see how he couldn't keep from glancing over at Abby during dinner?"

"Aye," Sophie said. "I couldn't tell if he wanted to kiss her or tell her to leave the table. Or perhaps, to leave Scotland altogether." She laughed.

"Exactly. It's all going to work out fine." He gave her a quick kiss on the lips. "Let me feed the mongrels and then let's head up to bed."

"Do ye have an early morn?" she asked with a sly smile.

"Ye know full-well what I have on my mind. I want some much-needed alone time with my wife." He patted her on the bum.

"We're on the same page, husband. You feed the hounds while I wipe down the counters. Then I'll race ye upstairs."

Hugh chuckled. "I'm the luckiest man in all of Scotland."

"Aye," she teased. "Ye definitely are."

Chapter 5

ABBY'S FIRST NIGHT in Scotland was full of vivid dreams—strange and randomly mixed-up. For whatever reason, one of her dreams had her mother and ex-fiancé showing up in Scotland, where her mother didn't mince words: *You're ridiculous for moving to the land of kilts. And why are you dressed that way? That pantsuit isn't flattering on you at all. It makes you look fat.* Abby woke up feeling a heavy dose of dread. She'd gone way out on a limb without a safety net.

Imminent failure was a real possibility.

Conor had had a starring role in her dreams, as well. He was blaming her for the ruined wedding shawl which had gotten tangled up in the weaving loom, just like he'd gotten tangled up with her. For some reason, she wanted his approval, needed it like she needed air. She kept trying to tell him that it wasn't her fault that he had to help her at the bridal shows. But he wouldn't listen. He just kept walking away. When she woke, she felt like her miserable dreams had been foreshadowing her future and hinting at the truth. Conor would never be happy with her.

While lying in bed and not wanting to get up, a text came in from Hugh. MEET ME AT MY OFFICE AT 9 AM. Abby checked the time. She had an hour, which would allow for a shower, makeup, and breakfast. Thank goodness, someone had stocked her fridge and left dry goods on the rustic shelf above the counter. Abby was grateful. At least one thing was going her way.

She went to the standing wardrobe in the corner of her bedroom and skipped over the pantsuit from her dream that her mother said made her look fat. Instead, she chose a festive fall dress and warm tights to wear before heading off to the bathroom for a shower.

At eight minutes to nine, she slipped on her Merrell boots and zipped them up. She was ready ... at least in appearance. She grabbed her bag and a heavy poncho to throw over her dress, locked her front door, and then headed to Hugh's office, determined to be a few minutes early. It was important for her to start off on the right foot here in Scotland, so being prompt was crucial, especially on her first full day. When she exited her cottage, she looked this way and that, but then abruptly stopped herself. She'd been looking for Conor, which was ridiculous. But she decided to cut herself some slack. Conor had been appointed her guide and it was only natural she would look for him now. She put her excuses aside and focused on her surroundings, cataloguing the sights as she walked along.

The stone cottages were so quaint and cute. She could imagine the splash of color in the flower beds during the spring and summer. She bet the locals would choose to get married outside their own cottage to personalize their big day because it would make the perfect backdrop for wedding photos.

Sitting near the wool mill was a small wooden bridge arching over a stream, which would make a perfect place to take wedding photos. In fact, she could envision the bride making the short journey over the bridge to meet her groom, who would be waiting with the best man and maid of honor on the other side. It made a nice image. She pulled out her pad of paper and made some quick notes.

Arriving at the castle last night, she'd gotten only a glimpse of the gardens. They would work nicely from many vantage points for weddings and she looked forward to examining them further. She was really beginning to warm to Whussendale. The village oozed charm every which way she looked. But there was still the problem of the long commute from the major cities to the middle of nowhere, though Hugh said he would be tackling that problem. And she'd have to ask him about the timeline for the accommodations he'd mentioned.

She glanced at her watch. She'd lingered too long and knew she had to hurry or lest she'd be late.

As she neared Hugh's office building, she caught sight of Sophie and Hugh sitting on a white circular bench that surrounded the base of a beautiful oak tree. Another picture-perfect place for a bride and groom's photo op. The two love-birds had their heads together, speaking quietly, with mugs resting on the bench beside them. A pang of jealousy overtook Abby. At one time, she and Aaron had been a couple like that. *But not exactly.* To be honest, she and Aaron had never looked at each other the way Sophie and Hugh were gazing at each other now. Abby shook off the pang of grief. She'd thought her relationship with Aaron would last forever. They'd dated for four-plus years. Engaged the last two. However, she'd worked hard every day of those final two years to ignore the niggle that something was wrong between them. When her wedding day came, she could ignore it no longer. When she was told it was time to walk down the aisle, she walked out of the venue instead. Actually, she'd jogged. Yes, she'd become that cliché, a runaway bride.

Her mother was furious. Aaron was puzzled, clueless as to why she'd run. The truth was that neither Mother nor Aaron, nor Belle, actually—had known Abby at all. She hadn't known herself either. Which was something that she'd been trying to rectify every day since. For the last four weeks, she'd been examining her every action, but only in retrospect. Exhibit A: coming to Scotland without thinking it through. When she saw Hugh's ad, she'd jumped at the opportunity to leave her mother and Aaron behind, and the guilt for leaving Belle's Weddings. After Abby had quit, Belle had made it clear in a spiteful text that she was fired. Here in Scotland, there were no physical reminders of the ones she'd left behind.

Belle had been the one to set her up with her son, Aaron, a successful fertility lawyer and ten years Abby's senior. The same fertility lawyer that her mother had recently used for her clinic. Mother had described him as pragmatic in the most glowing of terms. Pragmatism had never been one of Abby's requirements for a relationship. Looking back, maybe it should have been. The only reason she'd gone out with Aaron was in the hope of getting her mother off her back with the added bonus of making Belle happy, too. But it'd been all for naught.

As it turned out, Abby had been a closet-romantic and wanted something akin to what Sophie and Hugh had. Theirs looked like a once-in-a-generation love story. Abby took a cleansing breath and decided to get real for the sake of her sanity. When thinking of herself, she had to banish the romantic fairytale, and instead, focus on her clients and their happiness. Hugh and Sophie's relationship was the outlier, as most people never found a love like theirs. Most people settled for something comfortable, and if not finding that exactly, they resigned themselves to finding someone at least tolerable to spend their lives with.

Abby glanced around, looking for someone or some way to

intervene. She didn't want to be the one to interrupt the pair. But at that moment, Hugh looked up. "Abby!"

Sophie glanced up, too, looking a little flushed, which made Abby wonder what the two of them had been intimating to one another. Sophie straightened and waved to Abby. "Are you ready for the grand tour?"

Abby glanced at her boots, hoping she'd made the right selection as Hugh hadn't said anything about a tour. "Yes. I look forward to it." Abby waved her pen and paper. "I'm ready to take notes."

"Good," Hugh said.

But before they took off, Abby needed to say what had been on her mind since last night. "I wondered if we could speak about Conor. He seemed unhappy about being assigned to me. I'll be fine working the bridal shows on my own."

Hugh shook his head. "Nay. He'll get over it. Just think of Conor as your bellhop, your muscle to carry your luggage, and your help to set up the booth—"

"And to attract women to the booth by showing off his legs in his kilt," Sophie cut in.

Abby opened her mouth to argue but Sophie continued. "Originally, Hugh and I planned to go to the bridal shows with you, but now ..." She trailed off, looking at Hugh.

Hugh took over from there. "Can you keep a secret? Sophie's parents know but my aunt Davinia doesn't know just yet."

Sophie smiled shyly. "I'm pregnant."

"Congratulations!" Abby was happy for Sophie, but wistful as well. It wasn't until after she'd left Aaron at the altar that she realized it meant giving up on having children. Some would suggest doing what her mother had done and opt for artificial insemination. But Abby couldn't do that. Growing up without a father had left an empty space inside her that would never be filled. For the sake of her new life here, she shook off the sadness and put a smile on her face. "When are you due?"

"Early April," Sophie said, laying a protective hand on her stomach.

Hugh wrapped his arm around his wife, beaming at her. "We're very excited. But what do you say? Should we get started on the tour?"

"Great idea," Abby replied.

As Hugh stood, he picked up a clipboard that Abby hadn't seen on the other side of him. He offered Abby a sheet from it. "This is a list of locations that we thought would be of most interest to you and to your brides and grooms."

"Thanks," Abby said, looking down at it. "I don't see the loch, the one that I saw last night near your castle. I think it would be a perfect location to exchange vows."

Hugh and Sophie shared a look, making Abby wonder if she'd stumbled upon an old wound. Hugh gave Sophie a sad smile and then nodded, before turning back to Abby. "Ye're right. The loch would make a nice backdrop for weddings. Let's add that to the list."

Sophie gazed at Hugh and squeezed his arm.

Abby felt fairly certain that she shouldn't ask what that had been about. Instead, she glanced at the list again. There were about ten places, beginning with the waterwheel, which she'd already seen in person yesterday, and online when she'd briefly looked up Whussendale Woollens. The waterwheel would be great for photographs—something unique from all the other wedding destinations. "This list ... were you thinking that the waterwheel could be a place where couples might get married, or just for photos?"

"Both," Sophie answered. "We wondered what you thought about us building a trellis archway that could be moved from one location to another on the estate, wherever the bride and groom would like to get *hitched*."

"That's an excellent idea." Abby pulled out her phone and took several photos from different angles than the ones that were on the website.

Hugh held up his hand. "Don't worry about getting pictures. I had a professional photographer come when the flowers were in full bloom. I'll give you a flash drive so you'll have a copy of the photos."

Abby pocketed her camera. "Okay. Sounds good."

"This way," Hugh said. Sophie took his arm once again as they walked to an area not far from the wool compound that looked to have been cleared of bushes. "I have a big surprise for you."

"What's that?" Abby asked.

"We're having a train car delivered soon."

"Yes," Sophie said excitedly. "A caboose. We thought it would make a nice showpiece, not something you see everywhere else in Scotland. We're thinking of converting it into a small restaurant. Hugh has a line on a Michelin star chef, who has been wanting to get out of the rat race and set up in a small town."

Abby could see a bride and groom waving from the back of the train. "Could we offer it as a place to hold small weddings, too, when the restaurant isn't in use?"

"Aye. What a great idea," Hugh said. Sophie nodded in agreement, then the two of them beamed at each other. Once again, Abby was hit with a pang of grief that she had no one to share special moments with anymore.

"We'll have the caboose fixed up however you think is best," Sophie said to Abby, "so yere weddings could happen either inside or out."

"Oh, that sounds wonderful!" Abby was surprised how they were going *all in.*

"When I get back to the office," Hugh said, "I'll send you pictures of the interior. I think it looks grand, but, Abby, of course, you'll have the final say of how the interior is to be decorated."

Abby thought this was a good time to get one of the big questions answered. "What are you thinking about as far as timeline? When would you like the first wedding to take place?"

"Certainly for the high season, which starts in June," Hugh answered.

Sophie shook her head. "I think the weddings can begin almost immediately. We don't need everything in place for Hitched in Scotland to be active."

Abby nodded. "If this were my venture, I would want to start making money as soon as possible, especially since there has already been an outlay of money." And the fact that Hugh said the wedding planner would be on the payroll from the moment she arrived.

"Abby, I do want you to think of this as yeres," Hugh said.

Sophie bobbed her head. "One of the things that Hugh asks and encourages is that everyone in Whussendale own their work, from the weavers to café workers to shop clerks. We're all in this together. We're a working community."

"I get it. I think it's great." Abby had never been part of a tight community and she was looking forward to being one of them.

"This way." Hugh pointed to an empty field.

"Hugh is having a small herd of coos brought in for the wedding venture, too," Sophie added. "Everyone loves High-land cattle. Lots of photo opportunities with them, too."

"Oh, yes," Abby said. She'd long been a fan of the hairy cows and followed several social media accounts that posted the *coos* on a regular basis.

"Davey McBain, owner of McBain Distillery, told me that their hairy coos have been quite the draw for tourists so I thought we might as well have some of them, too. Just so ye know, we do have a herd of sheep on the estate for the wedding guests to gawk at and to take pictures with, too."

"Plus, ye can always get more sheep from yere cousin Ewan," Sophie added. "He lives on the next estate over from ours."

Hugh nodded and pointed to the road. "Our next stop is the chapel at Kilheath Castle. I'm anxious to see what ye think of it. But we'll cut through the gardens so ye can get a read on them, too."

When they arrived at the castle, Sophie ran up the steps and let out the Wallace and the Bruce. The dogs greeted them with wagging tails and whines of enthusiasm for getting petted.

"The little moochers are always looking for attention," Hugh said as Sophie petted her guardians, who were each vying for her love by sticking their muzzles in her hand.

"Come on, ye two," Hugh said. "Let's take a walk through the garden."

This time, Abby got more than a little glimpse of the gardens; she got the full view of the topiaries and the lay of the land. Sophie explained how it was much prettier in the spring and summer, while pointing out any number of places where couples might want to get married. Abby drew a quick map and made notes of her favorite spots. She especially got a kick out of the dogs, who chased each other, then chased a butterfly, nipping at the air, but never catching it.

"On to the chapel," Hugh announced and the dogs took the lead, tearing off for the castle. "Ye'll see that the chapel is attached to the castle and has two entrances—one from the outside and one from inside Kilheath."

When they walked in, Abby was wowed by how magical and serene it was. Light streamed in through the stained-glass windows and danced across five small pews. The space was big enough for maybe twenty people. Abby turned to Sophie and Hugh. "It's absolutely lovely. What a treasure you have here."

"Let's head inside the castle and we'll show ye the largest spaces which would accommodate big wedding receptions," Hugh said.

The dogs followed as Sophie and Hugh showed Abby the ballroom, where a wedding dance would work. The dining room would be perfect for sit-down wedding feasts. Even the massive foyer would be a great place for couples to get married and then have their pictures taken at the apex of the double grand staircases to the second floor.

For the next hour or so, they explored the guest bedrooms and bathrooms upstairs where the wedding parties could stay. Abby was beginning to see that being in such a remote area wasn't a liability at all, especially since Whussendale had so much to offer as a wedding destination. The promotional material would write itself, in pictures alone.

"What about nightlife?" Abby asked. "Are there things for guests to do in the village? What about shopping?"

"The pub closed in my father's time, but I hope to have it reopened soon," Hugh said.

"We'd like to have someone open a shop selling Made in Scotland items," Sophie said, then added, "We're planning to have concerts in the castle's garden."

"Also, Ewan said he could offer up sheepdog exhibitions at certain times of the year."

"You mentioned something about a distillery?" Abby asked. "Is the distillery local? If so, I wondered if it would be okay if I mentioned a whisky tasting for the wedding guests?"

"Aye. McBain Distillery," Hugh replied. "I'll give you Davey's contact info and ye can speak with him directly. Tell him I sent you."

"Sounds good," Abby said.

Hugh pointed in the direction of the wool mill. "Let's head back and get you set up in your office." Once again, Hugh and Sophie shared a look, but this time, it wasn't as if they were remembering a funeral, but sharing a secret. Abby wondered whether with time she would be able to decode or decipher the looks they gave each other. Knowing what they were thinking would surely go a long way in making Abby feel more comfortable and at home.

Sophie gave Abby a sheepish look. "Sorry to leave ye. I have to head to the kiltmaker's building. So much work to do. And Willoughby will read me the riot act if I don't get back to it soon." But something about Sophie not meeting Abby's eye made it feel as if she wasn't exactly telling the whole truth.

Abby nodded to Sophie. "I appreciate you taking time out of your morning. Thank you."

Sophie gave Hugh a quick kiss on the lips. "Good luck." And she hurried away.

Abby couldn't help but wonder what Sophie meant.

Hugh pointed out the direction they were to go. "So what do you think? Will the village, the castle, and the area in general make a good place to have weddings?" He was grinning from ear to ear, making his question rhetorical.

"It's going to be great," Abby said honestly. "I can't wait to get started." For a brief moment, she remembered the bad dreams of last night. As it turned out, they weren't foreshadowing anything upsetting or unnerving. Apparently, her strange dreams had just been a biproduct of jetlag and not a bad omen at all. *Thank goodness.*

Hugh led Abby to the weaver's building. She knew it was the weaver's building because of the wooden sign hanging above the door. Presumably Hugh had to make a stop here before taking her to her office.

Just inside the door was a small foyer. Hugh grabbed a packet of earplugs from a cylindrical container hanging on the wall. Abby knew they were necessary as she could already hear the clanging and clanking of the machinery coming from the other side of the steel double doors. Obediently, she took the earplugs, tore open the package, and slipped them in. Hugh inserted the plugs that were hanging around his neck, something Abby had noticed earlier but hadn't given a second thought to since.

Once they were through the doors, Abby took in the humongous room filled with equipment. Several people worked the machines, but there was one person in particular who caught her eye ... Conor. Both Conor and Magnus were working on the same machine with wrenches in their hands.

Hugh pointed to them and yelled, "This way."

Abby followed but wondered why he hadn't told her to wait outside while he spoke to the weavers.

Hugh walked straight to the man she hadn't been able to take her eyes off of. "Conor, I'll need a word. Do ye have a minute?"

Conor looked up and nodded, and then he stopped cold, as if it had just registered that she was there, too. She didn't know what to make of his reaction but was sure that she wasn't his favorite person. He was probably still sore with her, or the laird who'd assigned him extra work because of her. "I'll be just a moment," Conor said above the noise.

"This way." Hugh walked to what looked like a smallish building constructed inside the bigger open floor weaver's building. The smaller building had a lower ceiling, a door on one wall, and windows on three sides. As they got near, Abby could make out a couple of desks and a filing cabinet within.

"In here," Hugh said, holding the door open for her.

She walked in and he shut the door, taking out his ear protection. She removed hers as well. For a moment, she took in the old, battered desks with neatly stacked wool remnants and files, but then she returned her gaze to Conor who was still beside the loom. He laid down the wrench, wiped his hands on a rag, and then walked over to the office. Once he was inside, he gave a nod of deference to Hugh. "Laird." But he was frowning. "What can I do for ye?"

"I just wanted to give you a heads up that we're putting Abby in here with ye in yere office."

What? Surely, she hadn't heard him correctly. Maybe he meant that he was here to show her Conor's office. She shifted her gaze to Conor. But his frown was on her now, as if she'd been the one to suggest that they share an office!

"I knew nothing about this," Abby blurted, unable to hold it in. But she was able to stop herself from asking if the laird had lost his *ever-lovin' mind!*

Conor shifted his frown back to Hugh.

"Calm down," Hugh said. "I'm not kicking ye out. Ye have plenty of room in here, enough for Abby to have her own desk and wall space for shelves or whatever she might need."

Conor's glower never wavered as he returned to her.

"Conor, this is my idea," Hugh said, "not Abby's."

If it wasn't so awkward, Abby might have thought the whole thing was comical. Conor looked as astonished as if the laird had suggested he share his office with a swarm of killer bees.

Only moments ago, Abby had felt excited about her job, anticipating all the good things to come. Now she wanted to skulk from the building. Later, when she got Conor alone, she'd have to remind him once again that it wasn't her idea that he was stuck with her.

Conor rolled his eyes and then said, "Fine. Is it all right if I get back to work?" He sounded belligerent.

"Sure," Hugh said.

Conor didn't look at her again as he marched out of the office and back to the machine he'd been working on.

"What do you think of yere new office? Do you think there's enough space?" Hugh asked.

Abby was still struck speechless. Finally, she came up with a suitable question, one that wouldn't have her being paraded from the wool mill with her walking papers. "Um, Hugh, why is my office in this particular building?" The only reason she could think of was that she and Conor were supposed to work together sometimes. But it still didn't make a lot of sense to her.

Hugh blew right past her question. "I'll have Declan and Tavon bring you a desk from the castle this afternoon. We have an extra one in the attic." He glanced at the doorway as if he didn't dare ask Conor to help. Not surprisingly, since she still felt Conor's veiled rage from where she stood. He certainly wouldn't like it when she scooted his desk back to the far wall to make room for hers.

Finally, she said, "Thank you." Every bit of her wanted to plead with the laird to plant her somewhere else. Anywhere. It didn't matter where, as long as there was plenty of space between her and Conor.

"Is there anything else you think you might need, besides a chair?" Hugh asked.

"Yes, I would like to hang a couple of cork boards on which to lay out wedding designs and seating charts for the receptions."

"Just give me the specifications and I'll have Declan make them for you."

"Sure. Thank you." But Abby was distracted, her thoughts no longer on design boards. Or hauling a desk into this office. She'd made the mistake of looking through the office window to check on Conor. Unfortunately, he was staring back. Not in an I'm-attracted-to-you way either. But one that said getting Conor to work with her willingly—or at all—was going to be an uphill battle.

Chapter 6

HUGH FOLLOWED ABBY outside. He'd give her time and space to get used to the idea of sharing an office with Conor. Everyone in Whussendale made sacrifices; he would not make Abby and Conor the exception. Though if he was being honest, playing fast and furious with a couple's love life was beyond the normal purview of a laird. But Hugh had agreed when Sophie came up with the idea to stick those two together in Conor's office. But he didn't agree with Sophie when she'd said he was conducting himself like his meddling Aunt Davinia.

Hugh watched as Abby's mouth opened, and he felt relatively sure she was going to protest the arrangement. But then a familiar, female voice—craggy and old—hollered at him.

"Laird! Wait up!" He turned to see the two old women hustling toward them. He'd known them for years since his cousin Amy had moved to Gandiegow with her husband, Coll. The women were waving at him—one was short and squat, the other, tall and slim, both had white hair. The short one was frowning, while the tall one was giving him a kind smile. Typical

Deydie and Bethia, best friends who couldn't be more different from each other if they tried.

"Who's that?" Abby asked before the old ladies were near enough to hear her.

"Aye. Right. The one wearing the army boots with her skirt is Deydie and the one who is smiling is Bethia." Hugh might have been answering Abby, but his thoughts were consumed with *why in the devil these two were here* ... and so soon. They joined them before he could explain more.

"Is this *she*? The wedding planner?" Deydie bellowed, which made Abby take a half-step back.

"Deydie, let me introduce Abby Potter. Abby, this is Deydie McCracken and Bethia Lennox, our dear friends—" he hoped he'd get some points for that "—and quilters from Gandiegow, our sister village, a fishing village on the coast."

Deydie yanked on his arm. "Have ye told her yet?"

"Told me what?" Abby asked, turning to face him.

Bethia took Abby's hand and patted it. "I'm so glad to meet ye. We made an impromptu stop on our way back from Inverness. We were shopping, ye see, picking up supplies for our next quilting retreat. Do you sew, Abby?"

"Yes." Abby answered. "Why do you ask?"

The old woman Deydie cackled. "It's damn near a requirement to sew and quilt, lassie, if ye want to live in Gandiegow or Whussendale." Deydie let go of him and grabbed Abby's arm. "We best be going."

Surprisingly, Abby dug her heels in. "Going where?"

He'd thought he would tell her tomorrow or the next day that he'd agreed to share Abby with Gandiegow. "Deydie, I thought we decided that we were going to wait until she got settled."

Deydie slammed her hands on her wide hips. "Ye may have decided, laird, but I surely didn't."

Bethia smiled sweetly at him. "Laird, it's such a beautiful day. We thought it'd be a good time for the wedding planner to take some pictures in Gandiegow."

Hugh should've thought of sending the professional photographer there when he'd set up the shoot in Whussendale.

Deydie picked up the thread of the conversation. "She might want to get some shots of the fishermen returning from the morning run. It's quite the sight to see."

"Hugh, please, I don't understand," Abby said in earnest.

"Well, it's like this. When the folks of Gandiegow got wind that Whussendale was setting up the wedding venture, Gandiegow wanted a piece of the action, too."

Deydie tugged on Abby again, but this time, Bethia gently removed Deydie's hand before speaking. "We were hoping ye would come back to Gandiegow with us. We want ye to look around and make recommendations as to what we need to do to hold weddings like the ones that Laird Hugh has planned for Whussendale."

"Don't forget," Deydie added, "that Diana and the DCI are getting married in two shakes of a lamb's tail, on St. Andrews Day. We could use the wedding planner's input with that, too."

Abby gave him a help-me look. Aye, he'd promised he'd share the wedding planner. He just hadn't expected Gandiegow to come calling so soon. Hugh knew from past experience that Deydie always got her way. He might as well show Abby that they all caved when it came to Deydie McCracken. But he would give Abby a small reprieve. "Ladies, uh, listen. Abby needs to head to her cottage and get her notebook, if she is to take notes about Gandiegow." Even though he knew her notebook was in her bag; she'd used it all morning. "How about if you and I head over to the café for a cuppa. Then Abby can meet us there in thirty minutes or so?" He pointed to the building at the end.

"The lass doesna need thirty minutes," Deydie complained.

Abby's expression said she did.

Hugh nodded to Abby. "Take yere time." It was the best he could do for her.

Abby hesitated for a moment but then nodded. "All right."

Hugh turned back to Deydie and Bethia. "Get whatever pastry ye like at the café. My treat."

"Well …" Deydie said begrudgingly. "I guess that'd be all right, since ye're buying." Then the old woman hollered to Abby's retreating backside, "Don't be long! My quilters are gathering today and are anxious to meet ye. We're going to plan out the next quilt retreat."

Abby didn't turn back but put her hand up in a wave.

Hugh really hated throwing Abby to the wolves, but suddenly an idea came to him. "I need to take care of something. Ye two go on ahead without me." Deydie and Bethia nodded and walked toward the café, while Hugh pulled out his phone and texted Conor. DO YOU HAVE TIME TO GO TO GANDIEGOW? That way, Abby wouldn't have to ride with Deydie and be overwhelmed; Deydie excelled at being a bit much. If Conor drove Abby, she would have a friendly face during the ride there, plus Conor could be her ride back to Whussendale.

Before Hugh could slide his phone back in his pocket, a reply came in from Conor. SORRY. TOO BUSY.

Hugh had made the mistake of asking. He wondered if Conor's answer would've been different if he'd told Conor he would be chauffeuring Abby. Too late now. He pulled up Declan's number, tapped, deciding it was better this time to talk instead of texting. "Hey. I need ye to take the wedding planner to Gandiegow so she'll have a ride back to Whussendale when the Gandiegow quilters are done with her."

"Sure," Declan said. "When?"

"Now. Meet us at the café."

"I'll be right there."

For a moment, Hugh wished Declan was the weaver instead of Conor. It might've been a smoother transition for Abby. But Declan was going to be on the road and very busy soon. He'd recently become certified as a Scottish Blue Badge tour guide. The whole village was proud of him. Declan had been working with Kit, the matchmaker from Gandiegow, to put together a special tour for singles looking for love. There was even talk of tours specifically for the over-fifty crowd. He had confided in Hugh that he wasn't too keen on what Kit planned to call the tour: the Love Coach. Each tour would consist of golfers and quilters. Hugh could see why he wouldn't be thrilled about the name, but he sure hoped the idea was successful for both Kit and Declan's sake. Hugh could recommend a few old-timers who should go on that tour for the sole purpose of smoothing off their rough edges by spending extended time with the opposite sex.

Hugh arrived at the café just as Deydie and Bethia's pastries and small teapots made it to the table. He waved to Lara, who ran the café. Although she was young, she was very competent. "Can I get a small coffee?" Lara nodded and went to fetch the heated carafe.

Deydie tapped the large men's watch strapped to her ample wrist. "Where is the lass?"

Bethia touched Deydie's arm. "It's only been a few minutes. She'll be here in due time." Bethia was definitely the friendlier of the two.

At that moment, Declan came through the door. Hugh sighed with relief. Declan had the gift of gab and would be able to entertain the Gandiegow women better than he could, or was willing to do at this point.

Declan took a seat beside Bethia and proceeded to tell them all about the latest developments for his first tour. Next, he kept the conversation going by asking about the quilt retreat the ladies had planned for when he dropped off the quilters from the Love Coach. He explained that while the women were quilting, he would keep the men busy by playing a round of golf with them. With the help of Declan, time flew by. At exactly twenty-nine minutes from the time Abby had rushed off to her cottage, she appeared in the doorway of the café.

"There she is," Bethia said. "Right on time."

Hugh and Declan stood, and when Abby drew near, Hugh introduced her driver. "Abby, this is Declan Brown. He is going to be your chauffeur today."

Abby looked circumspect. Hugh couldn't blame her. From almost her first moment here, he'd been making Conor her keeper. But now, he wasn't giving her a choice about who was driving her to Gandiegow.

Declan took her look in stride. "I promise. No accidents. No speeding tickets. I'm a safe driver. Ask anyone."

"Aye, he is what he says he is," Hugh said.

"Nay," Deydie said with the shake of her head. "She'll ride with us. We've got a lot to say to the wedding planner."

Bethia smiled sweetly at all of them. "We want to discuss the upcoming wedding of Diana McKellen and DCI Rory Crannach. As Deydie mentioned, we could use yere input on the finishing touches for the celebration."

Deydie bobbed her head so much that Hugh was afraid she was going to dislocate her noggin.

Abby, though, looked a bit stunned, as if she were a ragdoll being tugged between the sister cities of Whussendale and Gandiegow.

"Listen—" Hugh started, but Deydie cut him off.

"We'll get Abby back to ye when we're done with her." But that sounded as if Deydie was going to keep Abby until after

Rory and Diana's wedding!

Hugh cleared his throat, ready to remind them who he was. "Abby can go to Gandiegow now—*with Declan*—then they will return by evening time. She and Conor have much to do for the upcoming bridal show and they need to prepare. Besides, she'll need to lay out a marketing plan for *both* Gandiegow and Whussendale."

Sophie saved him by walking through the door. "Hugh, there ye are." She had a way of knowing when he needed her. "Oh, hey, Deydie, Bethia." Sophie rushed over and hugged them both with her arms around each of their shoulders. "I've missed you!"

"We've missed ye, too," Bethia said. "All of Gandiegow misses you."

"So what's going on?" Sophie asked, looking to Abby and then Hugh.

"Declan is going to take Abby to Gandiegow to see what can be done about having destination weddings there," Hugh said.

Sophie nodded. "But she'll have to be back by this evening. We have a lot to go over with her and Conor about the booth we've rented for the upcoming bridal show."

Hugh loved his wife. She'd backed him up without him even needing to ask. "Aye. That's what I've been saying."

"Should we head out?" Declan asked rhetorically as he put his arms out, as if to guide the sheep. Abby, Deydie, and Bethia complied and walked to the door and then outside.

Hugh kissed his wife. "Thanks."

"When I saw through the window that Deydie was heading to the café, I had a feeling you might need me," Sophie whispered.

They followed the Gandiegowan entourage outside.

Hugh took her hand and squeezed. "Ye sure are a bright

one." He waved to Declan and Abby. "We'll see you later." They waved back.

"I feel bad for her," Hugh said to his wife.

"Abby?"

"Aye," he said. "She's been bombarded with a lot since she's arrived, with no time to regroup or to even get her bearings."

"Och, Hugh, don't fash. Abby will adapt soon enough. She may be in shock now, but she seems like a strong lass."

"Maybe." Hugh wrapped his arm around his wife as they watched the two vehicles pull out of Whussendale. "Remember, Abby's an American lass, luv. She's not accustomed to the likes of us. As ye know, we Scots tend to be … a handful."

Abby didn't have to say much, as Declan kept up a one-sided stream of information, pointing out castle ruins and other historical sites as he drove. He related all kinds of interesting Scottish tales. The man sure had the gift of gab. Or maybe Declan instinctively knew that she didn't feel like talking. While he chatted, she learned a lot about him, which was a great contrast to the Scot she'd been assigned to. Strangely, she hadn't been able to keep Conor off her mind since she'd seen him in his office … now, her office, too. She was certain he was upset with her over that development. When she got Sophie alone, she would ask why she was to work out of the weaver's building. Maybe ask Conor if he knew why, too. Yes, she could ask Hugh, but Abby got the feeling that questioning the laird's decisions was something people did not do here in Scotland.

If she had to set up a shop in the weaver's building, wasn't there some other corner to put her desk? She shook her head, trying to rid her brain of her circular thoughts. But it was to no avail.

She was still trying to process the other revelation of the morning. She was to serve another Scottish village? She couldn't quite get over the shock of it. She hadn't even gotten her bearings yet in Whussendale!

She heard Declan say something about shearing. "What?" she asked.

He laughed. "In my younger days, I sheared sheep at Here Again Farm, the next estate over from Whussendale, which is owned by Laird Hugh's cousin, Laird Ewan McGillivray. Eventually I moved to Whussendale to do maintenance at the wool mill. I'm good with my hands." So the man had several gifts besides small talk.

"And now?" Abby asked, so he'd keep talking.

"I'm starting a new career as a tour guide. I love to travel. I love Scotland. And I'm fond of talking, in case ye haven't noticed. So being a tour guide is perfect for me, don't ye think?"

She chuckled. "Yes. I guess it is."

"Och. Look at that!" Declan exclaimed. "Coos! I have to admit that I never tire of seeing these gentle, noble creatures. Not since I was a wee bairn."

A line of shaggy Highland cows ambled into the road, forcing Declan to bring the vehicle to a stop. There had to be at least twenty of the long-haired beasts, all of them brown, except one lone black one, which was a bit smaller than the others.

"This would be great for the website." Abby pulled out her phone and snapped pictures of the coos. "How exciting!"

"Go ahead and step out to take yere photos, if ye like. Ye'll get better shots that way."

"Thanks." Abby got out and took a ton of pictures. She could've reasoned that she was only taking them for Hitched in Scotland, but she was also taking them for herself.

When the *coos* had crossed the road and were too far away to get any more up-close-and-personal photos, she got back in the car.

Declan laughed. "The *Heilan' coos* have *moo-ved* on, right?"

"Yes, they have." Abby smiled. Seeing the Highland cows had really lifted her spirits and she decided that being in Scotland was quite the rollercoaster of emotions.

Getting to know Declan made her think that if she'd ever had a brother, she might like to have one like him. Which made her think of another Scottish male. The one who'd pretty much taken up residence in her every thought. There was no way that she could ever think of Conor as a brother. Declan might be as good looking as Conor. But there was something about Conor that made sparks ignite in her.

Not long afterward, Declan pulled onto an unmarked road and declared, "We're almost there."

On one side of the narrow road was a drop, seemingly off the edge of the world. Further down below, she saw the red and gray rooftops of stone buildings. Then she gazed out at the North Sea stretching toward the horizon, which seemed to go on forever as their vehicle made the descent down a precipitous slope to the parking lot adjacent to the village. Abby wondered what it was like to live in Gandiegow in the winter with steep, icy roads and the cold sea at its doorstep. Treacherous, definitely. Only strong people would choose to live with that danger every day.

Declan brought the vehicle to a stop and shut off the engine. "Gandiegow is a walking village. No cars beyond this point."

"Really?" She glanced around and saw there was no road leading into town. She'd thought Whussendale was old-timey! But if vehicles weren't allowed within the village, apparently Gandiegow had cornered the market on being archaic. She gathered her things, stepped from the car, and then pulled out her phone for taking pictures and her pad of paper for taking notes.

The village was perfect with the sea as its backdrop. From here, the pier looked ideal for a destination wedding. She snapped a couple of photos before shutting her door and following Declan. Her senses had come alive. The smell of the salty air and the crashing of the waves gave the place an aura of magic. She couldn't wait to see everything. But first, she examined the parking lot further and noticed there was a total of six other vehicles. One of them was the vehicle that Deydie and Bethia had driven. *They beat us here.* Which Abby guessed wasn't too surprising since she and Declan had stopped for the parade of Highland cattle.

"Aye, ye're checking out the parking lot. All of Gandiegow share their vehicles and sign them out from the General Store," Declan said. "What are ye writing in yere notebook?"

"It's a to-do list of sorts. There are just a few things I need to check into." Abby wondered how much of a hassle it was to carry all the flowers, decorations, and food from the parking lot to where the wedding and reception would be held. The first building they passed was a pub, the name The Fishman painted on the storefront windows in large letters. Abby made a note of it, too. Perhaps that would be a good place to hold a bachelor party or a *stag party* as it was called in Scotland.

Now she could see the village better. It arced around the water as if the small town was an arm hugging the sea. "Do you know if Gandiegow has enough space to host the wedding guests? I'm afraid that a lack of accommodations could be a huge hiccup for Deydie and Bethia's plans to hold weddings here."

"Don't worry," Declan said, smiling at her. "There are two quilting dorms here in the village, plus Partridge House, which is a B & B. Also, sometimes the people of Gandiegow open their homes up to out-of-town guests when all the other spots are full."

"I see." But as they walked into the village, Abby saw that most of the cottages were not very big, making her wonder how out-of-towners would feel about being crammed into a small living space with people they didn't know.

In the middle of the arc, a steeple rose above the cottages. "I hope Deydie and Bethia will show me the church."

Declan tsked at her. "*Kirk*. We Scots call them kirks."

Speak of the devil, Deydie came out of a building that was near the ... *kirk*. Abby was amazed how spry the old woman was as she hurried in their direction.

"What took ye so long?" Deydie hollered when she got near enough.

"A typical Highland traffic jam," Declan deadpanned.

"Sheep or coos?" Deydie asked.

"Coos. Abby got out and took pictures while we waited," Declan said. It felt a little like he was throwing her under the bus.

"Well, ye're here now," Deydie groused. "Come. Bethia has made a list of places to show ye. But first, I'll introduce ye to the quilting ladies. I'll also make sure ye get some time with Diana, the bride-to-be. She and her intended did us quite a service a while back. We're indebted to them both so we want to throw them a helluva wedding."

"Is Kit at Quilting Central?" Declan asked. "I'd like to bend her ear for a bit about the details of the Love Coach."

"She was here with us earlier, helping Moira iron blocks for the Thistle Wedding quilt."

"Good," Declan said.

"But she went home to have lunch with Ramsay."

"Can I leave Abby in your capable hands, then?" he asked.

Bethia gave Deydie a look. "Let me text Kit first to make sure she isn't in the middle of something." Bethia pulled out her phone and dictated her text into it. "Is it okay to send Declan to your cottage now?"

A moment later, Bethia's phone pinged. She smiled at the reply. "She said she's busy at the moment." She looked at Abby. "Ye see, Kit and her husband are still newlyweds. They're usually *busy* at this time of day." Her old cheeks turned a ruddy pink.

"Not exactly newlyweds, those two just act like it," Deydie grumbled. She turned on Declan. "Get on with ye now. Go to the pub. Or the restaurant. Or head over to the fishing boats." She shooed him away with her old flabby arms. "I have the wedding planner under control."

Declan seemed a bit embarrassed. "Maybe I should wait for Kit at Quilting Central?"

"Nay," Bethia said. "Ye should do as Deydie suggests. I'm sure Kit will text ye in a bit."

"Oh. Aye." Declan nodded and lumbered away.

"Abby, in case ye're hungry, we've got biscuits and tea at Quilting Central," Bethia added.

Deydie grabbed Abby's arm and nearly dragged her to the building with a Quilting Central sign—decorated with a beautiful painted quilt block—hanging above the door.

When Bethia opened the door, the bell above it jingled. She continued to hold it open for their small group to enter. "We're so glad ye're here, Abby."

Once inside, Abby took in the sights. Tables with sewing machines took up space in the center of the large open room. Racks of fabric lined half of one of the walls. Over to one side was a library of sorts—shelves of books and a comfy couch resting nearby. At the back of the room were several longarm quilting machines. The women who were working at them stopped and stared at Abby. The rest of the room went still, too. Those at the ironing boards put down their irons and gaped. Those putting blocks on the design wall came to a standstill. Those cutting fabric halted. All chattering ceased. Abby felt like a lamb who had been brought to the lion's den for a dinner party.

"Stop yere gawking," Deydie commanded, "and get back to work. Ye act as if ye've never seen a newcomer before." Abby was surprised by the old woman's words and also comforted by them, too. When she'd met Deydie, Abby never imagined that she'd like her. But in this moment, she did.

Deydie grabbed Abby's arm once again and didn't waste any time taking her to each area of the room and introducing her to every woman there. Abby hoped there wouldn't be a pop quiz afterward as there was no way she could memorize all of their names and whatever tidbit Deydie mentioned about each one, especially since Abby was still trying to get used to Deydie's Scottish burr.

The door opened with another jingle and Deydie clapped her hands. "Oh, that's me granddaughter, Cait, and me great-grandson, Hamish." Deydie pulled Abby along to greet the woman and the boy, who looked to be about two. The boy ran to Deydie with a squeal. The old woman hugged him to her ample bosom.

When Cait made it to them, she stuck out her hand. "Hi, I'm Cait Buchanan."

Abby was surprised that Cait sounded a bit like an American. "I'm Abby Potter, the wedding planner."

"We're so glad you could visit us. Gran and the rest of the village are excited to have weddings come to our village, too." Cait leaned in conspiratorially. "Don't let them bamboozle you into doing more than you're comfortable with. I know the village has a habit of taking advantage of people who are new to town."

"Thanks. I'll keep that in mind." Abby was comforted by her words.

"So what is the plan?" Cait asked Bethia.

"We're going to show Abby all the sights," Bethia said. Deydie, surprisingly, was tossing Hamish in the air while he giggled. "Plus we want to get her input on Diana and Rory's wedding."

Cait nodded. "Well, then, Gran, let me take Hamish from ye so you can get on with the tour."

Deydie glanced over at Cait and set the boy on his feet. "I guess ye're right. Business before pleasure. Come back here and give me a *schwunch*, wee lad."

Hamish nearly tumbled trying to get back to Deydie's outstretched arms. He quickly hugged her and then went back to his mother.

Cait smiled at Abby. "I look forward to spending more time with you."

"Same here," Abby said, hoping to get Cait's backstory at a later time.

The first stop on the Gandiegow tour was at the top of the bluff. Abby was out of breath before they were even halfway up. Deydie and Bethia had no such problem. "Hurry it up," groused Deydie, and Abby wondered how a woman her age could have such pep in her step. Bethia, too. But she was much kinder and turned back occasionally to smile at Abby. The hike made Abby's mind wander between her huffing and puffing. She wondered what Conor was up to this afternoon. She also wondered if he thought about her as much as she thought about him. But then she remembered his look of frustration that she was being moved into his office. Her mind went over and over it again until they reached the ruins of what the ladies called Monadail Castle. At that point, Bethia seemed subdued and Deydie gave no explanation as to why.

"Take yere pictures." Deydie held onto and patted Bethia's hand while Abby framed several shots. She wondered how brides and grooms would feel about hiking up this practically vertical trail to get to the beautiful castle ruins. And the view of the North Sea from here was spectacular!

Outdoorsy couples would love it. But for others, maybe the village could invest in a couple of four-wheelers or sturdy golf carts for this purpose only.

Abby noticed that near the ruins there was a large mansion, nothing like the cottages at the bottom of the bluff. "Who lives there?" She lifted her phone, ready to take more pictures.

"Nay! Put that camera down!" Deydie hustled over to her. "No pictures. And never ye mind who lives there. Let's get ye to the kirk."

The trip back down the bluff was much nicer than hiking up. The Episcopal church was absolutely charming and would be the perfect spot for religious wedding ceremonies. "I assume the pastor will be available to perform weddings here?" Abby asked.

"Of course he would," Deydie answered.

"Father Andrew would be the one to decide," Bethia interjected. "Episcopal Diocese probably has certain requirements for couples to wed in the kirk."

Abby nodded and made a note to check into it. Being here also reminded her of Diana and Rory's upcoming wedding. "Where will Diana's wedding be held?"

Deydie turned and gestured. "They're getting married on the pier."

Abby looked to where she was pointing and saw a group of people building a railing around the wooden structure.

"The railing will be painted white," Bethia added. "It's going to be beautiful when it's done."

Abby agreed but thought she should mention what would be obvious to any wedding planner. "Do you have a backup plan in case the weather is bad on their wedding day?"

Deydie frowned at her. "Don't be bringing bad luck to Gandiegow by mentioning such things." But now the old woman looked worried.

"We hadn't given a thought to bad weather," Bethia said.

"I'm not trying to be a pessimist. I know from experience that it's important to be prepared for every eventuality." She glanced off into the distance and saw dark clouds. "Do storms ever catch the village off guard?"

Bethia touched Abby's arm. "We'll come up with a contingency plan. Right, Deydie?"

"Nay." Deydie said. "We'll have to speak with Diana and Rory. The weather can get especially nasty here in November. They'll have to change their minds. The old people in town won't want to stand out in the cold while they tie the knot. Besides, they should have a kirk wedding anyway!"

"Tell them that they can still have plenty of pictures taken on the pier. It is a beautiful location and will look even nicer once the improvements are completed," Abby said.

"Aye," Deydie groused, "now let's get to the restaurant."

When they arrived at Pasta & Pastries, Abby couldn't believe how good it smelled—the aroma of fresh-baked bread, garlic, and Italian sauce lingered in the air. Deydie and Bethia introduced Abby to Dominic and Claire, the owners, who seemed very friendly.

"Abby, don't worry about bringing outsiders to cater the

weddings," Deydie said. "Dominic and Claire make the best damn food in the Highlands." The old woman gave Abby a frightening smile.

"We've had no complaints." Dominic put his arm around Claire. "My wife is a pastry chef and makes wonderful wedding cakes."

"That's good to know." That solves the problem of getting the food from the parking lot to the wedding venue. Especially if the wedding receptions were upstairs.

"We have a dumb waiter," Dominic added as if he'd guessed what Abby was thinking.

"Excellent," Abby said.

"It was nice to meet you," Claire was saying as Deydie dragged Abby to the staircase that was leading up to the second floor and to the Grand Dining Room.

The space was aptly named. This was the largest indoor area that they'd seen. Abby was pretty sure that it would hold 100 to 125 people, but she'd have to check with the owners to be sure.

"This is where we're holding the wedding reception for Rory and Diana," Bethia said.

"It's a great space. Perhaps, if Rory and Diana don't want to get married at the church, you could hold the ceremony over there on the stage if the weather doesn't cooperate."

"They're getting married at the kirk!" Deydie declared.

"Regardless, we could make a kind of archway wrapped with silk flowers," Bethia suggested. "For picture-taking."

Abby thought it was best to have a professional make the trellis or maybe there was someone in the village who was a talented florist. She added that to her list, too.

Deydie looked at her watch. "Tour's over. We better get ye over to Quilting Central. Laird Hugh said he wanted ye back in time to do some planning for the bridal shows."

At Quilting Central, Declan was talking to an older man working on one of the longarm quilting machines. Abby joined them. "I believe it's time to head back to Whussendale."

Declan frowned, the first frown she'd seen from him. "Kit had to take a call so I came here. I was hoping she would make it to Quilting Central before we left. I wanted to ask her one more thing."

As he pulled out his phone—presumably to send her a text— the bell over the door tinkled, and in walked a petite, dark-haired woman.

Declan laughed. "Well, speak of the devil. Come, Abby. I'll introduce you." He lifted his head in greeting to Kit. "I was afraid ye'd flown off to Alaska."

"No. I don't leave for another two weeks," Kit stuck out her hand to Abby. "I'm Kit Armstrong. I hear from Deydie and the gang that you started up Hitched in Scotland. I love the name, by the way."

Abby shook her hand. "I'm Abby. Nice to meet you." She was puzzled. Kit had an American accent. And the fact that she had ties to Alaska? What was she doing in Scotland?

"Whussendale is a beautiful locale for weddings," Kit said.

"And Gandiegow!" Deydie injected from halfway across the room.

"Wow. She's got great hearing," Abby remarked.

"Don't I know it," Kit said, laughing. "I definitely have to watch what I say here in Gandiegow."

"I heard that, too, lass," Deydie said.

"Of course, you did," Kit shot back. Abby was surprised that Kit didn't seem afraid of Deydie in the least.

"What are your ties to Alaska?" Abby asked. "I was just there in July, helping with a double wedding."

Kit looked surprised. "Really? A double wedding? Surely,

you weren't the planner for the St. James sisters ... Tori and McKenna?"

"Oh my goodness!" Abby said. "Yes, that's the wedding. Their uncle hired Belle Weddings and I was thrilled to be sent to Sweet Home, Alaska, to manage all the arrangements. Of course, I was happy to be there the day of, also."

"It's a small world, isn't it?" Kit said in wonder. "I started my matchmaking business in Alaska—The Real Men of Alaska. I've held a couple of matchmaking events in Sweet Home. It's such a charming place." She leaned in close and half-whispered. "Scotland isn't half-bad either. I came to Scotland to expand my matchmaking services and was fortunate enough to find my own happily-ever-after." Kit looked at Declan, then. "Speaking of finding happily-ever-afters ... I know we need to finish planning for the Love Coach, but more pressing, I need an extra bachelor for our Hogmanay mixer for when my clients get here from the U.S. Of course I thought of you. You'll be around for New Year's Eve, won't you?"

"Not interested," Declan said. "You know I don't have time for anything more than I'm already doing. It's important to get my touring business off the ground. Besides, I've been having way too much fun playing the field. The way ye talk about yere socialite clients, those lassies are ready to settle down. And I'm not."

"We'll keep talking about it," Kit said firmly.

Declan's response was a grimace.

Kit turned to her. "Listen, Abby, I have an idea. I never thought about partnering with a wedding planner before. What do you think about me matching up the couples here in Scotland and then you help get them hitched?"

Abby's wheels began spinning. "I think it's a great idea." Just another avenue to get couples signed up for Hitched in Scotland beyond advertising at the bridal shows. "Let's brainstorm about it sometime after Rory and Diana's wedding."

"That works for me."

Bethia joined them. "Can I nab Abby for one more minute? Deydie and I want to give her the information about Rory and Diana's wedding."

Kit pulled out her card and handed it to her. "All my contact info is on there."

"Thanks," Abby said.

Declan nodded. "When ye're done, we'll head out." He went back to speaking to Kit.

Abby followed Bethia over to where Deydie stood by a printer. The ladies had already given her a lot of details about the upcoming wedding and she'd promised to get back to them with any other ideas that she came up with.

The printer kicked on and ejected two pieces of paper. Deydie handed them to Abby. "This one lists the itinerary and details about the day. The second piece of paper is a drawing of Rory and Diana's Thistle Wedding quilt."

"Thank you." Abby scanned the details page and noted what had been marked as completed. Really, most of the work was done, but maybe she should add the wedding shawl idea to the list ... the shawl that she and Conor were to work on. "I'll look everything over and get back to you."

"Make it soon, lassie," Deydie said.

Bethia touched Abby's arm. "It looks as if Declan and Kit are wrapping things up, too. It's been so lovely to meet you." She looked at Abby as if she were a precious granddaughter.

Which was both lovely and strange. Abby had never met her mother's mother. And of course, she didn't know her father's mother, being a test tube baby and all. Her mother had never doted on her. Never encouraged her. Only criticized. Bethia made Abby feel wanted. But to feel wanted now only felt unfamiliar and weirdly uncomfortable.

For Abby, not belonging was the norm. Her therapist had tried to help her see that what she'd experienced was not normal at all. And that nothing was wrong with Abby; that this issue wasn't Abby's issue, but her mother's. *'Your mother is to be pitied,'* the therapist had told her. *'She missed out on having a loving relationship with her only child.'*

Declan came up beside her. "Ready to go?"

Abby shook off the sadness that had filled her. "Yes. I'm ready."

She said goodbye to Deydie and Bethia—Bethia even gave her a hug. Plus, Abby waved to the others she'd met. As she and Declan walked to the parking lot, Declan asked, "Did ye have a good day? I know Deydie can be a lot but most everyone else in the village is nice."

"I took a lot of pictures. It looks like I'm going to be busy juggling responsibilities between the two towns. I'm not complaining. Being busy is a good thing. It's better than being idle and bored, at least to my way of thinking." Abby realized that she'd have to learn to drive on the opposite side of the road here. If she was to split her time between the two villages, she couldn't bother others to chauffeur her back and forth.

"Then ye're going to love it here in Scotland," Declan declared. "It seems as if something is always going on."

But Abby wasn't feeling as sure. Conor wasn't happy with her. If he continued to be irritated, then sharing an office with him, collaborating with him, and traveling with him to the bridal shows, let alone working the shows with him, wasn't going to be fun. So loving Scotland? It didn't exactly seem to be in the cards. "We'll see," was her only reply.

Declan handed her his phone. "Choose what you'd like to listen to for the trip back to Whussendale."

"Thanks." She chose a Lewis Capaldi album and hit play.

"Good choice," Declan said. "One of Scotland's own home-grown talents."

Back at home, she usually listened to Christian radio. Her mother wouldn't approve, if she knew; she didn't believe in religion. But Abby felt lucky to have stumbled upon a Christian station one day when she was scanning for something to listen to. The songs on the Christian radio stations were uplifting, and on most days, she needed something to give her a boost. Especially when dealing with her mother or when Aaron was trying to minimize Abby's love of being a wedding planner. He kept telling her that she could quit her job after they were married. He didn't understand that being a wedding planner was her passion. Gave her life meaning. She liked creating the perfect day for her couples. "We don't need your income," Aaron had said. "Besides, wedding planning isn't a career; it's only a job." Maybe she shouldn't have left Aaron at the altar, but every day since, she was glad she didn't have to justify her *career* choice to anyone but herself.

While Declan drove, she was able to enjoy the scenery out the window. The sheep. The horses. The hairy cows, *no, coos.* The fields and rolling hills. The patches of forest here and there. Scotland really was a beautiful place.

Suddenly, there was a pop, and a *blump, bump, bump.* "Did we just blow a tire?" she asked.

Declan maneuvered the car to the side of the road. "I'm afraid so." She thought how lucky they were to be able to pull onto the grass when just a moment ago there had been a long stretch of stone walls on either side of the road.

Declan got out and she did, too, following him to the back of the vehicle to see the flat tire.

He opened the back door and frowned. "There's no spare in the boot."

"What are we going to do?" She wondered if her AAA card would be good here in Scotland.

"I'll get someone to help us." He pulled out his phone saying, "Last week, I took the spare to McGuinty's auto shop in Lios to have it patched. I got so busy afterward that I forgot to pick it up the next day."

She opened her mouth to speak but he put his hand up. "Hold up while I make this call." He scrolled through his contacts, selected one, and put the phone to his ear. A few seconds later, Declan said, "Hey. I've got a flat tire. We're about twenty or so miles out of Gandiegow. Can ye pick up the spare from McGuinty's and bring it to me?" He listened for a moment, then said, "Thanks." Another moment. "No, there are no farmhouses nearby. I'll be fine right here."

But at that moment, it began to rain ... hard. Abby wished for one of those uplifting songs right now because she was beginning to wonder if the sudden rainstorm was a sign of bad things to come.

Chapter 7

WITH THE SPARE TIRE in the back of his uncle's vehicle, Conor drove through the rain to get to Declan. It gave him time to think about the predicament the laird had put him in. He didn't want to share his office with Abby or any other female. He only wanted to be left alone. Correction: Needed to be left alone. If he had to put a positive spin on things ... well, Abby did smell great. But that only made Conor feel more uncomfortable, knowing he was stuck with her. Which brought to the forefront that more and more, he was having trouble denying that he was drawn to her.

At least one good thing happened today; the laird had returned and finally listened to his ideas to improve the wool mill. Thank goodness Magnus was off taking a break at the time or else he would've grumbled through every proposal. It wasn't lost on Conor that Hugh hadn't given him the go-ahead to make any of the changes. But he had taken the list with him back to his office and said he would think about it. Conor decided to be optimistic. He'd wait until Hugh made up his mind before telling Uncle Magnus about the discussion.

An hour later, when he pulled up to Declan's vehicle, Conor saw that someone else was sitting in the passenger seat. Someone familiar. The person who seemed to be consuming his thoughts of late. It was Abby. *Abby!* What was she doing with Declan? Declan had a reputation for attracting women from every shire in the area. Conor suspected it had something to do with Declan being *dreamy,* or so he'd overheard many women of the village describe Whussendale's longtime resident.

Well, Conor wouldn't give a *shite* as to whether Abby and Declan were together. She certainly was a fast mover, though, to have put two men on the hook in so short a time. She'd certainly knocked him for a loop, if he was being honest, and now she apparently was making a play for Declan, too. He wondered if she had insisted that Declan drive her to Gandiegow. But then Conor remembered. He'd been the one to turn down the laird when asked to go to Gandiegow earlier today.

Well, the laird hadn't said a damn word about chauffeuring the American lass!

Conor had to rein in his anger and remind himself that he wasn't interested in her or in any other random woman.

Reluctantly, he waved to Declan as the man exited his car. Conor got out of his vehicle, too, and went to the boot to retrieve the tire.

"Hey, thanks for this," Declan said, taking the tire from Conor.

Conor knew he was going to act impulsively right now, and he just couldn't stop himself. "I'm going to take Abby back to Whussendale while ye change the tire. The laird needs her back for, uh, a planning session or something."

Declan looked at him a little strangely but then acquiesced with a nod. "I'll see ye back at the village."

Conor stalked over to Abby's side of the car to give her the news, but she was already out of the vehicle before he got there. "Grab yere bag and whatever else you have with ye. You'll be headed back to Whussendale with me." He sounded a bit possessive but there was nothing he could do about that.

Abby stopped and stared at him for a long moment as if looking at a complicated puzzle that needed to be assembled.

Conor walked back to his uncle's vehicle and opened the door for her. He would stay silent on the drive back to the village, he decided, because who knew what he might say or do next? Something about this woman got under his skin.

He slid into the driver's seat and started the car. "Are ye buckled?"

"Yes," she said.

"Good." But not a minute later, after he'd turned the car around and was driving away, he opened his big, fat mouth again. "Tell me the real reason why the laird put ye in my office. Was it yere idea or is the laird and his missus playing matchmaker again?" The second he said it, he realized his tone was less than friendly, so he added, "Please."

She frowned at him and said nothing. He was pretty sure that she was done talking to him. But surprisingly, she said, "Take your grievances up with the laird. You heard him. It was his idea; not mine." She stared out the window. "If it's any consolation, I don't want to share an office with you either." She glanced over at him but quickly looked away. "Just so you know, a desk is being delivered for me tomorrow."

But he was hung up on the first thing she'd said. He opened his mouth to ask *Why don't you want to share an office with me?* He shouldn't care about the *why* of it. The bigger question in his mind was the turmoil that was roiling through him. Why did *he* care what she thought of him anyway? *Aye,* she was attractive; anyone could see that. But he wasn't in the market for a relationship. Not even a casual fling. Period.

The other question that was nagging him, and not for the first time either, was why the laird was pushing him and Abby together. Hugh wasn't his aunt Davinia, who had a reputation for playing matchmaker. She'd even tried, one time, to set him up with Tally, the bookkeeper. But Conor had shut that nonsense down fast.

Regardless, Conor would have to make an effort with the wedding planner. At least to get along with her. But he'd have to keep his hormones in check, which might be the biggest hurdle of all, because he certainly felt drawn to her.

He glanced over at Abby. He didn't like how she was looking at him right now, as if he were the most disagreeable man on the planet. If that's what she really believed, then no wonder she didn't want to share an office with him. "I understand how ye're feeling. Ye're stuck with me, and I'm stuck with you."

"Then shouldn't we try to make the most of it?" asked Abby.

"Yeah, ye're right. When I think about it, I guess it makes sense that the laird wanted ye to plant yereself in my office. Since we are to work together. Actually, Magnus shares the office, too." Though his uncle never spent any real time in there. When Conor arrived back in Whussendale, Magnus had turned over the management of the orders for the weaving building so Conor could keep track of inventory and costs. His uncle said the numbers made his eyes hurt but Conor knew that it wasn't just his eyesight. The stress of keeping the books was daunting, especially since the weaving part of the mill wasn't as efficient and profitable as it once was. He hoped that would all change.

From nowhere, Conor had a flash of what it might be like for him and Abby to put their heads together while working in close proximity. An unfamiliar heat rose in his chest. He felt oddly uncomfortable as his imagination went into hyperdrive and got the best of him. He had the crazy urge to pull her to his side of the vehicle and kiss her.

He missed what Abby was saying. He forced himself to quit fantasizing about something that would never happen. "I'm sorry, what?"

"I thought we could use this car ride to get started," Abby said. "A meeting of sorts. Since we're *stuck together*."

She'd used his words against him and it made him smile. She was smart. He liked that in a ... *person*. Aye, it was better if he looked upon her as a generic human, no gender, and put aside that she was female. Woman. Attractive. That should keep his mind from wandering down paths that it shouldn't.

"Good idea. A meeting. Just so ye know, I've pulled together twenty or so tartan samples for the wedding shawls."

"Hmm," Abby said. "That seems like too many choices. How about you pick the top five to seven tartans?"

"Seven, then," Conor said. "And if the couple wants a custom tartan?"

She shrugged. "They'll have to pay for it. We'll make it an add-on in the pricelist."

For the rest of the trip, Abby took notes as they discussed the cost of time and materials in making the shawls.

Finally, she said, "This looks good. Knowing the cost of the shawls will help me price out the weddings in Whussendale."

Suddenly the scope of the work involved in bringing weddings to the village hit Conor. Abby had quite the undertaking to fulfill—a mountain of responsibilities—and he could now see that she was going to need all the help she could get. He had to suck it up and stop being an obstacle to bringing the wedding venture to fruition. Especially since she was doing the hard work and thinking through all the angles. He sure hoped Hugh was paying her well. Abby, after all, had left behind her country and everything she knew to come to Scotland and be their wedding planner.

He would shape up. He would be willing to travel with her as the laird wanted. Between now and then, Conor would promote Tavon, who had been apprenticing in the weaver's shop for some time now. He was a capable man and Magnus thought the world of Tavon, too. Conor would also make sure that Tavon looked after his uncle while he was gone. Before the first bridal show, Conor would have everything arranged to make the transition as smooth as possible. He would shift his priorities and his mindset. By the time he had to leave his uncle and the weaving building, Conor would be okay with it all. The wedding shawls. His time away. And even Abby.

He glanced over and noticed that she wore neither an engagement ring nor a wedding band. He wondered if she had a beau back in the States. Or maybe someone here in Scotland? Maybe that's the reason she decided to move to his homeland. "About us traveling together ..." he let his words trail off as he wasn't sure how to broach the subject of whether she was attached or not.

She beat him to the punch, though, with a question of her own. "Will your girlfriend be okay with you and me doing the bridal shows together? Also, there's the issue of the women at the bridals shows who will be fawning over you in your kilt. You'll have to prepare your girlfriend for that, too."

"No girlfriend. No attachments. I'm the most single man in all of Scotland." And he intended to stay that way, though the appeal seemed to be fading somewhat. Probably because he could still smell her flowery perfume. Or shampoo? Or was he changing his mind because he was spending more time with her? "Besides, I doubt there will be any fawning going on." He glanced over and was surprised to see that Abby was scanning his person.

"Oh, believe me," she started and then chuckled. Her laugh

sounded like the tinkling of the *Heilan' coo* wind chimes outside his cottage window, something frivolous he'd hung there when he first arrived. His father had something similar—his were sheep chimes—outside his wool shop in Glasgow when Conor was a kid.

She continued. "I guarantee women will be fawning. Look at you! You better prepare yourself for them to be pawing you, too."

He wanted to ask if that went for her, also. Probably not.

But hadn't she just checked him out? Though he didn't want a relationship, he wouldn't mind if she pawed him a wee bit. And the thought that she was attracted to him heated up his insides as if she'd put fresh tinder on the fire. Another thought crossed his mind, making him uneasy, especially since he was taking a break from women. He really shouldn't be thinking about it, but he couldn't help himself.

He wouldn't mind pawing *her* a wee bit, too.

Abby probably shouldn't have warned him about how the women at the bridal shows would be all over him. She definitely shouldn't have gawked at him as if she'd never seen a ruggedly handsome man before. Her phone rang and saved her. But then she glanced at the screen. "It's my mother." Conor undoubtedly thought she was awful because she didn't mask her tone, not even a little.

"You should take the call," Conor said. "At least let yere mum know that ye're in Scotland." His voice was filled with reprimand.

But he didn't have the right to judge her. Except he probably wished he could speak to his mother one more time.

Reluctantly, Abby took the call. "Hello, Mother."

"I told you not to call me that. My name's Joann. Where are you? I stopped by your apartment today but you weren't home." Her mother's tone was one that Abby had heard often—one of accusation. Accusing her *of what* depended on the day or whim. *Joann's* other natural tone was disappointment.

"I'm … I'm in Scotland," Abby confessed.

"What?" Her screech hurt Abby's ear. "Why are you in Scotland?" This was exactly what she expected from Joann. "Once again, I'm sure you made some kind of irrational and ill-fated decision. First, you refused to pursue a career in medicine or law, and instead you got a degree in anthropology. Abigail, you were smart enough to do anything! Then, instead of continuing on to get your PhD so you could teach at the university level, you made the asinine decision to keep working at that wedding planning company, which was only supposed to be a temporary, part-time job while you were in college. Most recently, *daughter*—" she made it sound like a dirty word "—you dumped Aaron at the altar. And now this! Abigail, what are you thinking?"

What Abby was thinking was that she shouldn't have answered her phone. She bet Conor had heard every word shouted at her over the airwaves. "I needed a change of scenery." Actually, the scenery had nothing to do with her decision, though it was pretty damned beautiful! It was only because Scotland was far, far away from her mother! And from Aaron, too.

"When will you be home from this *vacation*?" Joann made *vacation* sound caustic and untenable.

"I'm not on vacation, *Mom*." Abby knew her mother hated it when she used such a familiar endearment. "I saw this ad online and I took a job here. End of story." She tried to sound confident and firm, but inside she felt like a shrinking violet.

"A job? What job?"

"You know I'm a wedding planner. Now, I'm working for a town that wants to hold destination weddings. It's beautiful here," she added lamely.

"What? Have you gone round the bend?" This was another of Joann's *oldies but goodies.* Along with, *"Have you lost your mind?"*

Abby had no immediate response. She knew this was hard on her mother. Joann was meticulous about everything she did. She never would've made a split-second decision, the way Abby was prone to do. Joann Eileen Potter ran the top fertility clinic in St. Louis. She had everything under control, 24/7. She'd never been a loving mother and Abby often wondered why Joann had her in the first place. The only thing that Joann had true feelings for was her cat, Romeo. Romeo hated Abby ... and Abby had to admit that the feeling was mutual. The only time Romeo didn't hiss at Abby was when she had to take care of him while Joann went to a conference out of town.

When Abby was a child, she used to fantasize about her real parents coming to get her. From where Abby stood, the only logical reason that Abby ended up with Joann was that there'd been a mix-up at the hospital and Joann had gotten the wrong baby.

Joann cleared her throat—just another of her habits to get Abby to focus on her again.

Abby sighed. "No, Mother, I haven't lost my mind. I made the decision to come to Whussendale because I believe I can help them."

"Abigail, it's time to grow up. You're nearly thirty." Yes, *it's time to grow up* was another phrase Abby had heard for her whole life. "What do you have to say for yourself?"

"I have to go."

"Not before you tell me where you're staying?" Joann said.

"Whussendale, Scotland. Take care, Mother." With that, Abby hung up.

She slipped her phone into her bag. A moment later, her phone rang again. Abby didn't look at the screen. She knew it was Joann calling her again so she let it go to voicemail.

"Are you all right?" Conor asked.

"I'm fine." She could feel his gaze on her. She should tell him to keep his eyes on the road but was afraid the tremor in her voice—for surely there would be one—would give away the emotions roiling through her. Also, there was no way she was going to glance in his direction, because without a doubt, she'd see pity in his eyes. And he'd see her reddened cheeks. He'd know for sure, then, how embarrassed she was of her mother.

Conor reached over and squeezed her hand. "It's okay. We all have relatives that can drive us a bit crazy. Ye've met my Uncle Magnus, right? He and his old cronies in the village don't believe in progress. They give me grief for wanting to improve our processes. What they don't realize is that life is always changing. They want to keep everything the same."

She squeezed his hand back, hoping to comfort him, the way he was comforting her. But it was as if that small gesture had flipped a switch and he dropped her hand. She wished he hadn't. She liked holding on to him in that way. It made her feel not so lonely in her very lonely world.

"Keep your chin up, Abby Potter. Living in Whussendale will fix everything," he proclaimed.

"Is that what Whussendale has done for you?" she braved. "Fix everything?"

Conor laughed. "Not exactly. I guess I was just entertaining a bit of wishful thinking."

"Thanks for trying to cheer me up," she said honestly. "I

really appreciate it." But Abby was worried about the next time she spoke to her mother. There would be repercussions for hanging up the way that she had. At least she couldn't get grounded like when she was a little girl. Or go without supper, which happened more times than she could count. And the worst her mother could do: *the silent treatment.* But surely, it wouldn't have the same devastating effect on her since she was here and her mother was back in St. Louis. She couldn't take much solace in that, though, as her mother had always been creative when it came to punishing her. Abby just didn't know what to expect next.

For the rest of the trip, they both remained silent. Conor seemed to be mulling over what he'd said to her. And she was trying to come up with a way to get her mood out of the rut her mother had put her in.

Conor wasn't sure why he'd said that *Whussendale would fix everything.* Had he been directing that comment toward Abby, or had he really been directing it toward himself? He didn't believe in fate or destiny. Or that the village had magical powers to make his world right again. He did, however, believe in the Almighty to change a miserable life into something better. But a change like that could take a lifetime and Conor was an impatient man.

It was dark by the time Whussendale came into sight. He glanced over at Abby again. "Do ye want me to take ye up to the castle to meet with Sophie and Hugh, or do ye need to stop by yere cottage first?"

"My cottage, please. To freshen up," she said. "I'll text Hugh after I finish writing up a few more notes about Gandiegow."

As Conor pulled into the crescent-shaped lane where the cottages were, he instantly recognized the man sitting on his front stoop, although he hadn't seen his older brother in a year. The Irish setter lying beside his brother was new to him, however.

Abby was eyeing his brother, too, which wasn't a surprise; most females fancied Kieran, and couldn't help but stare. Kieran was generally known to be the good-looking one in the family. She glanced over at Conor but he didn't give any explanation. Instead, he parked and hopped out before she could say a word. "What are ye doing here, big brother? Why didn't ye call first?" Conor outstretched his hand but it was the dog who came over first and greeted him with its tail wagging.

Kieran stood and wiped the dust from his pants. "I forgot my charger. Who is that with ye?" Abby was just now getting out of the vehicle.

Conor wasn't thrilled that his brother had noticed her that quickly, but he couldn't exactly blame him because Abby was *verra* attractive. "Abby, come here." She came to him and stood by his side. "Abby Potter, meet my brother, Kieran Masterson. Abby is Whussendale's new wedding planner."

Abby stuck out her hand and shook Kieran's. Conor loved his brother but didn't like the way Abby was ogling him, a typical female response. Kieran looked like their Irish mother— dark red hair and piercing blue eyes that always had a twinkle of mischief in them. His brother might be considered the fun one, but sometimes it wasn't fun to be Kieran's brother.

Kieran gave Abby an approving smile. "I hope ye're being good to my baby brother. I'm eight years his elder and it's my job to look after him."

There were all kinds of problems with what Kieran had just said. First, he and Abby weren't together and would never be a couple so Abby *being good* to him didn't make any sense at all.

Secondly, Kieran had never really looked after Conor, at least when it would've meant the most to him. Shortly after Mum left Dad to return to Ireland when Conor was only ten, Kieran wasted no time in signing up for the military. His brother left him all alone to deal with their Da's sadness over his broken marriage and broken heart. Conor often wondered if Da's car accident eight years later had been an *accident* at all. Maybe he got tired of living a half-life and pining over the mother of his children, who never returned home.

Instead, Conor kept quiet on all fronts. He tamped down those old feelings of abandonment—first his mum, then Kieran, and finally his da. He could throw Morag in the mix now for good measure, too, if he really wanted to succumb to being maudlin. As an alternative, though, he pivoted to a safe subject. "What's yere dog's name?"

"Dublin. She's a good girl," Kieran said. The dog obediently ran to Kieran's side and sat like a well-trained pet.

"Great name. Where did you get her?" Conor asked. He'd been thinking of getting a dog himself. A companion. Someone to greet him when he returned to the cottage for lunch or when he arrived home each night after work.

"I got her from SSPCA. She's a rescue. Two years old."

Conor turned to Abby. "Kieran is in the military." Conor said it proudly because he *was* proud of his brother for serving his country. But that feeling of pride was always tangled up with Kieran's letting him down ... and leaving him behind.

"Aye, the military," Kieran said. "That's why I'm here to see ye. I'm shipping out on a short deployment and I need a babysitter for Dublin." He laughed. "I figured ye'd do it. Mum used to say that yere name means *lover of hounds*."

Conor hated it when Kieran talked about their mum. She'd died in Ireland not long after walking out on them. *Hit by a bus in Galway.* Conor was a little fuzzy on exactly how long she'd been gone, but he did know that she'd never contacted him once after she'd left. The memory of her walking out with her suitcase in her hand still haunted him. If Conor thought about it rationally, Kieran would have known their mum better than he did. He guessed that was the reason Kieran seemed to bring her up every time that they talked.

At that moment, Dublin came over and nuzzled Conor's hand. Maybe the dog sensed that he was feeling a little down and off kilter. Automatically, Conor scratched the dog behind the ears. "Is the mutt house-trained?"

"Of course. But beware. She likes to hog the bed." Kieran smiled over at Abby before looking back at Conor. "Ye'll do it, then?"

"Aye. We should get along famously," Conor said.

"I should be back in three to four weeks. I don't have an exact date. But as I said, it's a short tour."

Conor knew better than to ask Kieran where he would be stationed or question anything else about his brother's assignment. Ever since he was a kid, Conor had been shut down quickly when he asked his brother where he was going, so he certainly wasn't going to ask now. But he could say one thing. "Ye'll be careful?" He was always concerned for his brother's safety.

"Aye. Ye know I will." Kieran pounded Conor on the back in a brotherly fashion.

"Keir, do ye want to come in for a bit?" Conor asked.

"Nay. I thought I'd better say hello to Uncle Magnus and Uncle Willoughby before I go. I assume the wool brothers are in their same respective spots at the mill?"

"Aye. Nothing changes with those two," Conor said.

"I'll be back in a few minutes. It was nice to meet you, Abby. As I said earlier, take care of my brother for me." Conor could say that Abby wasn't his keeper, but Kieran had already turned away. Dublin trotted after him, but Conor called her back. Neither Magnus nor Willoughby would want a dog near the wool.

"So … that's your brother," Abby said.

"Aye. He looks like our mum. I take after our da," Conor said.

"I assume your brother isn't married or in a significant relationship, then?"

"What makes ye ask that?" Conor was irritated with how forward Abby was being. It must be the *American* in her. Most women would have at least disguised their questions about Kieran's relationship status, instead of asking outright like Abby had. Was she lusting over Kieran like every other woman in the world? Had she no shame?

Abby reached down and patted Dublin. "No real reason. I figured that if your brother was married or had a partner, he probably would've left the dog with them, right?" she said matter-of-factly.

Yeah, that made sense. "Nay, he's not married." Kieran had done well to dodge the marriage bullet. Conor figured it also had to do with his girlfriend dying while they were in secondary school. A car accident was all his da would tell him. "But my brother never lacks for female companionship." Conor wasn't sure why he was warning Abby off Kieran; his brother really was a good guy.

She hugged the dog before running a hand down Dublin's back. "I've always wanted a dog. My mother wouldn't allow it. She used to say, *There's no way I'm going to have a slobbering, flea-bitten canine in my house.*"

"Is yere mum a cat person?"

"Yes, unfortunately. She's had various cats over the years."

"Cats aren't yere thing, huh?"

"First, I'm allergic, though that never stopped Mother from having at least one feline around when I was growing up. She said that having a cat would help me get over my allergies."

"And secondly?" he asked, curious to know more about her.

"Secondly, Romeo, her current cat, hates me. Sometimes, he looks at me as if he has some vendetta against me, for reasons unknown." She shuddered and laughed sardonically. "Ridiculous. I know. But that cat likes to trip me at least once whenever I'm around him. He's definitely out to get me."

Conor grinned. "Paranoid much?"

"Yeah. It's possible I'm anthropomorphizing Romeo and giving him too much credit." She shrugged. "I better get inside and finish my notes. I expect that Sophie and Hugh have a lot for me to do."

"Aye," Conor said, walking Abby to her door. "And I better get back to the weaver's building. Magnus is probably fit to be tied that I was gone so long."

A concerned expression came over her face.

"Don't worry. My uncle is always up in arms about something or other."

"Except, I might be the reason this time."

"A flat tire is not yere fault."

She smiled. "Okay. You're right. Thanks for bringing me back." She seemed sincere.

He wondered if she was as hesitant to part from him as he was from her. Which was a strange feeling for him to have. Especially since he didn't want to have a female in his life for the foreseeable future. Possibly forever. "Any time ye have a flat tire, I'm yere man." *Dumb ass.* Why had he said such a thing?

She laughed. "Thanks. I'll keep that in mind." As she opened her cottage door, Dublin tore inside.

"Dublin. Come!" Conor said from the doorway. But the dog

wasn't listening. She immediately jumped up on Abby's bed and plopped down as if this was her domain. She looked quite pleased with herself, and not ready in the least to leave Abby's quarters.

There's some irony in that.

Conor stepped into the cottage—not to climb into bed—but to get his brother's dog back.

Chapter 8

ABBY CALMLY WENT to the open shelf where the glasses, bowls, and plates sat. "Conor, may I offer you something to drink?"

He looked a little taken aback, probably because she wasn't shocked or upset that the dog had made herself at home on her bed. He nodded to her. "Water would be great."

"You got it." While she was at it, she pulled down a bowl and made Dublin a drink as well. She set the dog's dish on the floor first, before handing Conor his glass.

As Abby took her first sip of water, Dublin jumped off the bed and ran to her bowl. She slurped so loudly that it made Abby laugh. "Not much on table manners, is she?"

"Not much on *any* manners, as far as I can see," Conor said.

"She seems to do as Kieran wishes," Abby defended.

"Yeah. Most women do," Conor said begrudgingly.

"Makes sense," Abby said honestly. Kieran was a good-looking man, and she imagined he was a heck of a flirt, too, because of that smile he gave her.

Dublin boldly glanced over at Conor before heading back to her place on Abby's bed. A trail of residual water followed her, possibly some drool, too, dripping from her muzzle.

Conor grabbed the roll of paper towels and began cleaning up the mess. "I'll have to get her leash from Kieran." He frowned over at the dog.

Abby threw Conor a bone. "I expect, in no time at all, that Dublin will be following you around like a puppy. She seems to like you a lot, too." As he wiped up the wet spot on the bed, Dublin licked Conor's hand.

"*Like me* ... aye. *Listens to me* ... not so much." He dropped the soiled paper towels in the garbage can. "I expect I'll have to invest in some dog biscuits to make her behave."

Dublin's ears perked up at *dog biscuits*. She jumped down, ran over to Conor, and plopped her behind down as if she'd performed this trick for him a hundred times. She stared up at him with puppy eyes, waiting patiently for a treat.

"I think you've said the magic words." Abby saw Conor glancing at his watch. "Do you need to check in with your uncle? Dublin can hang out with me while I make my notes on Gandiegow. It'll also give you a couple more minutes to visit with your brother before he leaves."

Conor gazed at her for a long second before answering. "If ye're sure."

"Of course I'm sure. Ms. Dublin will be no trouble at all." The dog glanced over at Abby first before stretching out in front of Conor and then lying down. Apparently, being a dog was exhausting. Or perhaps Dublin thought humans were boring.

But before Conor could leave, there was a tap at the door. Since Conor was closest, he answered it. Kieran was back with a dog bed, a couple of bags of dog food, and a leash. Of course, no one had to inform the dog that they had company, as she tore to her master and plopped her behind down again in front of him this time.

"That didn't take long," Conor said.

"Aye. Sophie said Uncle Willoughby went home early. She suspected he was going to bed early so I didn't bother him."

"And Magnus?" Conor asked.

"He was headed out the door. It sounds like he had a hot date with Coira," Kieran said, laughing. "How long's that been going on?"

"It's hard to say," Conor said. "Coira is in charge of the quilting retreats here. He spends a lot of time with her these days."

Kieran nodded. "I'll have to meet her when I get back."

Since Abby was curious about Conor, it made sense that she wanted to know more about his brother. She directed her next comment to Kieran. "Conor said he spent his holidays here as a boy. Did you work here, too?"

"No. Not really," Kieran said. "Con spent a lot of time here, according to Uncle Magnus. When I was a boy, I mostly worked in my father's kilt shop in Glasgow. I never had the privilege to learn much about the weaving business like my baby brother." Kieran seemed sad about that. Abby wanted to tell him that it was never too late. Before she could, Kieran handed Conor a piece of paper. "I know ye don't really need this, but it's a list of things to do for my girl, Dublin."

Dublin rubbed her body against her master's leg and was rewarded with another good scratching behind her ears.

"Follow me to the car?" Kieran asked his brother.

Conor opened his mouth, but his phone dinged before he could answer. He glanced at the message, looked Abby's way, then frowned.

"What have I done now?" she asked directly. Her response made Kieran laugh.

But Conor wasn't. "It's Hugh. We're needed at the castle."

For a second, she thought he meant himself and Dublin, but that was silly, as they surely didn't know that Conor would be watching the dog for the foreseeable future. Plus, he was staring at her. "Bring along yere notebook and things." Yes, he definitely hadn't meant the dog.

"Did the text say why we're needed at the castle?" She assumed she was to meet up with them at Hugh's office to go over things.

"Dinner," was Conor's one-word reply. A second ding rang out from his phone. Conor read the note before looking over at Kieran this time. "We'll walk ye to yere car, but first, we have to make a quick stop at the weaver's building. Ye don't mind, do ye? It'll only take a second."

"That's fine."

The four of them, which included the dog, walked to the weaver's building. It had already grown dark outside. She waited with Kieran and Dublin while Conor ran inside alone.

"American, huh?" Kieran asked.

"Yes. I'm from St. Louis, Missouri," she answered.

"Well, I, for one, am glad Conor's found someone. He doesn't do well on his own. None of us Mastersons do," Kieran said with more seriousness than she'd seen from him.

She opened her mouth to argue with him—that she and Conor weren't together—but Conor reappeared, carrying a large paper bag. "Ye ready?"

"Aye," Kieran said, laying a hand on his brother's shoulder. "What do ye have there?"

"Samples," Conor said. "The laird requested them."

As they walked to the car, Abby mulled over the thought that

Kieran had gotten it all wrong. She and Conor weren't a thing. She wanted to say something but the brothers were talking and she couldn't find an opening to correct Kieran. Also, it would be awkward to do so, especially since Conor was here.

When they arrived at the car, Kieran squatted down and spoke to his dog. "You be a good lass for yere Uncle Conor and Aunt Abby." He glanced up at them and winked. Abby felt more embarrassed than before. If she knew Kieran better, and if Conor was somewhere else, she would've set him straight. Instead, she gawked at Conor, trying to use telepathy to get him to correct his brother. But he wouldn't meet her gaze.

At least Conor was frowning. "Yere dog will be fine. *I* will take good care of her." Emphasis on the singular *I*. Apparently, no *Abby* needed!

Kieran put out his hand and the brothers shook, then half-hugged as men were known to do. "God willing, I'll see ye in three to four weeks."

"Aye," Conor said. "Three to four weeks."

Kieran got in his car. Conor held the leash tight to keep a lunging Dublin from chasing the vehicle as it pulled away.

"It's okay, girl," Conor said soothingly. "Yere da will be back. In the meantime, would ye like to meet a couple of fellows ... the Wallace and the Bruce?"

Dublin looked up at him and cocked her head to the side as if she understood she was going to make some new doggy friends.

"Let's go," Conor said as he and Dublin prepared to take off.

Abby reached out and pulled him to a stop. "Hold up."

Conor came to a standstill and waited.

Abby let go, dropping her hand. "Why didn't you say something?"

"About what?"

"You know what. Your brother thought that we were a couple."

Conor turned a pair of understanding eyes on her. "Listen. There's something ye need to know about Kieran. It's best not to protest when it comes to things like that."

"Why?"

"Because he'll dig in more. His teasing can be relentless. It's best to pretend that it doesn't faze either of us."

"Are you sure? He totally has the wrong idea."

"Ye've got to develop a thick skin, lassie. Or else ye won't survive here in Scotland."

She didn't like it, but she nodded anyway. "Thick skin. Got it."

"Now, can we head up to the castle, like the laird requested?"

"Yes." She was surprised that he didn't seem angry or annoyed that he wasn't able to get back to work right now. She wasn't sure what had happened to cause this change of heart. But she wasn't going to question it. A willing Conor was better than a stonewalling Conor.

Dublin entertained them by running zigzags on the lane leading to Kilheath. Abby was thankful for using the gym in the last year as she had no problem jogging alongside Conor. She'd never been a gym person before, but both her mother and Aaron had insisted that she needed to stay in shape if she were to fit into her wedding dress ... the same wedding dress that no one saw, besides the Lyft driver who picked her up at the venue and whisked her away.

Dublin arrived at Kilheath Castle first. Sophie must've been waiting for them because when she opened the door, the Wallace and the Bruce tore out like a couple of tornadoes. Oh, how those dogs made Abby laugh! Instead of the Wallace and the Bruce greeting the humans, the boys introduced themselves to Dublin with a couple of yips and lots of wagging of tails. Dublin seemed to like them instantly, too.

Sophie was chuckling as Dublin chased the boys around the grounds. "Come in, ye two. Wallace! Bruce! Come, boys!" She hollered the last bit. Dublin chased them all the way indoors. "Conor, Abby, we've got tea set up in the parlor. Follow me."

As Abby stepped through the doorway, she felt a light touch to her back as if Conor was guiding her. But in the next second, the touch was gone. She turned around to see if he was still there. He was, with no sign on his face that he'd made contact with her back. Which made her wonder, *Did I imagine it? No. It was probably wishful thinking on my part.*

When they entered the parlor, Abby saw that a small, four-person table had been erected for an intimate setting. Once again, she couldn't help but look at Conor. He glanced over at her, too, making her wonder what he was thinking. Was he, too, wondering if their knees would graze each other under the table while they ate? *Gads!* Why was she thinking so much about what Conor would or would not do?

"Hello, Conor. Hello, Abby," Hugh said cheerfully. "I have something for ye both." He handed them each a sheet of paper. "It's the schedule of the bridal shows ye'll be attending in the foreseeable future."

Abby scanned the paper and saw five events, one for each month except for December. Once the wedding venture got going, she might have to send someone else in her place, especially if Whussendale had a wedding scheduled during a bridal show weekend. But she was getting ahead of herself and decided to cool her jets. "This looks good. Thank you."

Hugh handed her a folder next. "All your hotel arrangements have been made. Conor, ye'll be able to help Abby set up the booth, won't ye?"

"Aye. It'll be no problem," Conor said.

"And ye'll wear yere kilt?" Sophie prodded. "Whussendale is counting on ye to represent Hitched in Scotland."

Abby thought she saw Conor start to roll his eyes, but then he schooled his features.

"Aye. I'll wear my kilt." But he looked troubled. "I'm going to train Tavon to take my place in the weaver's building when I'm gone. But I am concerned about what happens if one of the weaving machines goes down while I'm away. Ye know, don't ye, that while I was at the conference, Magnus called me several times so we could talk through the issues that the machines were having. And that was for only two days." Conor glanced at his sheet. "I expect I'll be away more than that for the bridal shows."

"Och, 'tis all been arranged," Hugh said. "George Campbell, Gandiegow's tinker, has agreed to fill in for ye, if need be, where it concerns the machines."

Conor nodded, but he didn't seem convinced.

"I thank ye for thinking of Tavon. That's a good call," Hugh added.

Mrs. McNabb, the cook, clad in her apron, walked into the parlor, carrying a tray. The three dogs were the first to greet her and to find out what smelled so good. Hugh rushed over and retrieved it from her. "Sorry. I didn't expect ye to bring this in. I planned to do it."

"It's no problem, laird," Mrs. McNabb said kindly. "Let me know if ye need anything else. Come on dogs. I'll have a treat or two for ye in the kitchen."

The four of them sat. Abby was surprised when Hugh bowed his head and said grace again. Did that mean that he did it at all meals? Interesting. She probably should've bowed her head, too, but she was intrigued by the ritual. Yes, she liked to listen to Christian music, but religion in her mother's household was nonexistent. Abby had been fascinated with religion since she was a little girl. At the library, she would read Bible stories. When having sleepovers at friends' houses, she would partake in the customary prayers before bedtime. She often thought of religion as if it were magic and wondered how it worked at the heart of it. She glanced over to see if Conor bowed his head, too, while Hugh said the simple prayer of thanks.

"Amen," Hugh said, which was chorused by Sophie and Conor in unison. Abby felt a bit awkward about not taking part as they had, but no one seemed to judge her for not doing so.

While they ate, they chatted about the weather, the coos Hugh was purchasing, and a bit about the upcoming bridal show in Inverness.

Then Sophie said "Abby, you've got to tell me what ye thought of Gandiegow, my hometown? Did ye get to witness Deydie whacking anyone with her broom?" She chuckled before reaching over and squeezing Hugh's hand. "I miss them, ye know. The next time Abby goes to Gandiegow, I want to go with her if I can."

Hugh squeezed back. "That's a fine idea."

Once again, Abby was struck by these two lovebirds. She and Aaron had never behaved like them. They'd never shared an intimate moment or a loving gaze, or squeezed each other's hands the way these two did. She glanced at Conor again and was surprised that he was staring back at her. Then she remembered she'd been asked a question.

"Oh, yes, Gandiegow is quite beautiful, especially the way it sits on the ocean like a child sitting on the bottom step of a staircase."

"Quite poetic," Hugh commented.

"But it's true," Sophie said.

Abby smiled at them. "Also, I couldn't get over all the quilts at Quilting Central. Everyone was very nice to me ... even

Deydie. And no, I didn't see her hit anyone with her broom. Is that really a thing?" Abby didn't tell them how badly she wanted to design a new quilt while she was there. Quilting Central was so inspiring! But she didn't have time to make a quilt. Her wedding planner duties had to come first over her sewing hobby.

Sophie laughed. "I've seen Deydie and her broom in action before, but I've never been on the receiving end of it. All in all, Deydie really is a good person."

"We'll have to introduce you to Coira," Hugh said. "She's the one who heads up the quilt retreats here in Whussendale."

Sophie continued for him. "We have a wonderful group of quilters here. Having them has helped me not to miss Gandiegow as much."

Abby turned to Conor. "Do you quilt? I didn't see any male quilters at Quilting Central." Back in St. Louis, she knew several male tailors from the tuxedo shops who were quite good at sewing. Surely, there were some male quilters here. "I only wonder as you're a weaver."

Conor seemed a bit stunned but then answered, "I learned to hand stitch in my da's kilt shop. But I don't have time for sewing now. I remember Mum teaching Kieran how to use the sewing machine. She promised to teach me, too, when I was older. But, of course, that didn't happen." That particular wound, it seemed, would never heal.

She wished now that she hadn't asked, anything to keep him from looking so sad.

Hugh cleared his throat. "Aye, maybe we need to go through the samples, now that everyone is done eating."

"Good idea. I'm anxious to see what ye've brought us," Sophie added cheerfully, apparently trying to lift the mood.

Conor took the large paper bag to the loveseat and unpacked

a few tartans and laid them on the coffee table. Abby thought it was good that the dogs stayed in the kitchen. "We could offer the brides an array of styles. The traditional wedding shawl." He held up the tartan that was folded into a triangle with fringe on the edges. "Next, we have the wedding tartan sash." This one was cut into a long rectangle with short fringe on each end. "The bride would wear it over her shoulder like this." He demonstrated for Abby what he meant by fashioning it over his own shoulder, while not looking embarrassed in the least to be pretending to be the bride. "Or you can fashion it into a rosette." He showed Abby a picture of what he meant. "And lastly, we have the wedding stole." Which was again a rectangle, but wider than the sash. Conor looped the stole over his arms like a bride would wear it. Abby couldn't help but beam at Mr. Confident-with-his-masculinity.

"I think they're all wonderful," she said.

"There is nearly a style for each season," Conor added. "Well, at least three seasons. But, of course, yere brides could wear whichever one they fancied."

"Do we limit the number of tartan patterns or do you suggest they can choose any tartan on the registry?" Hugh asked.

"It wouldn't be economical to offer every tartan," Conor answered. "I've been thinking that we could partner with other wool mills, who are known for certain tartans, to fulfill special orders."

"That's an excellent idea," Hugh said. "And a way to build goodwill with others in the weaving community."

"Uncle Magnus won't like it," Conor said, frowning. "He'd think it too progressive to work with other mills in that way.

"Let's table that worry for now," Hugh said. "Abby, what do you think about the three options of wedding shawls?"

She picked up the first shawl. "They're beautiful and will make each wedding special. I'll need to get up to speed on how the shawls are integrated into the ceremony."

Sophie picked up the third shawl. "Some brides will simply wear their shawl and won't make it part of the celebration." She stroked the tartan.

Hugh went to his wife and put his arm around her. "My wife is remembering our own wedding, where she wore the traditional wedding shawl made from McGillivray tartan."

"It was a magical day," Sophie said.

It pleased Abby to see a marriage that was still going strong.

"There ye are," a woman said as she entered the parlor.

Hugh and Sophie waved to Abby. "Abby, come meet Coira."

"I just got off the phone with Deydie," Coira said. "She said I should speak with you about the wedding quilts and how ye want to proceed."

Abby nodded. "We decided the wedding quilt will be an add-on. Not every couple will want one. I would appreciate it if you and the other quilters would come up with three designs for the couples to choose from."

"Aye. We can do that," Coira said, nodding her head.

Sophie took over then. "It'll be a lovely keepsake for the couple." She looked lovingly at her husband. "Whussendale made one for us and we treasure it."

"Yes, I've occasionally seen that back in the States," Abby said, "but usually it's made by family members or close friends. I never thought about the venue providing one."

"Besides having three designs, we'll have a few colorways for the bride to choose from," Coira said. "I'll get our quilters to come up with small samples. Ye can take pictures of them to put on the website."

"That's a great idea." Abby couldn't believe how Whussendale was going the extra mile for their future customers. "We'll have pictures of the three styles of wedding shawls, too."

She nodded at Conor as a way of remembering to do that task later.

"Actually," Coira said, "if ye'd like to come, we're having a sew-in this evening to work on Diana and Rory's quilt."

"I thought Gandiegow was working on their quilt." Abby had been shown some of the blocks while she was there.

"Both villages are working on their quilt as everyone wanted to be involved," Coira said. "So will ye join us?"

"Sure." Though Abby wasn't certain what they would expect from her.

There was a knock on the doorway and Abby turned to see who it was. A group of women flooded in. "Oh, good, she's here." "Can she sew?" "Will she be helping with the quilts?" All the women were speaking at once.

Sophie held up her hand. "Aye, this is Abby Potter." She looked over at Coira. "Would ye like to introduce everyone?"

Abby should've taken out her notebook to take down everyone's name but instead she listened intently.

Three women stepped forward and Coira put her arm around the older of the three. "These are my daughters— Maggie, Rowena, and Sinnie. They live in Gandiegow but have been out shopping today, finding me the backing for Rory and Diana's wedding quilt. That's the reason ye didn't meet them in Gandiegow." Coira laughed. "I'm going to be in trouble with Deydie as she wanted to introduce them as her quilters."

Abby stuck out her hand and gave the obligatory *Nice to meet you* to each one. Next, Coira introduced another group of women. Abby took mental notes: Lara ran the café, Gunna helped out in the carding machine building, Hazel was married to Harold, and Mrs. Bates attached buckles to kilts in the kiltmaker's shop, where Sophie worked. The younger women seemed excited about Abby being there to bring weddings to

Whussendale, while the older women seemed to poo-poo the idea. But overall, they were welcoming, especially when Coira announced that Abby would be helping them with Rory and Diana's quilt, plus all the other wedding quilts for the Hitched in Scotland venture. The women all nodded approvingly at Abby for her willingness to pitch in. In truth, Abby wasn't sure how much time she would have to quilt, depending on how successful the wedding venture would be.

"We're missing a few quilters today," Coira said. "Like Tally, who's the wool mill's bookkeeper. She's visiting her gran and will be back after Christmas."

Hugh cleared his throat. "It's so nice that all of ye dropped by. But right now, Abby and Conor need to get to their office and make some decisions about the wedding shawls."

"Aye," Sophie seconded. "Abby will be meeting up with all of ye tonight, right?" She looked over at Abby.

She nodded.

"That's at seven o'clock in the ballroom, here at the castle," Coira said.

The women smiled at her once more, then filed out, leaving only Coira behind.

While Abby waited at the door until the last of them left, Conor gathered up the tartans. "Are ye ready to go then?"

"Sure." Abby turned to Sophie and Hugh. "Thank you for the lovely meal. And please give Mrs. McNabb my compliments. It was delicious."

"Seven tonight," Coira reminded her.

"Yes, seven." But Abby's mind was already wandering to the thought of being alone with Conor in his office ... *no, their office*. She followed him, thinking they were headed toward the door, but surprisingly, he went in the opposite direction.

"Where are we going?" she asked.

"To get Dublin."

When they got to the kitchen, Mrs. McNabb thrust a sack at Conor. "For yere pet. Just some bits she might like to have for later."

"Thank you, Mrs. McNabb. That's *verra* kind of ye."

"Let me carry that," Abby said. "You've got the tartans."

"Good idea." Conor knelt down and clipped on Dublin's leash. She seemed excited to have her leash on, until, that is, she realized she was leaving the Wallace and the Bruce behind. Dublin pulled back on the leash trying to stay with her new friends.

Abby opened the sack and pulled out a bite of beef and held it out to her. Dublin suddenly forgot all about her dog pals and obediently followed Abby toward the kitchen door.

Like a gentleman from a Scottish romance, Conor held it open for her as well. She couldn't help but feel gooey inside. Nothing was more satisfying than when *a man was a man*, which allowed her to be a woman. Yes, she was entertaining sappy thoughts, but they were true.

When they arrived back at the weaver's building and opened the door to the office, Dublin ran in first.

"You're going to have to get a dog bed for here as well," Abby remarked.

"Aye," Conor said.

As promised, the desk had been delivered. There was a Post It stuck to the top, which read, *Making design boards for you now. Declan.*

Conor leaned over, read the note, and ... growled. Or at least that's what it sounded like. Dublin must've recognized a kindred spirit as she glanced up at him, too. Abby decided then and there that perhaps Conor wasn't as domesticated as she thought he was. Yes, he'd been a gentleman earlier but underneath the exterior was a wild Scotsman … and she had to admit that the thought of him being wild with her was thrilling.

"Are you okay?" she asked, letting him know that she'd heard him. "Did you not get enough to eat? I assume that was your stomach growling."

Conor dropped the paper bag on the desktop. "Let's get this over with. I have real work that needs to be done." He tore the Post It note off the desk and crumpled it in his fist. Dublin went to the corner, curled up, and closed her eyes, while Conor retrieved a very large binder from one of the bookshelves. "We need to decide what tartans we're going to use." He flipped open the binder and she was amazed at all the plaid swatches within, organized alphabetically by the notes stapled to each one.

"You're flipping through them too fast," she complained. "Go slower. I want to get a good look."

He ignored her protest. Flipped a few more pages and stopped on a mostly red tartan. "This is the Royal Stewart. It's a universal tartan, and anyone who doesn't have a clan affiliation can wear it. I predict this will be our number one seller."

She leaned over his shoulder and gazed at the tartan that she'd seen plenty of times in the past. "I'll make a note of it. What other ones do you recommend?"

Next, he showed her the Black Watch tartan, then the Dress Stewart tartan that was mostly white. By the time they were done, Conor had picked out ten tartans.

"We'll make these our standard options and keep them in stock. So, the three styles of wedding shawls that I showed you at the castle, will they work?"

"Yes. They're great and will appeal to different personalities. I'm sure of it. Thank you for going to all this trouble," she said.

"Actually …" He paused for a long moment. "It really hasn't been any trouble. I've enjoyed narrowing down the styles and tartans to use. Next, I'll talk to the other wool mills who might be amenable to helping us fulfill any guest orders that are out of our purview."

"I know you didn't sign up to help me with the weddings, but your help is going to make all the difference. I really appreciate it." Maybe she'd gone too far because suddenly he seemed distant.

"Dublin, come," Conor said. The dog's head popped up and then she jumped to her feet. Apparently, a small catnap was all she needed before being ready for round two. She went to Conor's side and waited.

"I better check on my uncle now."

"Is everything all right?" she asked. She didn't like the frown lines that had formed between his eyebrows.

"Aye, but I have to go. Magnus is getting old. I can see he's slowing down. It's my job to take things off his plate so he has fewer responsibilities. He's worked hard his whole life. He deserves to have his load lessened."

No matter how much she enjoyed being around Conor, she didn't want to be the cause of burdening Conor's great-uncle. Hugh and Sophie had assigned Conor to do all this extra work for her, plus traveling with her to bridal shows. Now, though, she saw that it was not only unfair to Conor, but unfair to Magnus, too. She'd have to say something to Hugh. Surely there was someone else around here who could take Conor's place and help her. Maybe that *Tavon* person that Conor had mentioned.

But then another emotion hit her hard and almost toppled her conviction. It was confusing and at the same time she felt crystal clear. *I don't want anyone else. I only want Conor.*

Chapter 9

AFTER SAYING A quick hello to Magnus, Conor and Dublin walked back to the weaver's building. He was still tormented over the look on Abby's face when he'd left her. He hadn't meant to make her feel bad; he'd only been telling the truth. He owed it to Magnus to make his life easier. Aye, Tavon could help, but Conor was still the one responsible.

How was he going to be able to give both Abby and Uncle Magnus the attention that they deserved? It was like he would need to be in two places at once. Hell, three or four places, if he was adding up everything that had been put on his plate recently! The biggest kicker now, though, was how he could be true to himself—upgrading the wool mill's operation and making the weaver's building a more efficient place to work? Something as big as that could give a man a sense of worth. He had so much that needed to be done and he wasn't sure how to complete everything.

Plus, he wanted to make Abby happy.

That thought stopped him in his tracks. Somehow, Abby had

become the center of everything. Good and bad. She might be the thing to hinder him in all that he wanted to do and who he wanted to be. He felt honor bound to both his uncle and his clan, plus the things that he wanted to accomplish. The truth was that Abby shouldn't have anything to do with any of it, but now, for some reason, she did.

Even though it was late and he was feeling a bit wrung out, Conor went to the hit list hanging by Loom One to read the order sheet. His uncle had scrawled in two things that he had completed on the order and where he had left off. Conor appreciated the notes. Keeping busy would help Conor focus on the work instead of worrying like an old woman. Aye, he was feeling tormented. But he put it aside and set up the next color on the loom. After everything was aligned, he started the weaving machine.

He planned to make up for the hours he'd missed earlier in the day. An hour later, Uncle Magnus stopped by.

"I thought ye were in for the night," Conor said.

"I just wanted to make sure everything was all right here," Magnus said.

"Checking up on me, huh?"

"Nay. Just checking on the machinery. Is she having any troubles?" Magnus asked.

"She's humming along with no problems right now. If ye're done here, do ye mind taking Kieran's dog back with ye to yere cottage? She's asleep in the office. She shouldn't give ye any trouble." Though Conor worried about her listening skills when it came to *not* lying on a person's bed. "I'll pick her up when I'm done here."

"Aye. I'll be happy for her company," Magnus said, before shuffling away.

At eight o'clock, Conor left the weaver's building. He wondered if Abby had made it to the quilters' group as Coira requested. It would be an easy walk up to the castle to check on her. In fact, he now had a built-in excuse. Dublin needed her evening walk anyway. And Dublin would be thrilled to see Abby again … and the Wallace and the Bruce. Abby would be happy to see the dog … and perhaps she'd be happy to see the man who brought her. But Conor stopped this line of thinking. He'd made a promise to himself to not get involved with women, hadn't he? Morag had taught him a hard lesson and he meant to keep that lesson in the forefront of his mind, especially when he felt the slightest bit of weakness around a woman. Like he did around Abby.

Conor was proud of himself for ignoring his baser instincts and making it to Magnus's cottage without making a detour to find Abby. He found his uncle sitting in his old red and blue plaid recliner. Dublin seemed perfectly happy to be resting alongside the old man, getting her ears scratched. "Do ye want something to eat?" Magnus asked. "Leftovers are in the refrigerator."

"I'm not hungry. I finished the Thompson Camel tartan. In the morning, I'll work on the Mackenzie order." Good communication was important when working with others in the weaver's building.

"Ye're a good lad," Magnus said.

"Come on, Dublin. Let's get ye settled into your new, temporary home," Conor said.

The dog rose and stretched as if she were straightening out her old bones, acting like an old gal. Had Magnus rubbed off on her?

"Ye know," Magnus said, "ye could leave the mutt here with me, if she's too much trouble for ye."

"Thank ye for the offer but she needs to be walked. Plus, I plan to take her on a run in the morning to work off any excess energy before the day starts. Both of us need our exercise," Conor said lightly as he clipped Dublin into her halter leash. Dublin danced around, apparently excited about going on an adventure. Conor was determined not to take that adventure in the direction of the castle, where the quilters were sewing tonight. He'd make sure to head in the opposite direction.

But his uncle's offer to watch Dublin did give Conor pause. Maybe Uncle Magnus needed a full-time canine companion. Aye, his uncle had been spending time with Coira, but maybe a dog would be a better fit for him. Less heartache, in Conor's opinion. He could help Magnus with the dog—like lots of walks or visits to the veterinarian and such. Magnus wouldn't have to do anything that he didn't want to do, and Conor could pick up the slack. Getting his uncle a dog was something to think about, anyway.

Something else to think about was the number of dog beds Conor would have to get for Dublin. One for the office, one for Magnus's ... and one for Abby's cottage to keep the damned dog off her bed. Maybe he'd ask the quilting ladies if they could put something together from their scraps of fabric.

"Goodnight, uncle," Conor said at the doorway. "See ye in the morn."

"Goodnight, lad," Magnus said.

The second Dublin got a sniff of the outside, she turned into a rambunctious pup again, pulling hard on the leash. Conor laughed. "Ye can pull all ye want, but you won't be able to drag me along." He tried to get Dublin to head in the other direction, but she had a one-track mind. She wanted to go to the castle. Conor guessed she could smell the Wallace and the Bruce, even from this distance.

"All right, then, lass," Conor said, acquiescing, "we'll go see the boys." And it had nothing to do with the human wanting to see Abby.

With her tongue hanging out, Dublin turned back for a moment and smiled as if she'd understood every word he'd said. She certainly was an expressive animal.

They half-walked, half-trotted to the castle with Dublin's tail going a hundred RPMs. Before the castle came into sight, she began barking, yipping, and tugging harder on her leash. Conor assumed that Hugh was out walking his dogs and that Dublin had a notion of where they were. Not two seconds later, though, Abby came around the bend in the road...and stopped.

Conor stopped, too, pulling Dublin to heel. He just stared at Abby. He had decided while she was with the quilters, he wouldn't peek in on her. And he certainly hadn't expected her to appear out of thin air. It had just begun to mist. He must've relaxed his grip on the leash because Dublin pulled free and tore after Abby. Conor ran after the dog as the mist turned to droplets.

Abby squatted down to greet the dog as Dublin ran into her arms. Doggy kisses ensued. Conor wondered if Abby would greet him with open arms, too. Which was a ridiculous thought. He slowed down. "Hey. I thought ye were supposed to be sewing tonight with the quilters."

She grinned up at him. "Not sewing, exactly. But I did get inspired to design a new quilt. Coira said she'd help me pick out the fabrics. She showed me a flyer of some bright and beautiful Riley Blake batiks. I can't wait to get started. The only quilts I ever made were for a few friends in college. Lap quilts. Nothing fancy. Nothing like the blocks they had hanging on the design walls in the castle's quilting room." Abby stood and brushed her slightly wet hair away from her face. "If you must know, the reason I left early is because I got another call from my mother. I don't usually talk to her when I'm around others."

Apparently, she'd forgotten that she'd taken her mum's call while they'd been in the car together.

Abby screwed up her face. "Well, it's a trust thing. I don't usually feel comfortable speaking to my mother when others are around."

It was as if she'd read his mind … again! And it sounded as if she trusted him!

The droplets from a moment ago turned into a downpour. "Come," Conor said. "Let's get you out of the rain. Then, if ye want, ye tell me all about the call from yere mum."

"Getting out of the rain is a good idea." Abby grabbed the handle loop of Dublin's leash and took off with the dog at a quick jog. Conor followed and had the strange realization that he was once again chasing after a female. But this was different. He wasn't a teen, and Abby wasn't a girl like Morag had been. Abby was a woman. An attractive woman who got his blood pumping. It was especially surprising to him because he'd put the *kibosh* on the whole dating thing.

He easily caught up to her. "Come to my cottage and I'll build a fire. I'd like to see your quilt design." He shook his head at his own words. Hopefully, Abby hadn't heard his offer as the equivalent to the old cliché of asking a lass to come back to his place to check out his CD collection.

He had no intention of seducing Abby. Or dating her either. He could be her friend, which would be right charitable of him, since she had no one else here in Scotland. "That is, if you want to … share your design and all." He sounded lame.

"Sure, I'll come to yere cottage." She laughed then. "I'd rather have Dublin jump on your bed instead of mine, considering the rain and all."

He laughed, too. "Good point. I think I'll have to tie her up to the dining table to keep my bed dry."

"You know what?" Abby asked, a little out of breath.

"What?"

"You have a nice smile. You should do that more often." She gazed at him while she said it, then immediately turned away and picked up her speed.

"You have a nice smile, too," he called after her. She didn't respond, so he wasn't sure whether she'd heard him or not. He was in awe of Abby being so forthright and speaking her mind. What did people call it? Aye, Abby was transparent. Not like his ex-wife who seemed to say nothing of what she really felt; or worse, said nothing at all.

They ran the rest of the way through the rain without saying anything until they reached his door. "Go on in," he said. "I never keep it locked."

Abby went inside and did a good job of holding onto the leash.

"Thanks for keeping Dublin restrained. Wet dog residue and a goodnight's sleep aren't a good match up." He smiled at Abby and it felt good because she smiled back. "I'll return in a second. We all need some dry towels and then ye tell me about yere phone call with yere mum."

Abby didn't know how much of her mother's call to tell Conor. Unfortunately for her, she didn't have any girlfriends to vent to. She had been so busy over the last several years that there had been no time for extracurriculars, like making, strengthening, and maintaining friendships, beyond the people she worked with at Belle's Weddings. She'd barely had enough time to see Aaron, which was something he griped about often. He'd been selfish with her time, always monopolizing her. When a couple would ask them to dinner, he always balked at the invitation, so, invariably, they hadn't gone. Being with

Aaron, it turns out, had been isolating. But shouldn't a significant other have expanded her horizons, not limited them?

When Conor reappeared, she took the towel he offered and wiped down Dublin. The dog enjoyed the rubdown by sighing in pleasure. "You are one sweet girl," she said to the dog.

Conor held out another towel. "Here."

For a second, she wondered if he wanted her to rub *him* down like she had Dublin. Or maybe he was going to rub *her* down. That was a happy thought. She smiled, knowing she'd sigh in ecstasy, too, the way the dog had.

"Thanks." She took the towel to dry off her hair. Afterward, she used one of the dry ends to wipe down her bag.

"I'll start a fire," Conor said, "and while I do, ye can tell me all about yere phone call, okay?" He gave her a smile and looked away, almost as if he understood that she wouldn't be able to speak freely if he was staring at her. Yes, he already knew that she had a dysfunctional relationship with her mother, but she wanted to control what information she shared with him ... and with anyone else for that matter.

"Okay," she agreed, because God knew she needed to talk to someone. "My mother called me because she's on a mission to have me come back home." Which seemed odd and didn't make sense when Joann wasn't interested in having a strong mother-daughter relationship.

"I bet she's missing ye," he said, as he crumpled up newspaper and put it on the grate.

"You bet wrong." Abby grabbed another clean towel and rubbed down her clothes.

He did look at her then. "Let me grab you a dry shirt to put on. It'll swim on ye but it's the best I can do."

"Sure." She wouldn't point out that she could run next door

and get her own dry clothes. That might break the spell of them being together inside his cozy cottage, smiling at each other and on the verge of revealing confidences.

He hurried to the armoire next to his bed and returned with a blue plaid flannel shirt. "This should help warm ye up." He handed it over. "Ye can change in the bathroom."

She went into the bathroom, closed the door, and quickly slipped out of her wet shirt. She hung it over the showerhead and then put on his dry one. Instantly, she felt better. She wasn't sure whether it was from the shirt taking away the chill or the fact that it was his.

Once back in the living area, she watched as Conor stacked logs into the fireplace and then lit it. When he saw her, he pulled two chairs in front of the hearth. "Come, sit, and get warmed up. Then tell me why ye think that yere mum isn't missing you."

Abby took her seat and Conor took his, too. Sitting together like this was a strange sensation—not strange bad, but strange good. The atmosphere surrounding them was snug, familiar, as if they'd sat in front of a fire like this a thousand times before. To her bones, she felt like she'd known him forever. She wondered if he felt it, too.

"Yere mum?" he reminded her.

"Oh, yes, she actually called to tell me to send her my resume, that she had a line on several jobs for me."

"Wedding planner jobs?" he asked, gazing into the fire.

"No. Executive assistant jobs, mainly. She said that she called in several favors to get me interviews with her two top picks."

"So yere mum doesn't approve of you being a wedding planner?"

"Nothing truer was ever said." Abby frowned, which was something she did a lot when the subject was about her mother.

"My mother is quite embarrassed by me. I overheard her telling the people who work for her that I'm still trying to *find* myself. Which isn't me at all. I've never felt lost when it came to my profession."

Of course, Abby wouldn't tell Conor everything. Joann had said she'd talked to Aaron, too, and convinced him to take Abby back. Abby shuddered. She never should've stayed with Aaron for as long as she had. She especially shouldn't have agreed to marry him. At the time, though, she'd felt trapped. He'd asked her at Joann's Christmas party she threw each year for the employees at the fertility clinic. Everyone *oohed* and *ahhed* when Aaron got down on one knee like it was a Hallmark movie or something. What else could she have done but say yes? Her mother had wanted her to marry Aaron from the moment she'd met him. Abby saw a chance to gain her mother's approval, which had been futile up until that moment. She could give up her own happiness to make her mother happy, couldn't she? Not her most rational thought. At the time, it seemed like a no-brainer. But what it really was ... was a recipe for disaster.

Conor touched her arm. "I'm sorry. Parents can let us down like no one else can."

"That's an understatement." The only way Abby had been able to get her mother off the phone was to tell her that she'd think about the interviews. She glanced over at Conor's hand on her arm. She liked him touching her, but she shouldn't. She needed to stay fully focused on making a go of the wedding business here in Whussendale. She certainly couldn't be in another relationship—not that Conor was asking for one. Abby didn't have any confidence when it came to choosing the right man after she'd screwed up spectacularly by being with Aaron. She couldn't tell Conor that she was the worst when it came to relationships, so she deflected. "How did your parents let you down?" she asked bravely. She thought it only fair that he reciprocate her confession.

He dropped his hand. "My situation is a bit complicated," he said evasively.

"Hey, I told you mine so you have to tell me yours."

"All right," he conceded. "But at least your mum didn't run off to another country when ye were a bairn like mine did."

"What?"

"I think I told you my mum was from Ireland. Dad said she went back because she was homesick. Now that I'm older, I suspect there might have been more to it. Kieran probably knows the truth of what happened better than I do."

"You should ask him," Abby said gently. She thought it might help both of them to talk about it, but she wasn't a therapist. It was just a feeling.

"Nay, I'll not ask him. He doesn't like to talk about the past. Actually, because of the military, he's very closemouthed about everything."

"Oh. I guess that makes sense. But I think it would be great to have a sibling to commiserate with, especially since I don't understand why my mother had me in the first place. She's made it clear that I've been a nuisance from day one."

"As I said, parents can let us down like no other."

"Agreed," she said.

"How about we change the subject?" he offered.

"Change to what?" she asked.

"For the reason why I asked ye here. Do ye want to show me the quilt ye're going to make?" he said, smiling encouragingly.

"Sure." She stood and retrieved her bag and pulled out the drawing, feeling relieved that everything inside was dry. "I call the quilt *A Touch of Celtic*." She'd been a bit ambitious but was happy with how it looked on the graph paper—from the hearts across the top and bottom rows, the four thistles lined up in the middle, and the Scottie dogs guarding the stars. She touched the picture and couldn't wait to get started.

Standing, he took the notebook, scanned it, and then gazed at her in awe. "Oh, lass, this is excellent. It'll be something special when ye get it all sewed up."

"Thank you." She could feel herself blushing. If he asked her about her red cheeks, she could blame it on the fire that was quickly warming up his cottage.

Suddenly, the air between them felt electrically charged. Or maybe it was just her overactive imagination again. She stared at his lips, wondering what it would feel like to kiss him. She took her pipedream one step further, imagining how he would respond if she reached up and rested her hand on his bearded face? Or brushed his hair back so she could see his eyes better?

"Um, I should probably go," she almost squeaked, as if her voice had taken on the characteristics of a timid mouse. "Lots of work to do."

He took a step closer to her. "What kind of work?" Now he was staring at her lips, too; she was sure of it. Then he inched even closer.

"The list of Gandiegow things I told you about. Website stuff. *Lots* of website stuff. *Lots* to do." Lots to think about, too. She couldn't screw up this gig here in Scotland, because she couldn't go home with her tail between her legs. Thinking of home reminded her that she would have to set her mother straight about everything. She didn't want to get back together with Aaron. She didn't want to send her mother her resume. She most certainly didn't want to interview for jobs that wouldn't fulfill her.

She picked up her bag and shoved the quilt drawing inside. "Thank you for warming me up." *Oh my gosh, did I really just say that?* Embarrassed, she glanced down. But that only reminded her that she was wearing his shirt. His shirt! She wasn't ready to return it. She wanted to wear it a little while longer. Feel his clothes wrapped around her. And because she was a dreamer and had an active imagination, she pretended that it was him hugging her body and not his clothes.

She really should do more than return his shirt before she left. She should offer to wash and dry the damp towels—do some fluff and fold for him—but she had to get out of here. "See you later." She hurried to the door. Dublin must've been listening in her sleep because her doggie head popped up and she ran after her.

Abby halted and put her hand up as if she were a human stop sign. "Stay."

The dog whined.

Conor went to stand beside his brother's dog. "I'll see ye later, then?"

Her imagination went off the rails. Did he mean to see her later tonight? After all the other villagers went to bed? Something clandestine? Something hot and spicy?

"Goodnight," she said as firmly as she could muster, especially since she wanted to answer *yes* to all that her imagination had conjured up.

He grinned at her. She had the feeling that he'd read her mind as easily as if her lusty thoughts had been splashed across a billboard. "Goodnight, lass. I'll see ye in the morn."

She rushed out and ran next door. Her cottage was cold and damp and she was already missing Conor. No ... she missed his fireplace. She probably should've let Dublin come with her because the dog would've kept her company on this dark, damp, cold Scotland night. She went to the radiator, knelt down to get a good look at the controls, and then tried to turn it on. Nothing happened. She messed with the dials for several minutes more until finally giving up in defeat.

She gazed over at her empty hearth, longing for a roaring fire like Conor's. She wished now that she found Conor about as attractive as Mr. Potato Head. Then she wouldn't have any qualms about going next door and asking for help. But now she couldn't do that. She'd left things awkwardly between them.

She paced back and forth, searching for a solution to her problem. Maybe she should've gotten Declan's number. She'd had the whole trip to Gandiegow to get his digits but hadn't thought to ask.

She had Hugh's number; she could text him. But Hugh had told her to contact Conor if she needed anything. Actually, he'd said *Conor is your man.*

Her phone rang, making her jump. She picked it up even though she didn't recognize the number. "Hello," she said cautiously.

"Listen, lass," Conor started in immediately, "I forgot to tell ye that the radiator in yere cottage can be a little finicky. May I come over to make sure it's running all right for you? I would hate for ye to be cold tonight."

Her heart soared at hearing his voice, plus she felt relieved to hear his offer. Had he read her mind again, even though there were walls and space between them? But a second later, she felt embarrassed. She'd have to admit that she hadn't been able to get the radiator started on her own. She hated looking incompetent. Her mother had called her *incompetent* on more occasions than Abby could count. Oh, well. She decided that accepting Conor's help was better than turning into a human popsicle overnight. "Your offer is appreciated and I accept. I'll unlock the door so you can come on in." Maybe she should ask him to bring some dry firewood, too, just in case. But something more pressing came to mind; she better fix her unruly hair before he arrived. "Just give me a few minutes to get decent." Immediately, she wanted to pull the words back, because they hinted at something intimate ... like lingerie or nakedness. As she rushed to the restroom, she added, "I'm a little indisposed." She was brushing out her hair before she hung up.

As it turned out, she needn't have hurried. He gave her a full ten minutes, which gave her enough time to touch up her make-up, too.

Conor knocked, then stepped inside with Dublin on heel. "Sorry for the delay. Kieran called." Like always, Dublin's ears perked up at hearing her owner's name.

Conor stopped suddenly and stared, his expression dropping into a frown. Did she have a bit of spinach from dinner stuck in her teeth? "Lass, ye needn't have spruced up for me. Personally, I think ye look better without all that extra makeup on yere face."

She wasn't prepared for his admonishment and didn't appreciate him calling her out like that. She glanced down at his shirt. She wished now that she'd changed into her own clothes so she could lob his shirt at his ruggedly handsome face. She was definitely on the defensive. "No one asked for your opinion. Just so you know, I wasn't *sprucing up* for you! I was getting straightened up for myself. Women do that, you know?" She congratulated herself. She decided to dig in more. "Something for you to keep in mind, Conor ... women dress and primp for other women; not men. Remember that."

He deliberately dropped his gaze to his shirt hanging from her body and then raised an eyebrow.

"Well, I wasn't exactly done getting ready, now was I?" She crossed her arms over her chest and hugged herself. A shiver went through her.

He looked at Dublin, whose head had been going from one to the other like a tennis spectator. "Dublin, go lay down."

The dog did what she'd done before—jumped up on Abby's bed and collapsed with a sigh.

Conor shook his head at her. "Sorry about that. And never mind what I said. I apologize. It's none of my business how ye make yereself up. But I see that ye're cold. Let's get yere cottage warmed up."

She noticed he was looking at her chest. She glanced down and saw it, too. Immediately, she dropped her arms to keep his shirt from showing just how cold she really was.

He smiled as he walked to the radiator. She wondered if he enjoyed sparring with her. Or maybe it was the unintentional peep show her perky breasts had given him. She couldn't help that she had no control over her body. Or maybe he was proud of himself for getting the upper hand. At times like these, men could be infuriating!

"I'll go change so you can have your shirt back," she said with a pout.

"Nay, keep it," he said. "This is just the start of the cool weather and I expect you didn't bring the right clothes with ye to Scotland. I haven't seen you wearing anything warm since you got here."

"How did you get my phone number?" she asked coolly.

"Hugh. I texted him."

"Oh, well, that makes sense."

He glanced back at her. "Come on. Forgive me for being an *eegit*. I really do think you are more beautiful without all that makeup you women like to wear."

"What women are you speaking of? Your ex-wife?" She'd had one of her brave moments again. Maybe not brave exactly, as she was trying to get back at him for criticizing her.

"Aye. My ex-wife. Months before I knew what was going on and before she ran off with my best mate, she got a new haircut and spent hours primping in front of the mirror, caking the stuff on her face and lips as if she were a clown getting ready for the circus." He glanced down and then back up to look at her, his face serious now. "Turns out, I was the clown for believing that she would be faithful." He knelt down at the radiator, looking away. "My issues with makeup are my issues. I shouldn't have said anything about it. I'm really sorry."

Abby felt like a heel. The poor guy had some heavy baggage when it came to women. Hoping to comfort him—and only as a show of friendship—she went to him and laid a hand on his shoulder. He stilled so completely that she wondered if he'd turned into stone. He didn't even seem to be breathing. The good news was that he didn't pull away from her touch. She took his nonaction as a show of permission to bravely squeeze his shoulder—in an *I'm-here-for-you* kind of gesture. It was the least she could do for him. It was her fault for bringing up his ex. She had to apologize and say something to make him feel better. "I—"

She didn't get a chance to finish her sentence. He abruptly stood, pulled her into his arms and kissed her. Not some first-time kiss, tender and loving, but a hard, punishing kiss, as if the tension in his back had raced up to his lips. It both shocked and surprised her. But she didn't stay that way for long. She decided to seize the moment and kiss him back. She ran her hands up his chest, to his neck, and then threaded her fingers into his hair, holding onto him. There was no way to describe his kiss except thrilling. She'd been cold only moments ago but now she was burning up. He was holding her tightly, too, and it was exhilarating, which made her put more of herself into the kiss. She was hit with all kinds of sensations and felt like she was floating outside herself, soaring above the clouds. Nothing could hurt her from here. It was just her and Conor and nothing else mattered. As if from a distance she could hear a low growl coming from him. His hands went to her upper arms, gripping them, when without warning, he pushed her away, ending the kiss as suddenly as he'd started it.

She wasn't prepared for this about-face, and it made her dizzy. Or was the dizziness an aftereffect of that amazing kiss? Her own feelings were in direct conflict with the expression on his face. Two people on opposite ends of the spectrum. She'd been elated while in his arms, but now, she was confused. He looked as if she'd done something to punish him.

She couldn't verbalize what she was feeling. Disappointment was swirling around in this heady cocktail of lust and excitement, bombarding her. Why couldn't he be ready for another round of kissing? She certainly was!

And because she had no words—actions spoke louder than words anyway—she laid a hand on his chest, hoping to make him feel better. His heart was beating a mile a minute, which made her feel somewhat vindicated, blameless, and absolved. He looked down at her hand, and for the moment, he allowed it to remain there.

But then he stepped back, breaking the connection, making her hand fall. "I can't. I-I really can't."

She wondered if he was trying to convince himself. The warmth she'd felt was gone and once again she was cold. It was bad enough that she was shivering, but now she felt stupid, too. Let down. Somehow, this was all her fault. She thought she'd given him one helluva kiss. But apparently not, as he didn't want to go in for another. He definitely looked like he regretted starting something between them. Between taking her off guard with the kiss and then rejecting her, he had thrown her off her game.

"It's not you," he said hoarsely.

"Yeah, yeah. I know the drill," she said bitterly. "You say it's not me, but what you're really trying to say is that it is."

"No! That's not it at all. It really isn't you. It just shouldn't have happened." He said the last bit flatly.

Why shouldn't it have happened? She wasn't brave enough

to say it out loud, but the question was certainly echoing in her head. She wanted so badly to know. But she'd said enough. Argued enough. Done enough. She was supposed to be turning over a new leaf, not forcing things anymore. She needed to wear life as a loose shirt, and by God, she was going to do it.

"*C'est la vie.* Fine. Whatever." Abby had wanted to sound nonchalant, but she couldn't mask the anger and disappointment reverberating in her words. "But just so you know, Aaron and I never shared a kiss like that!"

Conor's eyebrows crashed together. "Who the hell is Aaron?"

Abby couldn't help herself. She gave Conor a satisfied smile. "Aaron's my fiancé."

Chapter 10

CONOR COULDN'T BELIEVE IT! He'd unwittingly attached himself to another unfaithful female! But while he was trying to sort out how he was going to get to the bottom of the bombshell that Abby had just dropped, she walked out the door ... wearing no coat, with only his plaid shirt for warmth. And then Kieran's damn dog jumped off the bed and followed her.

Conor stood there for a second, looking at the empty doorway. He wouldn't go after her. He had too much pride for that. But then he remembered how he hadn't gone after Morag when maybe he should have. His brain was telling him that he was comparing apples to oranges, but in the grand scheme of things, it didn't matter. Without thinking further, he ran after Abby.

He caught up to her quickly as she was stomping her way in the direction of the castle. Dublin was skipping and hopping, looking back at Abby often, acting like her new best friend.

"Hold up." He gently captured her arm and pulled her to a stop. "You have a fiancé?"

She crossed her arms, rolled her eyes upward, and shook her head. Clearly, the lass was irritated. And she was silent, making him wonder whether she was going to answer him or not. He decided to make his query clearer.

"Why didn't you tell me that you are engaged?" And why in the hell had she returned his kiss the way that she had? Conor could admit—only to himself—that he'd never had a kiss like that either. May the Almighty help him, but he had no clue how the kiss had happened. One moment he was examining the radiator controls, and in the next moment, he had pulled her into his arms and was ravishing her lips. "How long have you been engaged?" He slipped off his jacket and put it around her shoulders.

She sighed heavily, dropped her arms, and finally looked at him. Her frown didn't suit her otherwise friendly and outgoing face. "I'm not engaged, Conor, at least not anymore."

The imaginary vice-grips that had been clutching his chest loosened and he could breathe again. Dublin came up and stuck her head in his hand, looking for some affection. He obliged her and scratched her behind the ears. "Come back to the cottage, lass, and get warm. I promise not to be an arse again. On the way, ye can tell me about yere broken engagement." He wasn't sure when he'd turned into Abby's therapist—or some kind of girlfriend she could confide in—but he was certainly acting like it now. "Please?"

She rolled her eyes again. "Okay. But you're giving me mixed signals, you know?"

"Sorry." He meant it. "As I said, it won't happen again." But for the sake of being honest with himself, he did want to kiss her again ... and again. If he did, he wondered if that would get her out of his system. Perhaps the problem was that he'd been without a woman for too long. *Aye*, he'd been set up by the mothers, aunts, and grandmothers of the village. But he'd certainly not kissed any of them. The thought had never even crossed his mind.

Abby started jogging back to the cottage. Dublin chased after her.

Conor caught up to her in a couple of strides. "What happened with Aaron? Why didn't you marry him?" His need to know was unnerving. Normally, he didn't butt into other people's business. But Abby was making him do a lot of things that he normally wouldn't do.

"My mother is crazy about Aaron. When we started dating, she finally seemed happy with me. Not too long after we started seeing each other, my mother began dropping hints about us getting married. I'm pretty sure that during one of their late-night phone chats, she's the one who proposed the idea for Aaron to propose to me."

"But when he asked ye to marry him, you didn't have to say yes," Conor pointed out.

"That's where you're wrong. Of course, I had to say yes ... to keep the peace with my mother."

"What broke off the engagement?" Conor was certain that Abby couldn't be the villain in this story. She seemed sweet and kind. She was nothing like Morag. By now, they'd made it back to Abby's cottage. He opened the door and she and Dublin went in. "Why don't you wrap up in the quilt while I get the radiator going?"

"Good idea." She grabbed a quilt off the back of the chair, wrapped it around herself, and sat cross-legged on her bed.

Once again, he knelt down at the radiator and adjusted the knobs until he heard it kick on. "Go on. Tell me about what happened." He pulled a chair over to the bed so he could sit near her.

Abby hopped up as if she had excess energy and paced the

length of the cottage. "No big event happened. Basically, I had to admit to myself that I didn't love him ... at least not as much as my mother did." She laughed sardonically. "When it came down to it, I had to choose between what I wanted and what my mother wanted for me. Our two goals were not sympatico. They never have been and I've accepted that they never will be." Abby looked spent from saying it.

"That's rather heavy. You were very brave to make that decision." He approved of her scruples. Thinking of the unplanned kiss, he was glad she was single and relieved he hadn't put himself in the situation of being the *other man*. A strange thought hit him. Did he want to take her on a date ... or more? He knew he definitely wanted to kiss her again. Would the next kiss be as good as the first kiss? Or had that amazing first kiss been an anomaly?

She shook her head. "I wasn't really brave. I should've said something sooner. I didn't do anything about it until it was time for me to walk down the aisle."

"Ye left him at the altar?" Instantly, Conor was appalled and felt bad for that *bluidy* bastard, Aaron.

"You don't understand. I had no choice." She looked like she was going to cry. But he was having trouble reconciling his image of who Abby was with the awful truth of what she'd done to her fiancé. Basically, he'd inadvertently entangled himself with a *runaway bride*, after being duped by his own runaway wife. *I'm an effing idiot!*

"Say something," she pleaded.

She was looking for absolution and he was the last person on earth that could give it to her.

She pulled out one of the dining chairs, collapsed into it, and hung her head. "It's my fault. I imploded my life—my relationship with Aaron, my relationship with my mother, all the wedding plans, my whole life. Even my job, since Aaron's mom was my boss. It's the reason I'm here in Scotland. I just had to get away."

"Ran away," Conor said bitterly, knowing he didn't have the right to accuse her in that way.

"Don't judge me!" she shot back.

But he was judging her. She was exactly like Morag—selfish!—and she didn't give a whit about the pain she'd caused others.

"I tried to make it up to Aaron. I gave him the honeymoon trip that I paid for. My mother said he took one of the women from his law office to Hawaii."

But that didn't make it right in Conor's mind.

She shrugged off the quilt and started pacing again. "I also took on the unenviable task of writing an apology to every one of our guests. Then I packaged up and mailed back all the gifts." She was steadfast in her defensiveness. "I did the right thing, whether you, my mother, or anyone else thinks I did or not. This way, Aaron is free to find someone new."

That was an interesting thought. Did Morag believe that letting him go was opening up his own life to find someone new? A second later, he remembered her betrayal and didn't believe for a moment that her choices had anything to do with benevolence. But apparently, Abby's motives did, or at least she made it sound like they did.

"How about Hawaii? Did the trip work out for him?" Conor hoped so.

"Well ..." She trailed off.

"Well, what?" Conor asked, feeling like the other shoe was going to drop.

"My mother told me on the phone that she convinced Aaron to give me another chance."

There was a freight train roaring in his ears and those vice grips were back, crushing his chest more now than they had before. "Are ye going to? Give him another chance, then?"

It seemed like an eternity passed until she answered, where in truth, her reply was nearly instantaneous. "Absolutely not! We are not getting back together! End of story." She glanced at him and held his gaze. "The truth is that there was no spark between Aaron and me. I told you that I didn't love him. Yes, we had some things in common, but we were more suited to be brother and sister than husband and wife."

That last comment calmed Conor but he couldn't quite get back to where he was before. He'd trusted Abby from nearly the beginning. But now, his impression of her had turned realistic, making him realize how ill-placed his trust in her had been. He was disappointed in her. Knowing that she'd never loved Aaron and only agreed to marry him to appease her mum should have eased the condemnation that he now felt toward Abby. However, this feeling of disillusionment wasn't going anywhere anytime soon.

He had to admit that his thoughts were a jumbled mess. Maybe Abby was right that her ex was now free to find the right one. *A soulmate.* Conor had never given much credence to the idea. Or imagined he could have one for himself. When he was young, he'd stumbled along in life. Now, he was too much of a pragmatist to believe in such things as soulmates and true love.

When he married Morag, he was barely an adult, but even back then, he had steadfast principles to guide him. He'd been determined to honor the vows he'd made on their wedding day before the Almighty, Morag's family, and Kieran ... *till death do us part.* But so much for having scruples. Look what they'd gotten him. In the end, what he'd learned was that it really took two people to keep a relationship going and not just one dutybound man.

But Abby had him thinking. Maybe Morag had found her

soulmate in Steven. Were they meant to be together? Maybe that was Morag's only chance at true happiness. For a brief moment, he wondered if he should forgive Morag. Last week's sermon had been about how holding grudges consumed energy, took up space in our heads and in our hearts. The pastor had said that love and kindness were better ways to spend one's time. *Nay*, forgiveness for what Morag and Steven had done wouldn't happen today. But maybe in the future. Or perhaps not at all.

Abby glanced up and gazed at him just as Dublin began to snore. "Conor, do you see now that I wasn't being duplicitous in, uh, kissing you back?"

"Aye. Ye're unattached. Ye can kiss whomever ye want." He searched her face but apparently it was too much for her because she dropped her gaze again. She seemed shy now. For him, it felt good to say that she was unattached. But at the same time, it felt all wrong to put the notion in her head that she could kiss anyone she wanted! That chest-thumping Neanderthal voice in his head proclaimed that she should kiss only him! If they were never going to have another kiss, then he felt strongly that Abby should live like a nun. They'd be quite the pair since he'd virtually adopted a monk's life for himself.

Abby went to the bed, sat, and patted the space next to her. "Dublin, come sit by me and keep me warm." The dog—snoring one second and all action in the next—ran to Abby and settled herself beside her new friend.

Conor turned up the radiator as he listened to Abby whispering to the dog.

"He's the one who said it. That I can kiss whomever I want."

He looked over to see her kissing the dog. But her secretive smile hinted that she wanted to kiss someone other than her canine companion. He yearned to ask who she was thinking of. But he didn't want to know. Conor only knew he wanted to punch the man.

He stood and looked around. He had to get out of here or else he was going to take the dog's place on the bed so he could be Abby's *warm body*. The recipient of her hugs, kisses, and sweet nothings. While her arms were wrapped around him!

"Well, that's it," he said. "The place should be heated up in no time at all. Call me if ye have any more issues with keeping warm." It sounded like a proposition and he should've taken it back. Instead, he let his words lay where they were. Maybe she would take him up on the offer.

When she didn't, he headed for the door.

"Thank you, Conor."

"Aye," he said as he stepped past the threshold.

"Goodnight," she said.

He let the shutting door be his response. *Och,* he was in over his head. He didn't understand why he was so attracted to her. And had no idea how to get unstuck from the mess he'd made. He never should've kissed her. He'd given her the wrong idea by doing so. And he was certain that he'd given himself insomnia. For surely he'd lie awake all night thinking about that kiss. How it had been transformative. And how he'd like to do it again.

As predicted, that night Conor couldn't fall asleep. Aye, he might have dozed a little here and there, but the fifteen other men that Abby might find attractive enough to kiss within a twenty-mile radius haunted Conor. He *dinna* like it. Not one bit! And the Almighty knew he needed his rest. Conor had a lot going on before they headed to their first bridal show. He'd need his wits about him to be productive until they left. There were so many orders to be fulfilled. But thoughts of Abby distracted him and he was certain that images of her would continue to rob him of his nightly slumber.

Chapter 11

FOR THE NEXT FIVE DAYS, he worked nonstop, only returning to his cottage when he was sure the whole village was asleep, especially his American neighbor. Abby had the good sense not to use their office and Conor appreciated it. He got glimpses of her here and there, but he was never close enough to speak to her, let alone kiss her like he had before. However, his reprieve from Abby was coming to an end; the bridal show was coming up fast—days away. There were still many things they needed to decide before then. For himself, though, he'd have to come up with a new way to deal with seeing and talking to Abby, day in and day out, until the bridal show was done.

Conor had arrived at the weaver's building this morning holding a mug of hot tea, which he promptly spilled when he saw Abby in their office ... and she wasn't alone. She had company. Male company! And it wasn't Uncle Magnus either. His nightmare involving Abby surrounded by suitors was coming true.

But as Conor got closer, he saw it was Oliver Middleton,

Gandiegow's computer guy. *Aye,* Hugh had mentioned that Oliver would be helping Abby with the wedding website. But Conor hadn't been prepared to see her with another man—at least not yet. Of course, Conor knew that Oliver was engaged to Kirsty, Gandiegow's school teacher, but that knowledge did nothing to tame the jealousy that was consuming him.

He shook his head in disgust at himself. He'd definitely gone off the deep end. He had better get control of himself before he went into the office and did something stupid. Like pick a fight with Oliver instead of just picking up today's work orders.

Conor frowned at Oliver's physique. Oliver spent his days with computers, but apparently, he either worked out during his off time or he'd taken to doing manual labor around Gandiegow. Those muscles of his hadn't come about by typing. Conor wanted to know one thing: Why hadn't Hugh enlisted Ryn McBride—a graphics designer—to help Abby instead of Oliver? Nothing to be jealous of there. But Conor knew the answer. Ryn and Tuck's second child was due any day now and all new work for Ryn was being funneled to others.

Conor tried to calm himself. He didn't like how Abby was looking at Oliver—as if he'd invented the computer or internet or something—so Conor decided to break it up. Determinedly, he went to the office and slung open the door. "Abby, may I speak with ye a moment?"

She glanced up, looking surprised. "Speak to me about what?"

"Uh, the wedding shawls." But hadn't they already agreed on every aspect of them? He should've thought this through first. "I was thinking of paring down the tartans by one or two."

She looked conflicted. "Conor, if it's okay with you, can we do that in a bit? I'll only have Oliver for another twenty minutes before he heads back to Gandiegow."

Conor didn't like it, but he'd have to wait it out. Because, dammit, he couldn't come up with another excuse, lame or otherwise. "Okay."

Oliver looked up at him. "Why don't you come and see what we've been doing."

Excitedly, Abby motioned him over. "Oliver is setting up a way for couples to stream the wedding for those who can't make it here in person. Of course, we'll need a videographer. Is there anyone in the village with experience?" Abby was looking at Conor as if he had all the answers, which he didn't.

"We'll look into it," Conor said automatically. For whatever reason, he was trying to let her know that he and she were a team ... not she and Oliver!

Oliver looked thoughtful. "I have another idea. What about offering online weddings for couples on a budget who can't afford the trip to Scotland? The U.S. has tons of Scotland fans you could tap into." Oliver was an American who had recently moved to Gandiegow and he probably knew a lot about what would go in America and what wouldn't. "Whussendale could provide the virtual backdrop, the bagpipes, the Scottish charm, and all the traditions without actually traveling here."

"I love it!" Abby said. "And we could ship their wedding shawl and quilt to them in a decorative box."

Oliver pulled out a notebook and scribbled something down. "I'll look into it. Something this novel could really take off and be a treasure trove for Whussendale."

"And for Gandiegow, too, if you don't mind."

"I don't mind at all," Oliver said, as he jotted more in his notebook.

Conor frowned at Oliver for coming up with such a good suggestion.

Abby put her hand on Oliver's arm, which made Conor see red and want to punch him. "Yes, you look into it. I still need to familiarize myself with all the Scottish wedding traditions. Let me get a few in-person weddings under my belt before we offer online weddings."

Conor felt out of the loop. He was supposed to be the one helping Abby with the weddings, but the pretty boy American seemed to be horning his way in. Conor looked at his watch. "Ye better get going, mate. Kirsty's probably waiting on ye." Conor congratulated himself for reminding Oliver that he was engaged. He turned to Abby to explain. "Kirsty is Oliver's fiancée." Now Abby knew what-was-what.

"Congratulations!" Abby said. "Let me know if I can help with the wedding plans. I don't know if you've heard, but Deydie has made it clear that I'm to assist with Gandiegow's weddings from here on out. And I get the feeling that it's important to stay on Deydie's good side."

"You're right about that," Oliver said good-naturedly. He shut his laptop and stood. "Good to see you again, Conor. Hugh mentioned you might want to automate the order tickets. Just shoot me a text when you've got time to work on it. I've got some ideas."

"Thanks," Conor said. It was a relief to know that Hugh had been listening when he'd told the laird about the changes he wanted to make.

"Abby, I'll be in touch. I'll keep working on the website. Text if you think of anything you might like to add." Oliver gave a little wave before he left.

Conor had the urge to kiss Abby so she'd forget all about the charming and overly muscular Oliver. Conor also wanted her to forget that she and Oliver had other things in common, like the same birth country. But Conor couldn't kiss her here; anyone walking by would be able to see them through the office windows. Besides, he shouldn't want to kiss her. He'd vowed not to do that again. "Come to my place and have dinner with me tonight."

She seemed shocked by the offer. To be honest, he was shocked that he'd invited her, too. Had he no control over his mouth anymore? It was bad enough that he couldn't control his thoughts about her or the frequency … which was more times a day than he could count.

"It's not a date," he clarified. "I thought we could finalize the plans for our trip to the bridal show. We need to make sure that we have everything we'll need to set up the booth."

At that moment, he had a brilliant idea. Abby was right when she said that she needed to become more familiar with Scottish weddings. Conor could help. He'd need to make a few calls to see if any nuptials would be happening soon. That way she could really sell this Whussendale wedding thing when they were together at the bridal show.

Conor worked hard all morning on the orders until he broke for lunch. He used his meal time to call every kirk in the area to ask if there were any weddings over the coming weekend. By the seventh call, he was feeling hopeless and he was finding out the hard way that November weddings were uncommon. He felt like he was letting Abby down, even though she knew nothing of his plan.

He took Dublin out for a quick walk and then headed back to the weaver's building to work on the next batch of orders. His spirits lifted when he recalled that Abby would be coming for dinner tonight! Back at the loom, Conor threw himself into work and the afternoon flew by.

Hours later, he was home again, but this time, instead of making calls, he pulled out onions, carrots, leeks, and potatoes. He approached cooking like he did his work at the mill—being completely prepped and organized before starting. He even straightened the vegetables so they were lined up perfectly. Just as he grabbed the knife, ready to chop, his phone rang. He checked the screen. It was Keiran.

"Hey, little brother. I'm calling to see how my lass is doing."

Conor glanced over at Dublin who was sleeping on her bed. Apparently, she was dreaming about running through the fields, possibly with the Wallace and the Bruce, as her long legs were moving in her sleep. "She's all tuckered out. I think she's enjoying her vacation in Whussendale."

"Thanks for doing this favor for me. It's a relief to know she's in good hands," Keiran said.

"Hey, since you called: do you know of anyone getting married soon?" Conor asked. "I would like to take Abby to a real Scottish wedding before she starts planning ones here for Whussendale."

"Ye've got it bad for her, don't you?" Keiran teased.

Conor remained silent.

"Okay, okay. I'll let you know if I hear about anyone getting hitched."

"Thanks. I appreciate it," Conor said.

"I better hop off. I'm being hailed. Talk to ye later, little brother." And Kieran was gone.

Though Keiran had been ribbing him about the opposite sex since adolescence, it made Conor wonder if he'd been too obvious about his emotions, especially when it came to Abby. He didn't want to give her the wrong idea again, like he had when he'd kissed her. And he wasn't the kind of man who strung women along, either.

But he couldn't help but anticipate having her here this evening. He actually felt excited, which was something he hadn't experienced in a long time. *Och*, he shouldn't be looking forward to spending time alone with Abby, but he was. They'd be in his cottage away from prying eyes. But then he remembered his promise to himself that he wouldn't kiss her again. But he might break that promise because apparently, he was a weak man where Abby was concerned, and his willpower was dwindling.

As he picked up the knife again, the phone rang a second time. It was Magnus.

"Lad, do you mind stopping over for a cup of tea?"

"Are ye all right?" Conor worried like an old woman over Magnus and Willoughby, though the two elderly men were right as rain and sprier than men half their age.

"I'm fine. Just thought ye might have some free time."

"Uncle, can it wait? I'm in the middle of making dinner. For Abby." Conor didn't want to add the last but he had no choice. He had to come clean or else Magnus would insist that dinner could wait. Or his uncle would want Conor to come over for dinner at his place. Or worse, Magnus would invite himself over to Conor's and then his time alone with Abby would be a lost opportunity.

Opportunity for what? lingered in his mind. Unwittingly, some *verra* pleasant images popped into his head.

"Abby, eh?" Magnus said, breaking his musing. Conor could almost see the old man rubbing his chin in thought. "Do you fancy her? She's a right handsome young woman. I'm sure ye've noticed that."

"I better go," Conor said, not willing to admit anything. Not even to himself. "I'll speak with ye later."

"Aye, later." Magnus said it as if he expected a blow-by-blow of the evening with Abby.

Conor hung up, determined to ignore the next call that came in. Thirty minutes later, he had the soup simmering on the hob. Moments after that, there came a light knock on the door that kickstarted his heart. He stopped himself from racing to the door. Dublin had beat him to the punch, anyway; she was already there, whining. With mock calmness, he walked steadily to the door to let in his dinner companion.

But on the other side of the door was Uncle Willoughby. "We need to talk."

Conor loved his uncles, but seriously? Couldn't he get a break? At least for tonight? "Do ye want to come in?"

Willoughby waved his hand. "No. No. I need to say something. About Magnus. He's not a young man anymore," Willoughby said. "He's not as hale as he used to be."

"I know." Wasn't it the reason Conor had stayed in Whussendale? He stayed for both of his great uncles. He wanted to remind Willoughby that he was no spring chicken either—he was the older brother! Instead, he said, "How about some hot tea? It's awfully chilly outside. Plus, I need to stir the soup on the hob."

"Nay. I need to get home. I just wanted to say that ye need to spend more time with Magnus while ye still have the chance. Just don't tell him I said so."

"I promise I won't say a word," Conor said.

"Good lad," Willoughby said, which was high praise coming from him. Apparently, the discussion was over. His uncle gripped the railing as he went down the two steps and then shuffled away in the direction of his cottage.

It was perfect timing, since Abby walked out of her cottage at that moment. She watched Uncle Willoughby walk away. Dublin peered out and Conor grasped her collar just in time to keep her from running to Abby.

"Dublin, sit. And stop making a nuisance of yereself," he said, though in truth, he wanted to run to Abby, too.

When Abby got to them, she knelt down and kissed Dublin's nose. "She's not a nuisance. She only wanted to give me a proper hello." Abby shot him a look that said she'd like a proper hello from him, too.

But Conor didn't want to jump up and down and circle Abby like an eager puppy; he wanted to pull her into his arms and give her a proper kiss … or even better, an improper one! With her body crushed up against his. And with his mouth taking advantage of hers. He couldn't help but notice how wholesome she looked in her blue gingham dress. The epitome of the Scottish lass next door.

"Come on, Dublin," she said, breaking his reverie. "What smells so good?"

"Red lentil soup." Conor held the door wide for her and even stepped back because he wanted nothing more than to pull her into his arms. He wanted her to forget all about how clever Oliver was or the idea of her finding another man to kiss.

"What's wrong?" she asked. "Is this a bad time? Should we reschedule for another night?"

"No. We'll not reschedule." His voice was hoarse and raw. So were Conor's feelings. Hungrily, his eyes took her in. The sweetest, prettiest lass he knew. She made him forget what she'd done to her ex-fiancé. He was completely astounded by her. Which was the only reason he could think of for why he'd let himself give in to what he was feeling.

He shut the door and pulled her into his arms in one smooth movement. He kissed her; of course he kissed her. He had no choice. Just like he had no choice but to take his next breath. His pent-up need for her was nearly overwhelming.

Surprisingly, she didn't respond to him immediately. Worried that he'd scared her, he started to pull away, an act of Herculean effort. But then she snaked her arms around his neck and pulled him closer, fervently kissing him back. Which made him forget everything, until she shocked him by slipping her hands under his shirt and sliding them up his back.

"Gawd, lass," he exclaimed into the kiss.

"Shh. Just go with it," she said, laughing against his lips.

He growled, picked her up, and carried her to his bed without breaking the kiss. Then, with much disappointment, he had to stop kissing her so he could lie her down. For his effort, she rewarded him with an inviting smile, so he immediately positioned himself beside her to continue where he'd left off. But this time, he was kissing other places—her neck, her shoulder, everywhere he could reach. He didn't have to worry about whether he was going too fast; she seemed to be just as impatient as he was.

Somehow, she'd gotten his shirt off without him noticing, and now, she was unsnapping his jeans.

"I wish you were wearing a kilt," she said while wrestling with his zipper. "It would make this a whole lot easier!"

He grinned at her frustration. "Here. Let me." He made easy work of his jeans and kicked them to the floor.

While he'd been removing his clothing, she'd been working on her own, and was now waiting for him in her lacy pink bra and matching pink knickers. "Ye're so verra beautiful." He tried to cover how choked up he felt by leaning down to kiss her passionately again. But his kisses had surprisingly turned tender.

She clearly approved, because she scooted closer, crushing herself against him and moaning into his kiss. He was overwhelmed by her all over again. He could've made comparisons with past lovemakings but all other encounters seemed inconsequential compared to what was going on now. Plus, he wanted to be fully present with her.

"Do you have some protection?" Abby asked.

"Aye." He wanted to applaud her for thinking clearly because *that* had been furthest from his mind. He reached for his wallet and pulled out the condom that had been there for ages and set it beside her on the bed.

She laid a hand on his chest and rubbed tenderly as if she were caressing his heart. "I can't believe we're going to do this." Her smile felt like sunshine on a cold day. "And at the same time, I'm not surprised at all. We should have been doing this all along." She'd said the last bit in a whisper. What did she mean? Had she been attracted to him from the start, as he'd been for her?

Before he got caught up in her again, he'd better take a breath and admit the truth. "Lass, I'm a bit concerned this will go more quickly than I'd like." That wasn't exactly what he wanted to say. "What I mean is that it's been a long time since I've been with a woman." Probably close to two years, maybe longer. Morag had put a stop to their intimacy, always claiming a headache or that she was too tired. Which gave him some inkling now how long she and Steven had been carrying on. Or maybe Morag had been with others all through their marriage—they'd never had much of a sex life. Yet Conor had never thought to ask her if she'd been untrue. He'd always assumed she was as faithful to him as he'd been to her. What a fool he'd been.

He pulled away from Abby and sat up. Damn, he shouldn't be thinking about his time with Morag.

Abby sat up, too, and put her arms around him. "What's wrong?"

"Just a ghost from the past is all."

Last Christmas had been particularly hard. He was used to loud Christmas gatherings with Morag's family. But last year, he'd refused to leave his cottage even to have a meal with his uncles, though they'd practically begged him. Now, he was regretting the time he'd wasted being angry with Morag about what she'd done to him and their marriage.

Abby looked up and laid a hand on his cheek. "Come back to me."

He nodded and gazed into her eyes, thinking he saw so much there. But hadn't he'd learned that he couldn't trust himself when it came to women? He had no idea how to gauge what women were thinking. But the lass holding him right now really seemed to care about him. But maybe she was just using him to have a bit of fun.

She looked at him sadly. "It'll be okay if you're not up for this. I understand."

He glanced down between them. Being up wasn't the problem. It was his own blasted baggage that was so annoying. "No, lass, you don't understand. I've been unhappy for so long that I've forgotten how to enjoy myself."

"Come here." She pulled him down and snuggled into him with her arm around his waist. She threw her leg over his thighs, pinning him there. "We can just cuddle."

But he knew he couldn't settle for *cuddling*. Especially when this gorgeous woman was lying next to him in bed, nearly on top of him. "Ye know that ye're beautiful, wonderful ... something special." Her full body hug had erased all self-pitying thoughts and now he could get back with the program. He leaned over and kissed her, and within seconds, they both were eager for each other once again. She inched herself on top of him and was rubbing him in just the right way.

"Don't ye want to make this last?" Regardless of what she wanted, he needed to slow things down, and in a hurry, too, or it would be over before he could give her the same amount of pleasure that she was giving him. He started to roll on top of her but sat up instead to unclasp her bra. He leaned back to give her a good long look. Her breasts were just the right size. "Gawd, woman. Ye're so beautiful." She gave him an impish smile and he settled his body between her legs. He leaned down and kissed one breast while his hand teased the other.

Moaning, she wrapped her legs around him and wriggled

against him, nearly making him come undone. He put a hand against her hip. "Slow down, luv."

"No, I can't slow down." Her frustration made him smile. "You're driving me crazy, Conor. Can't you just put it in already?"

He laughed. "Ye're such an impatient lass."

She began blindly groping the bed with her hand.

"What are ye doing?" he asked as he moved over to her other breast.

"I'm looking for the condom." She must've hit paydirt because she said, "Aha!" He heard her rip open the package. "Here." She pushed him away from giving her lovely breasts more attention and then shoved the condom in his line of sight. His vision was somewhat blurry from lust.

"All right, then." He took the condom from her and rolled it on. Before he knew what-was-what, she'd grabbed ahold of him and was guiding him in. "Ye certainly know what ye want." Aye, he wanted *it* too, but he also was intent on making it last.

Abby had other plans. So did his body. Apparently, they were both on the same page now. He was acting like the one without any restraint. He was the one who was nearing the edge. But a moment later, it was Abby who came. Her muffled cry made him feel like the luckiest man in the world.

"Oh, lass, my lovely lass," he said as she clutched him. He clutched her, too, as emotions gripped him, emotions he'd never felt before. He wanted to tell her that he'd protect her with his life. He could never let anything bad happen to her, ever.

She opened her eyes and looked at him as if she could read his soul. "Thank you." She rocked against him and he couldn't help but meet her halfway. Two thrusts later, he came, while she held him tight, whispering sweet nothings to him.

He didn't want to end their connection, but he also didn't want to crush her either. He rolled away. "I'll be right back." He went to the bathroom to dispose of the condom and to slip into a clean pair of boxers from the laundry basket. After he washed his hands, he walked out of the bathroom. "Are ye hungry? The soup's been simmering." But he stopped short. She must've pulled her clothes on in record time because she was fully dressed. The quilt was haphazardly pulled up as if she'd attempted to make the bed in a hurry. He could feel himself getting angry and was sure she could tell his displeasure by his frown. "Sit down. Food's ready."

He didn't know what he'd been expecting in the aftermath of their lovemaking, but he certainly hadn't expected her to be racing for the door.

Chapter 12

ABBY STOPPED AND STARED at him. Yes, he was glorious, standing there in his boxers, but she shouldn't have made love to him! She was such an idiot. Sleeping with Conor had been rash, stupid. Yes, they had some kind of connection. A real connection. But it didn't matter. Once again, she'd mixed her wedding planner business with her personal life. Hadn't she done this with Aaron? She'd dated the boss' son, got engaged to boss' son, and then left the boss' son at the altar. And because she'd been such a fool, she had to burn every bridge back home. She'd had to change continents to distance herself from the disaster she'd caused. And for what? How could she have ignored the fact that Conor had been made her wedding planner sidekick? By Hugh, no less, the laird, the top dog! She'd ruined everything. When would she ever learn?

When things went down the toilet here, as they most certainly would, she'd have nowhere to go. Sleeping with Conor had even worse consequences than screwing things up with Aaron and her mother. The little voice in her head piped up:

But this time it's different.

"No, it isn't!" she whispered to herself. Conor pulled down a glass from the shelf and angrily filled it from the tap, all while talking to himself in bitter tones. She felt certain he hadn't heard her speak.

Her brain kept going over it again and again. She guessed she was trying to figure out how it could've gone differently ... or not happened at all. But she had no answers. She was shocked at herself for being impatient to *have* him. Miss Prim and Proper wasn't proper at all when it came to sleeping with the Scotsman. She blamed Conor! He was too sexy for his own good!

She glanced over at him and saw that he was staring back. He quickly looked away. It was clear that the air between them was awkward. Nearly unbearable. How could he expect her to stay and have dinner with him? Conor was delusional.

"I better go," she said feebly. She sounded as if she didn't possess a spine.

"Nay," he said gruffly. "Ye'll stay. That's the least ye can do." Stilted, as if he'd become a cardboard cutout of himself, Conor furiously stepped into his jeans and then yanked his tee shirt from the chair in the corner. He glared at her before he slipped it on. It was a shame to cover up such a beautiful body. Once he was zipped up and fully dressed, he pointed to the kitchen chair. "Sit."

Dublin plopped her butt on the floor and gazed up eagerly at Conor as though waiting for her reward. Abby wanted to tell Dublin that she needed to learn to read the room. Being so dang cute and clever would've been funny, if things weren't so strained in the cottage.

But since things were strained ...

"Conor, you can't order me around." Abby was glad for the anger and glad she'd finally found her voice.

He turned away from her. "Ye're right. Sorry." He pulled two bowls from the open shelves and set them on the counter. "Abby, please stay and eat with me."

This put her in a difficult position. He'd asked nicely, and if she stomped out now, she'd look like a shrew. Yeah, she would never be able to completely shake off her need to be a people-pleaser.

"All right." She didn't sit, though. Instead, she went to the sink and washed her hands while he placed the bowls on the table. He retrieved silverware from a drawer so she pulled two napkins from the holder and folded them in half before laying them beside the bowls.

"The soup is Mrs. McNabb's recipe," he said as if he couldn't bear for there to be any more silence between them. "I also made scones for us. Do you know Cait from Gandiegow? She calls the scones 'biscuits'. They aren't the typical scones that ye get at the café. Cait's are lighter and more buttery."

Abby didn't know what to say. She could be forthright and confess why she was regretting the best sex she'd ever had. How mixing business with pleasure had imploded her life once before. But she hadn't forgotten how bent out of shape he'd acted when she'd talked about her relationship with Aaron. She didn't want to make herself look worse in Conor's eyes than she already had. Anyway, compared to everything else, it was a small detail that she'd left Belle's Weddings without giving notice. Or that she hadn't responded to Belle's many texts, most of them berating her for jilting her son. The one thing that Abby did right was to give all her files and notes to her colleague at Belle's so that she could take over Abby's weddings.

Finally, Abby answered, "Yes, I met Cait."

He opened the oven door and pulled out the biscuits. "I kept the scones in here to keep them warm."

"They smell good." Feeling weird about just sitting here,

Abby grabbed the filled glasses and set them behind their bowls.

Conor brought the soup pot and ladle to the table. He walked over to the other chair and pulled it out. "For you."

As if they were at a fancy restaurant, she took her seat as he scooted in the chair, and then he sat, too. To her surprise, he held his hand out to her. She had no clue why he wanted to hold her hand. And she was regretting that she'd stayed and hadn't made her escape. She brought her questioning gaze up to meet his.

He wiggled his fingers. "To say grace, Abby. Nothing else. I promise. Our clans are God-fearing people, so we don't tempt fate. We thank the Almighty before we eat and before we sleep and many other times throughout the day as well. Just as the laird insists on saying grace at Kilheath Castle, I insist we do so in my humble cottage."

"Oh. Okay." She timidly put her hand in his. She had to fight hard not to notice how perfectly her hand fit in his. And how much comfort she got from the warmth of his grasp. For a moment, she wished things could be different. If Hugh hadn't assigned Conor to the wedding venture like he had.

Conor squeezed her hand before bowing his head. "Bless, O Lord, this food we are about to eat; and we pray you, O God, that it may be good for our body and soul." He squeezed her hand again. "Amen."

She repeated 'Amen' and then pulled her hand away.

Bravely, she glanced over at him; he was looking back at her as if he were peering into her soul. She immediately looked away. He didn't seem the type to have gooey sentiments like she did; one of the pitfalls of being a woman, she supposed.

She took a spoonful of the lentil soup and swallowed. The soup was thick, rich, and delicious. But if she ate quickly, she could get out of here, away from the bed in the corner that knew all her sins. Like how she'd complicated everything for a nice roll in the hay.

Dublin sidled up to Abby and whined, begging for a bit of human food. "Sorry, girl. I heard your daddy say you were not to have people food, only the dogfood he brought." Abby welcomed the distraction, appreciating that the dog could be a buffer while they ate. Also, Dublin had a way of relaxing her overly hyper nerves. She made a great therapy dog in that respect. Abby grabbed a biscuit, tore off a small piece, and discreetly fed it to her dog-friend under the table.

Conor pretended not to notice, while he ladled out a second helping of the soup. "I'll feed her when we're done." But just as the soup hit the bowl, his cell phone rang. "I better take this."

Abby thought it strange that he left the table before answering. But this evening had been full of strange things. Not the least of which was that she still wanted to be with Conor even though it would cost her everything.

She wasn't exactly the rebellious type to side against logic and forget all reason. If only she were a different person. Or if she had a different job. Maybe she could have him and to hell with the consequences.

But in the end, even if they were the perfect couple with no hoops to jump through and were together under the best of circumstances, there were no guarantees that *they* would work out. So why put her future in danger in the first place?

Abby ate the last bite of her red lentil soup and put her spoon down. Life was a complicated mess, and she wished that just once, she could get what she wanted. Instead, she stood decisively, choosing not to go after perhaps her one true love, but to leave Conor's cottage ... forever.

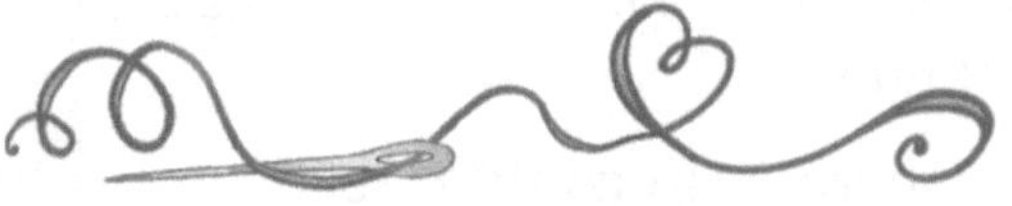

Conor stepped away from the table, feeling puzzled and wondering why Deydie McCracken was calling him. *What the devil does she want now?* That old woman had a way of insinuating herself into everyone's lives, even in Whussendale. Apparently, no one was safe when it came to Deydie.

Aye, it was rude to take a call during dinner, but Conor figured it couldn't make things any more awkward between him and Abby at this point. He had no idea why she was behaving as if she didn't know him at all, especially since they'd shared such an intimate moment not long ago in the bed in the corner. He was still puzzled by Abby's reaction. And he was especially puzzled by his own—having such romantic feelings about Abby.

The phone was on its third ring. For a second he thought about not answering, but he'd already walked away from the table. He turned so he wouldn't have to look at Abby while he spoke to Deydie. "Hullo."

"Conor? I was about ready to hang up!" Deydie hollered.

He walked to the fireplace to get a modicum of privacy. "Aye, I'm here."

Deydie harrumphed but then continued on. "Father Andrew said ye're looking for a Scottish wedding for the wedding planner to attend."

"Aye." Surely, Deydie wasn't going to offer up Rory and Diana's wedding. Abby had already been roped into helping them with it anyway.

"A couple from Lios and their families just arrived in town, hoping to use St. Henry's for their wedding. The water pipes burst at their kirk in Lios and they figured Gandiegow's kirk would be available on short notice. Father Andrew is with them now and asked me to call to let ye know that there'll be a wedding here in two hours. Do ye think ye can get the wedding planner here by then?"

"Aye. We'll be there." He couldn't believe his luck! Maybe

this would make Abby look kindly on him again. He glanced over and saw her feed another bite of scone to Dublin. He turned back around to speak to Deydie. "Don't worry. We'll be off shortly."

"It's no skin off me old back. Just hurry yere arses up!" With that Deydie hung up.

Conor pocketed his phone. When he spun around, Abby was at the door with her hand on the knob. He had to stop her. "We've had a change of plans." Convincing her felt paramount. "Ye look really lovely in yere gingham dress but I need you to head back to yere cottage and put on the best dress that you brought with you. I'm taking you someplace special." What a stupid thing to say! It made it sound like a date, and the lass was definitely acting skittish ever since they'd done the deed.

"Umm. . ." It sounded like she was considering how to let him down easy.

He cut her off. "This isn't a date. I promise ye're going to like this. Be sure to bring along yere notebook and something to write with."

"Why?"

Was that a look of disappointment on her face? Did she *want* this to be a date, after all? She was confusing him.

But she only said, "Tell me who was on the phone?"

"It was Deydie. We need to hurry to Gandiegow."

"What for?" Abby had a puzzled look on her face. "A quilt retreat? Why do I need to wear my best dress for a quilt retreat? Unless, of course, someone famous is coming to teach in Gandiegow."

"Nay. Not a quilt retreat. It's a surprise," he answered. He thought that would be the end of her hesitation. But it wasn't.

She frowned. "You don't know me very well but I'm not fond of surprises." A strange expression crossed her face as if she were reliving a painful memory.

He had to come clean and tell her what was up. "We're going to an impromptu wedding in Gandiegow. I thought ye might like to attend a real Scottish wedding before you have to coordinate one yourself. See what it's all about." Abby didn't need to know that he'd made more than thirty phone calls to find a Scottish wedding for her.

Her expression transformed into one of gratitude. "Oh, Conor, that's so considerate."

"Please hurry and change. Time is of the essence. I must change as well. I'll meet you at my vehicle. Okay?"

She nodded.

He made a mental note to ask her later why she didn't like surprises. He went to her in the opened doorway. With her eyes as big as saucers, he gently pushed a lock of her hair behind her ear to see her face better. And so that she could see him better, too. Especially since he was going to tell her something important.

"Lass, I do know you." He searched her eyes to see if she understood him. It was strange that he'd never known anyone as intimately as he knew her. Especially strange since they'd known each other for only a short period of time. Maybe he was reading what was going on between them wrong, but he didn't think so. *Aye*, he was feeling very sentimental about her. Perhaps, it was a mistake, because he might not have all the facts about her, but he sensed a deep connection between them. Soulmate kind of stuff. The kind of feelings that scared the hell out of him. He knew why those feelings were scaring him. He'd never felt this way about Morag. And still, it nearly destroyed him when she left him. He couldn't imagine the damage that Abby could do, because his heart was already fully invested in her. He could barely think above the pounding in his chest and he wondered if that was any indication of the depth of his feeling.

Then he did the stupidest thing. He leaned in and gave her a sound kiss on the lips. He was just as surprised by it as she was, even though it felt like the most natural thing to do. He was even more surprised that he didn't give a whit whether a Whussendalian passing by might have seen them.

"Head on over to yere cottage," he said hoarsely and maybe a little too harshly, though he hadn't meant it that way. Apparently, his voice knew it even before the realization hit his brain ... he was more affected by Abby than she was by him. *Clearly!* "I'll meet you at the car."

He dressed quickly in his wedding attire—kilt, sporran, jacket, waistcoat, dress shirt, tie, and kilt socks with garters. He texted Declan before dropping Dublin and her supplies off at Uncle Magnus's. When Conor arrived back at his doorstep, Abby was leaving her cottage next door. His breath caught at the sight of her and stole all oxygen away. To say she looked pretty in her red tartan dress beneath her open coat was an understatement. The dress fit her as snugly as a glove and Conor liked what he saw *verra* much! She had on a pair of tall black boots that he envisioned unzipping and slipping off before he got to the more interesting bits of her.

"You look very beautiful," he said, his throat feeling thick.

"Thank you. It's my Christmas dress."

"Nice choice for the wedding tonight," he said.

"I'm glad I brought it." She slowly scanned him from head to toe as if she were memorizing every inch of him and what he was wearing. "You don't look half-bad yourself." She smiled at him brightly as if she'd enjoyed what she saw. "Ready?"

Oh, *aye*, he was ready ... for more than just a car ride. He leaned in and gave her a quick kiss on the lips. He really needed to stop doing that. Especially out here in the open. Others would get the wrong idea. Hell, Abby would get the wrong idea, too. He needed to clear up what exactly was going on with him ... and with her. Before he did anything drastic. He cleared his throat. "Aye. Let's get going."

She glanced around. "Where's Dublin?"

"Uncle Magnus is babysitting tonight. Declan agreed to take her for a long walk before Magnus goes to bed." Conor asked Declan to look in on Uncle Willoughby, too. It was a habit that Conor had gotten into. His uncles were the last elders in their thinning family tree.

As they walked to the car, a thought hit Conor. Should he and Abby have packed a bag in case they didn't make it back tonight? Nay, surely, with an impromptu wedding, there wouldn't be a reception and céilidh. The evening would no doubt end early. Which made him feel oddly disappointed. Though they'd only gotten out of bed a while ago, he wouldn't mind taking another tumble with her away from Whussendale. As it was, he was concerned that the nosy villagers might have a clue to what they'd just done. Plus, he'd like a chance to dance with Abby, especially holding her close while dancing to a slow song. "We better hurry." He put his hand on her lower back and guided her to his car.

As soon as he got behind the steering wheel and she was buckled into her seat, he asked, "Tell me why you don't like surprises."

"Oh, that."

He glanced over to see her chewing her lip. "Go on." He drove but made sure to let her know he was listening.

"It has to do with how my mother and I differ when it comes to defining what a *surprise* means. When I was young, other kids would talk about the good surprises their parents would give them for their birthdays or Christmas. But my mother's surprises were more painful. Some were benign but still no fun for me."

"Like what?" he asked.

"She would make my doctor's appointments a surprise. *Surprise! You're going to get stuck with a needle!* Or like an unexpected trip to the funeral home to see my dead grandmother that I'd never met. Or when she'd schedule brunch or dinner but surprise me by including a man she wanted to set me up with—always a professional, boring and much older than me. For some reason, she thought I needed someone in my life to straighten me out. I don't know. Mother and I have never seen eye to eye."

"I see now why surprises aren't yere thing. But tell me why ye never met your grandmother before she passed on," he said.

Abby shook her head. "I've never met any of my relatives. My mother never talked about anyone in her family, even though I asked about them many times when I was a child. I used to wonder if we were in the Witness Protection Program or something. But no. My mother just doesn't believe in traditional family."

"What about your father?"

"Oh, yeah, him. Well, he was chosen from a binder for his attributes. My mother manages a fertility clinic in St. Louis. I'm a test tube baby."

Conor reached over and squeezed her hand. He hoped it conveyed how sorry he was for all she'd been through.

She squeezed his hand back. "Thank you for arranging this field trip."

"'Twas nothing."

"Tell me who is spontaneously getting married. I know Rory and Diana have been on the books for some time. How did this wedding just pop up?" she asked.

Conor didn't have much to tell. "I think Deydie said there'd been a flood in their kirk. We'll just have to hear the details when we get there." He was happy that the tension between them from earlier was gone. He pointed to his mobile that sat between them. "Would ye like to listen to some music?"

"Yes, that's a great idea."

"Your choice." He told her his passcode.

Abby chose a Celtic Thunder Christmas album from his music library and "It's Beginning to Look a Lot like Christmas" came through the car's speakers.

To his surprise, Conor was feeling great. By helping Abby, he'd inadvertently raised his own spirits. He sang along with the song and then Abby joined in.

After finishing two Christmas albums and starting a third, they finally rolled into Gandiegow's parking lot, where they were met by Moira who rushed them off to the kirk. People were lined up and processing in. The bagpipes were playing and the joviality of the wedding party and their families seemed to make Abby happy and more at ease.

They took a seat at the back of the kirk.

He glanced over when Abby pulled out her notebook and wrote, *Ushers wearing wool tartan pants, not kilts.*

Conor leaned over and whispered, "Ushers typically match the groom's party, wearing the same tartan for their kilts." At least that's what the ushers wore at his own wedding to Morag.

"Thanks." She wrote, 'Not typical' next to her last entry.

He watched as she scribbled *Bridesmaids wearing satin spaghetti strap dresses even though it's cold outside.* Then she wrote *Thistles in the bouquets.* When Father Andrew began to speak, she noted his *very long blue tartan stole.* She sketched the large hat of the woman who sat in front of them and wrote *Hats like at royal weddings.* Abby jotted down everything, filling several pages during the ceremony. She seemed especially interested when Father Andrew used his stole to perform the handfasting by wrapping the couple's hands together. She even looked over at him and smiled as if to say that coming here had been worthwhile.

Conor was enjoying watching Abby. But when the pastor started speaking about the duties of marriage, the commitment of marriage, and how marriage wasn't to be entered into lightly, Conor's happy mood faded and the bitterness of betrayal felt fresh once again.

He should've anticipated the setback in his mood. Hell, he should've thought twice before making all those phone calls, trying to find Abby a wedding to go to. Why hadn't he remembered that his own wedding had set him up for pain and disappointment? He tried to change his mood. Weddings were supposed to be celebrations. But he certainly wasn't feeling celebratory!

Abby slipped her hand into his and leaned over. "Are you okay?"

He glanced over and saw her look of concern. "I'm fine." But he wasn't. He wanted nothing more than to leave.

She squeezed his hand. "We don't have to stay if you don't want to."

"I wanted you to have this experience," he whispered back, trying to suppress the thought that it was better to get kicked in the head than to be married and divorced.

"I understand. And thank you. But you don't have to stay. I could meet up with you afterward."

He shook his head. "I'll be fine." He squeezed her hand back, then extricated himself from her grasp and faced forward.

But then Father Andrew had the couple repeat their vows. *"For better, for worse ..."*

For Conor, there had been plenty of *worse*, that was for sure.

"To love and to cherish until death do us part..." Conor scoffed internally. Coming to this wedding had been a monu-

mental mistake. It dredged up all the feelings he kept hidden, even from himself.

"And this is my solemn vow." Which Morag hadn't kept.

Conor endured the rest of the ceremony with gritted teeth. He couldn't wait until the registry was signed, the couple was leaving the kirk, and the bagpiper was leading the procession to the céilidh at Pastas & Pastries. They could skip the speeches and when the ties came off as the first drink was tipped up. They could skip all the fun because he wasn't in a fun mood.

His not fun mood followed him all the way to the restaurant.

"Let's head back to Whussendale," Abby said when they got to the doorway of Pastas & Pastries. "I can tell you're ready to get out of Gandiegow."

Either she was an intuitive lass or she could read his mind. He thought he'd been curbing his emotions. But he'd have to do better. "Nay. Ye need to eat. All you had was a cup of soup at my place." His place. Which conjured up rolling around in the sheets and steaming up the cottage's windows. A much more pleasant memory than the ones he'd been having. "We're going to stay."

She shook her head. "Really, Conor. I don't mind leaving."

"Well, I do. I'm hungry. I need sustenance." He was trying to lighten the mood. He was trying to let her know he was fine, or that he would be fine ... he wouldn't ruin this for Abby. He needed to suck it up because she needed to witness firsthand a real Scottish reception. "Here's something ye probably didn't know. It's said that if ye don't have a céilidh after a Scottish wedding then the marriage isn't actually legal."

She laughed. "Who says that?"

"Everyone. It's a well-known fact." He was glad he'd made her laugh, as her laughter was balm for his bad mood and he smiled back at her. "I'm glad ye enjoyed the wedding."

"Best time ever." She leaned up and kissed his cheek but quickly used her thumb to wipe away the lipstick left behind.

Though he wasn't quite sure where he stood with her, he wrapped his arm around her waist and kissed her back. A quick chaste kiss. It wasn't nearly enough for him and he wanted more. "Well, Abby Potter, ye should brace yourself. There are plenty of good times to come." She should count on it.

Chapter 13

ABBY WAS GLAD that the awkwardness was gone between her and Conor. She was also happy that he had refused her request to leave. It was plain to see that his bad mood had stemmed from memories of his wedding and consequently the marriage that hadn't worked out. Poor guy. It was sweet how he was giving her this experience even at the expense of his own peace of mind. She'd have to come up with some way to pay him back.

The first idea that popped into her head would probably get her put on the naughty list as she was imagining every steamy way to repay him, something akin to what they'd done in bed earlier. She could make round two something he'd never forget. It would start with a *lip-lock to end all lip-locks*! Then she'd run her hands over his chest and the rest of his body, just for good measure. Only if she was brave enough to make the first move. But hadn't she been brave earlier when she'd slid her hands under his shirt? And when she'd shed her clothes for him?

More realistically, she should return his generosity in the

same vein as the gift he'd given her. Perhaps she could arrange for them to tour a woolen mill while they were away at the bridal show. Yes, that would do nicely.

"What are ye smiling about?" he asked.

"Don't worry your pretty head over it," she said coyly. "But it might be something special for you."

His pupils dilated.

She laughed. "Clean up your thoughts, Masterson." Yet, she was grateful that he couldn't read her dirty mind. Or maybe he could. They had, after all, gone to bed together without having the typical conversations that happen before becoming intimate. She hoped her scold sounded like a schoolmarm and not the wanton woman in her uninhibited thoughts.

Once inside Pastas & Pastries, he followed her up the stairs to the second floor where the large Grand Dining Room was located. They'd been at the back of the line and the band was playing a soft tune, providing dinner music as people tucked into their meals.

"It's amazing what Dominic can whip up on short notice," Conor remarked. On Abby's previous visit, she'd learned all about how Claire had returned to her native Gandiegow a few years ago and opened Gandiegow's only restaurant, Pastas & Pastries, with her husband.

She and Conor filled their plates and found a small table where she could observe the Scots celebrating. Every once in a while, Conor would glance over at her; it felt as if he were making sure that she was happy and content. To show him that she was, besides smiling at him, she pulled out her notebook and continued to fill in the order and succession of the Scottish wedding and the celebration they were witnessing.

A few minutes later, the band leader announced it was time for the bride and groom to have their first dance. During the chorus, the parents of the couple joined them on the floor, then the rest of the members of the wedding party joined them, too. Abby watched as the bride's father cut in and danced with his daughter. Abby would never experience a father-daughter dance. Though she never gave thoughts like this much credence, she was surprised when sadness overtook her as she watched the bride smile up at her father. A sweet moment. A moment she'd never have, if she were to marry. But the likelihood of her ever getting hitched was nil. A pipe dream. She'd flushed her chances when she'd run out on Aaron at their own wedding. It took a moment for her to realize that the song had ended.

Conor took her hand. She glanced over at him and saw concern in his eyes. "Shall we dance, then?" He pulled her to her feet and guided her out on the floor.

She knew it was a pity dance—a slow dance at that—but she decided it was okay to soak him up, as if she were the Italian bread they'd dredged through the olive oil earlier. "Thank you," she said into Conor's shoulder. "You've made me feel better."

"As ye have done for me." He pulled her close and swayed to the music.

She had the awful feeling that she was falling for Conor. He was the wrong person for her. They worked together, plus this timing was the worst. She couldn't fall for someone so soon after her breakup with Aaron. Conor deserved more than to be her rebound. Yes, she was the one who'd broken things off with Aaron, but in some respect, she was still grieving the wedding she'd never have and the future companionship she'd hoped for. She was also mourning the truce with her mother that her relationship with Aaron had engendered. Now Abby was alone, with no chance of having children or a man she could call her own. Perhaps she was more like her mother than she'd thought. She might even have to go the same route as her mother and have a baby on her own since she didn't have a man in her life.

She'd come to Scotland feeling sure that she had too much baggage to ever settle down with someone. Yet here she was in the arms of the most incredible man. Alpha, through and through. Nothing like Aaron at all. Conor was the kind of man who ended up as a hero in a book— gorgeous, thoughtful, kind to dogs and the elderly ... and a fantastic kisser.

She looked up at him and found that he was gazing down at her. His eyes pierced the negative haze in her mind. The room fell away, leaving only the two of them. He leaned in and kissed her tenderly—

At that moment, Abby gave in and let herself fall.

Utterly and completely.

For him.

He'd spun some kind of magical web around them and there was nothing she could do about it. She'd been adamant about not jumping into another relationship, especially since she had the worst taste in men. Or the wrong type of men chose her. Why hadn't she had more self-esteem than to accept the breadcrumbs these men had given her? She'd found no romance with any of them, not like she'd found in the arms of the Scotsman. No validation. No satisfaction. No real love that she could sink her teeth into. Just shallow thinking. Money-seeking. The men she'd dated had more in common with her mother than they had with her.

Conor deepened the kiss and her automatic response was to embrace him and kiss him back with her whole being. After all, she thought, she might never get this opportunity again, since it was undoubtedly all the good feelings from the wedding and the romantic music that had put them under a spell. Her hands traveled upward and sunk themselves into his hair. Just when she was about to pull away and tell him they should find a more secluded place for what she was contemplating, her arm was nearly yanked from its socket.

"What are ye doing?" Deydie whispered harshly in Abby's face, a mere centimeter away. "Stop throwing yereself at that lad." Deydie smoothed down the front of her apron and then yanked Abby's arm again. This time, Conor had no choice but to let her go, making Abby miss his touch already. "Ye're coming with me," Deydie said vehemently.

"Where?" Abby asked. "Why?" She was so confused. A moment ago, she was perfectly happy in Conor's embrace. Now, she stepped away and hugged herself.

"Ye're coming with me to Quilting Central," Deydie said adamantly. "We need all-hands-on-deck to help finish Diana and Rory's quilt. And apparently, lass, ye need a chaperone."

Perhaps Deydie was right. If things kept on as they were, Abby would be back in Conor's bed again before the night was over. Abby had fallen into his bed earlier without thinking through all the ramifications. Maybe she did need a little space from him to screw her head on straight. "All right. I'll go with you." Abby really should spend some time examining why she let strong women push her around. But for now, she turned to Conor. "I'll see you later, okay?"

But he was glowering at Deydie and wouldn't meet her eye. "Aye. Later." He stalked off the dance floor and went straight to the open bar that had been set up in the corner of the room. A group of men had gathered there and he joined them.

"Stop looking at that lad as if he held dear all yere wishes and dreams," Deydie said. "Word is that he's still burning a candle for his ex-wife. That's not the kind of man ye need to involve yereself with. Ye know, Gandiegow and Whussendale are sister villages, and what goes on in one place is usually known immediately in the other." She nodded as if it were a fact. "He still carries a torch for *his Morag*, though she ran off with the local pub owner." The old woman gleamed as if gossiping were a sport, and she was on the winning team. "Put yere mind on more productive things. Like yere career, and of course, quilting. That lad there will never be yeres. Many have tried to get their hooks in him, but their efforts have all been in vain. Do ye ken?"

Deydie's words had a sobering effect on Abby's mood. Could it really be true that Conor was still hung up on his ex-wife? Abby couldn't believe it. Conor had kissed her repeatedly like no other man had done. Besides, he seemed angry about his marriage. But was that because he didn't want it to end? Maybe he was biding his time until he could win back his ex. *Well, crud.* She felt like a chump for thinking that their lovemaking had meant something.

But the question lingered in her mind: How could he kiss her the way that he had and still want his wife back? Why had he looked at her as if she—Abby Potter—was something special? Unfortunately, she knew the answer. The weight of it felt like a two-ton anchor. It crushed more than her feelings, it crushed whatever fantasy she'd been having about being with Conor.

He was just using her, and Abby had been an idiot.

She'd read his intentions completely wrong because it suited her. She'd thought that he liked her. Look at the trouble he'd gone to for her to witness this Scottish wedding. But the truth was that he'd been messing around with the new girl while he waited for his wife to reconsider. *Oh, hell*, Abby thought. He'd taken her to bed as a kind of anesthesia to dull the pain. Abby had been a sucker before when trying to read men. This time, apparently, was no different.

She couldn't give Conor the benefit of the doubt. Not if she intended to live in the same village he did after things between them cooled. For surely now they would. She wasn't going to put her future on the line for a few kisses and a satisfying roll in the hay. Now she would stop her heart from getting too involved.

"Come away with me, lass," Deydie said. If Abby wasn't mistaken, the old woman's voice now held a bit of tenderness. She sounded like a kind grandmother might sound if her granddaughter was hurting. "Ye've work to do and I'll be there right beside ye to help ye do it." And because Deydie was being kind, it made Abby think that maybe she was in more trouble than she'd imagined.

Abby followed Deydie out of the Grand Dining Room. With great effort, she kept her eyes on the floor in front of her instead of glancing back at Conor. More than anything, she wanted him to be looking at her with longing in his eyes. But she knew if she did cave and glance at him and he wasn't looking at her, it would kill her ... dead.

As she made her way down the steps, Abby thought it strange how life could turn on her without any warning. Until Deydie had said what she'd said, Abby had considered this the most remarkable day. Or at least some aspects of it had been remarkable. From kissing Conor to making love to him, then for him to have made arrangements for her to see firsthand a Scottish wedding? Mind-blowing! Yes, she'd had reservations about screwing up her professional life by getting tangled up with Conor. But as God as her witness, she'd been on cloud nine when he'd kissed her while they danced. So romantic. And it had been easy to ignore her reservations because it felt so good to be in his arms in that moment. But, as it turned out, she had just been a distraction for him. *Damn her rose-colored glasses!*

Well, the glasses were off now!

They'd reached the bottom step and Abby obediently followed Gandiegow's matriarch outside. A cold breeze blew through her. But it was only partly the weather's fault. Mostly, Abby was to blame. She should've guarded her heart more carefully. Abby tapped Deydie on the shoulder and spoke above the crashing waves and blustery winds. "What am I going to do now?"

"The quilters of Gandiegow will fix ye up." Which didn't answer Abby's question at all!

When they got to Quilting Central, Deydie held the door open for Abby so she could go in first. As if it were choreographed, all the quilters looked up at once; apparently, the tinkling of the bell over the door was their cue to react. Immediately, the quilters' faces went from curious to pitying looks. Abby had never been good about hiding her feelings and now was no exception.

"Everyone, gather around," Deydie said, motioning to the room. Abby thought she was going to make an announcement about what they were to work on next. But Abby was wrong. "Our wedding planner needs our help."

Abby gawked at Deydie as if she'd gone mad. "No. No. I don't need help!" Deydie had brought her here so that she could help them.

"That Conor Masterson has been using our poor wedding planner abysmally. We all know that he is still hankering for his wife to come to her senses and return to him."

The group nodded their heads enthusiastically as this truth was common knowledge.

"We need everyone to come up with ideas for Abby to get over him." Deydie slapped her own thigh. "Damn that lad!"

One of the quilters raised her hand.

"Go on, Amy," Deydie said.

"Abby needs to find a way to take her mind off him," Amy said, while giving Abby a sad smile.

"Damn straight!" Deydie said. "Quilting should do the trick!"

A very pretty woman wearing a tight, hot pink sweater stepped forward.

"What do you have to say, Bonnie?" Deydie asked.

"Abby should turn the tables on Conor by flirting with another man. That would show him for using her that way."

A couple of the women nodded, but most of the quilters were not on Bonnie's side when it came to this tactic. Abby didn't like it much either. She also wasn't comfortable with what her mother would call airing her dirty laundry in public. Her mother believed a woman should be a closed book, especially when it came to personal matters. Abby guessed some of her mother must've rubbed off on her, as she wanted the quilters to go back to their sewing machines and leave her to figure things out on her own.

Bethia cleared her throat and touched Abby's arm gently. "For your heart's sake, sweeting, you should give yereself plenty of space from Conor. If you and him are meant to be, love will find a way."

The group sighed out a collective, "Aye."

But those two thoughts tumbled around in Abby's brain. Take space from Conor and love will find a way. Those two things seemed incongruous and Abby wasn't sure what to do with them. Hugh had tasked Conor with helping Abby at the upcoming bridal show. How was she supposed to put space between them if they were together nearly all the time?

An idea hit her and she wondered why she hadn't thought of it before. She should ask Declan to take Conor's place. To outsiders, it might seem like Abby was trying to make Conor jealous, but the truth was that the only feelings she had for Declan were of the sisterly sort. Declan was charming and he could draw women into the booth with his kilt just as easily as Conor could. Abby couldn't wait to ask Declan if he would do it for her. Because she couldn't be around Conor without getting her heart even more broken than it already was.

"Everyone, get back to work," Deydie barked. "Abby, come with me and I'll get ye set up on Caitie's machine. Ye'll have three blocks to work on tonight. The Scottie dog, the heart block, and the thistle block."

Bethia had followed them over. "I'll hand-stitch this hankie for Diana while I sit with ye. It's her *something blue.* That way, if you have any questions, I'll be here to answer them."

"Thank you," Abby said. But what she really wanted was to be on her own. To think. To run through once more everything that had transpired on this rollercoaster day.

Following the instructions that Deydie had left, Abby laid out the pieces for the heart block first, then began sewing. What she found out was that there was a bit of magic in keeping her hands and brain busy. For as the block came together, so did Abby's plan. She wouldn't need to speak with Conor at all about the new arrangement. She would ask Declan to give Conor the news. And when Declan asked why he had to do it, she would explain that she just wasn't comfortable being around Conor. Declan seemed like the type of guy who went out of his way to please everyone. And if Abby had to resort to flirting with Declan to get her way, then so be it. For a moment, she let it play out in her mind. The consensus was that Bonnie hadn't given Abby good advice, but the more Abby thought about it, she was game when it came to flirting if the act would ultimately be a way to protect her heart. And if Conor suffered? All the better. It would be payback for the heartache he was giving her now.

For the next hour, Conor stood with the other men at the open bar, feeling disgusted. He couldn't believe Deydie could be such a pain in the arse. He'd finally gotten Abby back to normal after the awkwardness in his cottage. Bringing Abby to the wedding had done its magic. He was so glad to have her back in his arms, and even gladder when he got to kiss her again. But damn Deydie! She had no right to butt in and take Abby away. Conor downed his fizzy juice—as he was the one driving—and decided it was time to find Abby and take her home. Away from Gandiegow, and away from Deydie's meddling ways.

As he started to say goodnight to John Armstrong and Rory Crannach, the two he'd been standing with, Father Andrew walked up.

"I need volunteers to take wedding guests to Lios and Fairge where they have secured rooms for the night. Can you lads help?"

Conor really didn't want to volunteer but he felt dutybound; he needed to repay Father Andrew for remembering to invite Abby to the wedding tonight. "Aye. I'll help." He set his empty glass on the bar. "I haven't touched a drop of whisky as I knew I'd be driving tonight. Who do I need to taxi and where do I need to take them?"

Andrew looked at his clipboard. "Please take the groom's grandmother and aunt to the B and B in Lios." He handed him a sheet with the address written on it.

Conor typed the address into his phone. "Got it." At least he could be useful to someone. He rounded up the grandmother and aunt, took them to Lios, and on the way back, Andrew texted the info for him to taxi more people to their destinations. Three hours later, Conor was nearly back from his final trip. He wondered if Abby had gone back to the reception, for surely it was still going on. Or maybe Abby was still helping Deydie and the quilters with Diana and Rory's wedding quilt.

After Conor parked in Gandiegow's lot, he went to the Grand Dining Room but Abby wasn't there. He hurried down the walkway toward Quilting Central, anxious to see her and to figure out their next steps—either find a place to stay here in Gandiegow for the night or make the trip back to Whussendale. He expected Abby would be happy to see him, but when he opened the door to Quilting Central, all the women turned to look at him except for the one he'd come to see. Gandiegow's women were gawking as if he'd committed a crime. No welcoming *It's-great-to-see-you* looks, but a whole lot of *What-the-hell-are-you-doing-here?* glares. Abby glanced over for a moment—the briefest of glances—but then went immediately back to sewing. What the devil had Abby told them about him? Actually, Abby was probably innocent—this scene had Deydie written all over it!

Deydie barreled toward him. "Why are ye here?"

He rolled his eyes heavenward before answering. "I've come to speak with Abby." And that was all he was going to say to Deydie on the matter. He sidestepped the old woman and the broom she was wielding. Deydie had a reputation for swatting whomever crossed her, and he didn't plan to be her next victim. He walked straight to Abby and touched her shoulder. "Are ye ready to head back to Whussendale, lass?"

"No." Abby didn't look up at him.

"What's going on?" he asked.

"Nothing's going on," Deydie answered for her. The old woman had made it across the room as quietly as a cat and in record time. "Abby's busy helping us." Deydie glanced around. "She'll be staying in Gandiegow tonight. We have plenty for her to do for Rory and Diana's upcoming nuptials."

"Where will ye stay?" he asked.

"None of yere damned business!" Deydie barked, giving him such a fierce glower that most men might have shrunk from it. But he didn't.

Bethia stood and laid a hand on Deydie's shoulder as if to calm her. "We'll set Abby up in Thistle Glen Lodge. We really do need her help with Diana's wedding."

Bethia's gentle voice put Conor at ease. But he didn't want to strand Abby here. "Abby can't stay. She didn't bring extra clothes." He was grasping at straws and Abby turned to give him an incredulous look.

"Please stop talking as if I'm not here," she said.

"Sorry, lass," Bethia said contritely.

"Aye, sorry," Conor said immediately, not wanting to look like the insensitive ogre in the room. He glanced at Deydie as if she'd cornered the market on ogre-status. But then he turned back to his charge. "Abby, would you like for me to fetch your things from Whussendale?"

"Absolutely not!" She looked horrified.

"Ye'll not be rummaging through her things," Deydie said. "That wouldn't be proper." She squinted at him as if he were a bit of small print. "Conor, tell me the truth. Have ye taken liberties with our wedding planner?"

Gads! What was on his face or in his demeanor that let Deydie know the truth? He schooled his features. "I haven't taken liberties with anyone. Not a'tall." He felt his cheeks flush and hoped he wouldn't go to hell for lying. Maybe he should find Father Andrew for the rite of reconciliation before he left town.

But back to the business at hand. He turned to Abby. "If ye like, I'd be happy to run ye back to Whussendale to pack for yourself. I've been driving all kinds of folks this evening. What's one more?" He congratulated himself for being nonchalant. And while he was back in Whussendale, he could pack a duffel for himself, too. He could let Magnus and Tavon handle the looms tomorrow, couldn't he? He could bring Dublin back with him to stay in the room above The Fisherman, Gandiegow's pub.

Abby turned off her sewing machine and stood, shaking her head. "Listen, I better get back to Whussendale tonight. There's so many arrangements I need to make before the upcoming bridal show."

Aye! Right! The bridal show! Where I'll have time with Abby without the prying eyes of Whussendale or Gandiegow to contend with. Conor's mood lifted and he felt like high fiving himself. He was anxious to get Abby alone—whether in the car tonight or on their getaway to the bridal show.

He reached out to touch Abby but she backed away, which made his mood plummet. "Is everything all right?"

Deydie glowered at him. "No funny business on the trip back! Do ye ken?"

Conor refused to answer. What he and Abby were up to was none of the old fishwife's business.

Abby looked as if she wanted to change her plans but gathered up her things anyway.

Well, at least he'd have the ride back to Whussendale to get to the bottom of her altered mood. For surely he could fix things between them. He had to. He wanted nothing more than to sneak over to Abby's cottage for round two tonight.

Chapter 14

AS SHE AND CONOR stepped from Quilting Central, Abby was desperately looking for an escape plan. She didn't like how Conor kept gazing at her: as if he wanted to talk. She didn't. She suspected he was going to wait until they were in his vehicle before grilling her as to why she was pulling the plug on the two of them. She needed time and space from him to bring herself back into alignment. There was no way she was going to make the same dumb mistakes she'd made in the past, which meant she wasn't going to continue the mistake that was Conor.

Surprisingly, Declan exited the grocery store as they approached. Abby wondered if her silent prayer had been answered. "Hey, Abby. Hey, Con."

Abby smiled at him. "What are you doing here?"

"I had a meeting with Kit about the Love Coach tour. We had to nail down the itinerary. It was a now-or-never kind of meeting. Reservations for lodging and activities need to be made months in advance. Kit had a spreadsheet for us to go over. After this is finalized, we can start advertising for the first Love Coach adventure. We're thinking April of next year would be the perfect time."

Abby should seriously consider signing up for one of Declan's future Love Coach trips. Maybe it would help her get over Conor. But she wouldn't mention it now with Conor present. Her primary objective was to completely disconnect from Conor, not to make him jealous. At least not at this time.

"Are you headed back to Whussendale?" Abby asked bravely. She kept her eyes forward so she wouldn't see Conor's reaction.

"Aye." Declan tossed his keys into the air. "This very minute."

It was time for her to double down and be brave. "Can I catch a ride with you?" Abby stepped closer to Declan because she could almost feel steam rolling off Conor.

"Sure." But then Declan looked concerned. "Are ye all right, mate?"

"Fine," Conor said through gritted teeth.

Abby had to come up with a reason fast. "I, uh, need to speak with Declan because Kit wants her business to partner up with the wedding venture. And, uh, since Declan is partnering with Kit, then I need to speak to him about ways the wedding venture could partner with him, too." Though the temperature had dropped to just about freezing, she was burning up. "Declan, maybe there's an opportunity for you to do a wedding party tour of Scotland for our Hitched in Scotland business?" Her idea sounded lame to her own ears.

Declan frowned at her. "Yeah, I guess."

Conor gently touched Abby's arm, and it almost broke her heart because the gesture transmitted more than words could. Or at least her overactive imagination thought so. "Lass, we have much to discuss on our way home."

She steeled herself, especially her voice, because she was

sure it would quaver and give away how she was feeling. "What I need to discuss with Declan takes precedence," she said stiffly, as if channeling her mother.

"Very well." Stoically, and with some attitude, Conor huffed off, a soldier who'd been given his marching orders that weren't to his liking.

When Conor was out of earshot, Declan cautiously looked down at her. "Are ye putting me in the middle of something between you and Conor? He's a decent person and a good friend. He doesn't deserve to be toyed with."

"I'm not toying with him or anybody else, for that matter." Abby stood her ground, but it felt like she was walking a tightrope and could fall any second. She needed both villages to see her as a wedding professional. At the same time, she had to protect herself. "I need to ask you a favor. Actually, two favors."

Declan crossed his arms and gave her a stern look, which looked weird on him as he normally seemed like a happy-go-lucky guy. "Go on then. What is it?"

"Can we talk about it in your car? I'm freezing."

"Sure." He waited for her to walk ahead of him. He didn't try to put his hand to her back and guide her along as Conor had done. And she was grateful. "While we walk, though, tell me what's going on between you and Con."

"Do I have to?" Abby said. "It's complicated."

"Aye. Ye have to, if you don't want me to text Conor to tell him that you'd changed your mind and that ye want to catch a ride with *him* instead of me back to Whussendale."

"I'm not going to get into details, but something happened. And it shouldn't have."

"Why shouldn't it have happened?" Declan looked as if he'd guessed the extent of the *complication*.

"Hugh has paired Conor and me professionally. Conor is supposed to help me with the wedding shawls and work the bridal shows with me."

"So ... things got complicated because things got personal, right?"

She'd give it to Declan; the Scot was astute. She nodded as answer to his query.

"I don't see how I can help, lass. Especially since I refuse to get in the middle of anything personal." He clicked the key fob and unlocked the car before they actually reached it. "I won't play games, like making him jealous just to get a rise out of him."

Abby shook her head. "No. Nothing like that." She opened her door and slid inside.

Declan did the same and started the car. "Then, what?"

"It's a big ask," she hedged.

"Go on." He kept his eyes forward, which was good for her, because this was so embarrassing.

"I thought you might replace Conor at the bridal shows."

Declan was silent but she noticed he was gripping the steering wheel tighter than before. "What's the other favor?"

"You didn't answer the first request."

"Go on and tell me the rest," he said.

Boy, this was going to be hard. "I was, uh, wondering, um ... if you do say yes to the first request, that is, uh ..." She didn't want to say it but she had come this far. "I thought if you do say *yes* to helping me at the bridal shows that you could be the one to let Conor know that he's been replaced. He might take it better coming from you."

Out of her peripheral vision, she saw his head snap her way and the incredulous look he was giving her. He immediately put his eyes back on the road as he put the car in gear and headed for the steep, curvy road that led them away from Gandiegow.

"I don't think it'll be better coming from me," Declan said shaking his head. "Or from anyone else for that matter!" He made it sound as if she were crazy for even mentioning it. But she wasn't crazy … just desperate.

"How can I make you understand?" she asked rhetorically. She paused, wondering if she had anything to barter with. Finally, she said, "Name your price?"

Declan exhaled heavily. She'd fractured their easy brother-sister relationship with her requests. "Okay. If I'm going to do these things for you, here is my condition. Get Kit off my back about being part of her Scottish meat market next month."

"What?" She had no idea what he was talking about.

"Kit said she's short one bachelor for her Hogmanay matchmaking event. When all her ladies come over to Scotland, they expect to find a husband, not just a bit of fun while they're here."

"Don't you want to get married?"

"I'm not husband material. Plus, I don't have the time or the inclination to bandy with her U.S. lassies. I'm focusing on getting my tourism business off the ground right now."

"Okay," Abby said. "I understand. I'll do it." But she had no idea how to make Kit back off. Maybe she could offer up Conor as Declan's stand-in. A Scot for a Scot. As if those two were completely interchangeable. But they weren't. Maybe being set up with an American socialite would make Conor forget about his ex-wife, but what good would that do for Abby's broken heart? "I just need some time to figure it out. Okay?"

"Aye. But sooner would be better than later."

"And that goes for you, too," Abby said. "The bridal show is coming up fast so you'll have to break it to Conor before then."

They remained quiet for the rest of the trip. Abby's brain was in high gear with all she needed to accomplish this next week. At least she had more time to fix Declan's problem than he had to fix hers.

When they got to Whussendale, she half-expected Conor to be waiting for her outside her cottage. But he was nowhere in sight, and the lights next door in *his* cottage were off. It was probably for the best that he wasn't around.

Over the next few days, Conor was noticeably absent. She assumed Declan had spoken to him, and thus it seemed reasonable that Conor would stay out of sight and ignore her. But she didn't see Declan either, and he wasn't responding to her texts. She was beginning to wonder if the two of them had been spirited away.

While Abby prepped for the bridal show, it was Sophie and Hugh who helped her. They made sure she had plenty of brochures, tulle for decorating the booth, and an iPad to gather emails for the giveaway and for the contact info of couples who might like to get married in Whussendale. The one thing Abby was worried about was the wedding shawl samples that Conor had promised to bring. She texted Declan one last time to ask if Conor had given him the wedding shawls, which were supposed to be a highlight of their booth. She got no response.

On Thursday morning at the appointed time, Abby stepped anxiously out of her cottage. On her front step was one of the missing Scots! Her Scot. But she banished that thought. Conor wasn't hers.

Confused, she glanced around, looking for Declan, but he was nowhere in sight. Her confusion was compounded by how happy it made her to see Conor. Where had he been these last few days?

Conor held out a folded piece of paper. "This is for you. From Declan." He'd said Declan's name as if it were an unwanted knot in a woven scarf.

She took the paper and opened it. There were only two words written: I TRIED.

She rolled her eyes. Apparently, Declan hadn't tried hard enough.

"I'm ready to go if you are," Conor said as he took her suitcase from her. "I already have the rest of the things from Hugh and Sophie in the SUV."

Well, Hugh and Sophie could've given her a heads up that Conor was still participating in the bridal show. But, then again, Abby hadn't given them the heads up that she had asked Declan to sub for Conor. She just hadn't been able to get up enough courage to ask them where Conor was, especially since it was Hugh who had assigned Conor to help her.

But her plan had been for naught and it would take a while for her to adjust.

"The wedding shawls are already packed as well. Ye needn't have worried." Conor's right eyebrow lifted. Not in a quizzical way, but the way a know-it-all might. Apparently, Declan had shared her texts with Conor. The next time she saw Declan, she would give him *what-for* for not keeping his end of the bargain. Also, for not telling her that he'd failed to convince Conor of the switcheroo.

Well, at least she wouldn't have to worry about keeping up her end either. She hadn't come up with a clever way to get Declan out of Kit's event. Because Abby was feeling a little vengeful, she hoped some socialite would lay it on thick and make Declan feel as uncomfortable as Abby was feeling now.

"Just so you know," Conor started, "I expect you to tell me why you didn't want me to escort you to the bridal show." He put his free hand up in an effort to halt her response. "But not right now. We'll have the whole way to Inverness to discuss why ye were trying to replace me."

Abby looked out at a copse of trees, anywhere to keep from looking into his blue-gray eyes ... eyes that made her melt. She couldn't acknowledge him in any way. What could she say that wouldn't be mortifying? *Deydie told me that you're still hung up on your ex-wife.* Abby was done moving heaven and earth to make a man like her; especially since she was gaga over this man. She didn't want to admit it, but she might even love Conor ... for she'd never felt this kind of connection with Aaron, and they were engaged!

She rolled her eyes heavenward as if saying a prayer. For the zillionth time, she reminded herself she could never mix business with pleasure again! This weekend at the bridal show would give her the perfect opportunity to prove that she could keep her resolve.

Except, she and Conor would be spending all their time together.

They would be staying at the same hotel.

Lord help her, but she couldn't stop herself from wanting to be in his bed again. If for no other reason than to say goodbye to the relationship that they would never have.

But she shelved that thought.

It was best to nip things in the bud now. "Listen, Conor, I'm not in the mood to talk. So if you don't mind—"

"I do mind," he said, cutting her off. "You've left me hanging for days now without an explanation."

She glanced around to see if anyone was in earshot. "Okay. I could lie to you and tell you that I didn't want you to come along to the bridal show because I thought Magnus needed you more than I did. But that's not even close to the truth."

"Aye. I've arranged for plenty of people to help Magnus while I'm gone."

"So here is the unvarnished truth. You are a complication I can't afford right now. Whussendale is a small town. A small community, which is just like working in an office. I won't complicate my new life here for an *office romance*, if you catch my meaning. I've mixed business with pleasure before and it didn't work out." She'd mentioned it before but it felt like she really needed to drive home the point so he would understand.

He looked hurt, which was ridiculous. She hadn't even mentioned how he was still hung up on his ex-wife. Abby certainly wouldn't tell him that she was falling for him. There was no way she was revealing *that* truth!

He opened the back of the SUV and set her suitcase next to all the things they were bringing to the bridal show. After he shut the back, he turned to her. "Okay. I hear you. I understand."

Which wasn't what she expected. "Then you can let it drop?"

"If that's what you want." He opened the passenger door for her.

"Yes." But that wasn't what she really wanted. She wanted all the complications to go away. She wanted him and his feelings to be unattached from his ex-wife. She wanted Conor to want her as much as she wanted him. She also needed to get over the fact that Conor had used her and her body to distract himself from the heartache of losing his marriage. Abby assumed Morag was a beauty, while Abby felt as attractive as an old, burlap sack.

Also, dammit, Abby wanted a happily-ever-after for herself. But she'd just have to settle for having a front row seat to others' happily-ever-afters. As a wedding planner, she curated happily-ever-afters, she didn't receive them.

Once they were settled in the vehicle, Conor drove them away from Whussendale. She wondered if they would listen to the wedding playlists that she'd sent to him or possibly an audiobook. Or just talk? But the vehicle remained quiet.

Conor was mute. Abby was sad. Awkwardness filled the SUV. Abby was starting to doubt she would ever feel happy again.

With his brain buzzing, Conor drove through the countryside thinking about what Abby had said. He was still angry and reeling that she'd tried to replace him. Didn't she understand that being replaced was one of his hot buttons? Hadn't Morag replaced him with Steven? And did Abby know that Declan was lucky Conor hadn't decked him when he'd shared Abby's cockamamie plan to make a switch.

Conor would have to let it go. He did understand what she meant about having a romance with someone in a small town. As a lad spending the summer in Whussendale, he'd had a romance with Tally. After they broke up, Whussendale was nearly unbearable, and he'd been glad to leave when summer ended. Now that he was a man, it would be that much worse. If things didn't turn out well between himself and Abby, he wouldn't be able to run from this failed relationship as he'd done before. Abby was stuck in Whussendale, too. They would both be miserable. They would see each other all the time, especially since their cottages were side-by-side! And if some other man came a-calling at Abby's door—as would surely happen—Conor would have a front row seat to her new rela-tionship, which would kill him.

Aye, he had to hand it to her; she was the one who was being mature about this whole thing. But he couldn't just let it go. Apparently, she didn't feel about him the way he felt about her.

What was he going to do with the strong desire he had for

her?

It was going to be an awkward couple of days! But he could get past this. He knew it. As a boy, when he'd come back to Whussendale the following summer, he and Tally had become great friends and were friends to this day. A realization suddenly hit him. Morag's betrayal no longer caused him the level of devastating pain that it once had. He wasn't completely past it, but he was definitely healing. He guessed Abby could take the credit for that. Spending time with her, kissing her, making love, and dancing with her had distracted him and helped to heal the hurt. *Aye*, Abby was the reason. He never would've come this far if it hadn't been for her.

He glanced over at Abby; she was staring at something out her window as if it was the most interesting thing in the world. He wouldn't disturb her. He turned on some Christmas music and focused on the road ahead. When they finally got to the hotel, they walked to the elevator together.

"So, you're on the fourth floor?" he asked, lamely.

"Yes." She didn't look at him.

"Do you want to meet down here for dinner?" he tried.

She shook her head. "I'm beat. I think I'll go to bed early."

Her tone was clear; she didn't want his company. Nowhere in her words was there a hint of an invitation to join her in her bed. "I'll see you at breakfast, then." The elevator dinged, the doors opened, and he went to his room alone.

Thankfully, the next day was busy. The demands of setting up banners, moving tables, and getting the booth in working order was a nice distraction from Abby's rejection. It might've been even better if Abby wasn't there at all as he couldn't help but notice how cute she looked in her jeans and Red Hot Chilli Pipers tee-shirt. He decided to say something. "Nice shirt."

"Yeah. I ordered it right after I arrived. I needed something casual and Scottish." She glanced down at it. "I saw the band on YouTube and thought this would make the perfect shirt for setting up and tearing down the booth until we can get Hitched in Scotland polos. You know, for promotion."

"Aye. That's a great idea. What do you say to us having dinner in the hotel's pub tonight?" He saw the flash of angst shoot across her features. "It'll give us a chance to go over tomorrow's schedule."

"Oh, okay," she said quietly.

Once again, he wondered at the change in *them*. For a while there, they had been in perfect tune with each other. He couldn't help but relive how easy things had been between them. Not just the best-sex-ever but all the other times they'd been together of just *being*. Now Abby was quiet and things were strained between them. It couldn't just be that they'd mixed business with pleasure. Maybe something else was bothering her. Her change of mood had started in Gandiegow, and the image of Deydie's glower popped into Conor's mind. The mean old quilter might be the one at fault here. At dinner tonight, whether Abby liked it or not, he would get to the truth. His mind flashed forward to a time when things were good between them again, after they'd straightened everything out. He'd walk her to her room after dinner. She'd let him give her a kiss goodnight. She'd invite him in for a sleepover. Everything would go back to normal. His mood lifted and by the time they were done setting up, he was feeling better.

But not ten minutes after getting back to his room, Abby shot down any grand plans he'd been dreaming of. His mobile dinged with a text from Abby. I'M TIRED AND NEED TO SLEEP, MORE THAN I NEED FOOD. WE'LL HAVE TIME TO GO OVER THE

BRIDAL SHOW TOMORROW MORNING AT BREAKFAST.

It felt like a load of bull. Just another excuse not to talk to him. For a while there, he'd been certain that he and Abby could talk about anything. Apparently, he'd been wrong.

Well, hell. He'd have to get honest with himself and admit he'd been wrong about a lot of things lately.

Chapter 15

ABBY KNEW SHE'D taken the coward's way out last night, but she'd been honest when she texted that she was tired; setting up the booth had been a lot of work. But instead of sleeping, she ruminated on Conor. About how she had gotten him all wrong. About how he was pining over Morag. She tried to muster up regret for going to bed with him, but she couldn't quite pull it off. She cared for Conor, and their time together had been. . .she hated to admit such a silly sentiment, but their time together had been *magical*.

When she crawled out of bed, she knew the black circles under her eyes were going to be dreadful ... and telling. Conor would instantly know that she'd been up all night worrying over him. Over them!

After her shower, she plastered on concealer until the damning evidence was masked. She dressed in her cream-colored dress and stylish black boots, ready to sign up brides for Hitched in Scotland.

When she arrived downstairs at the restaurant, Conor wasn't

there, and she breathed a sigh of relief. While she picked out her food from the buffet, she tried to steady her nerves. Her brain knew she was being ridiculous but her heart couldn't help pounding every time someone new came into the dining room.

When Conor sauntered into the room, her heart did triple somersaults. He was dressed in his kilt and the sight of him knocked the breath from her. She fanned herself with the stack of flyers she'd brought downstairs. How could she have forgotten how amazing he looked in his kilt? Abby noticed other women noticing Conor as well. She was certain that several of the brides-to-be were comparing their grooms to Conor, thinking how their future husbands didn't measure up to the man at breakfast.

He walked directly over and set the tartan samples in the chair across from her. He took the chair perpendicular to her, which was considerably closer and more disarming. "'Morning."

"Good morning." She gestured to the samples. "Why did you bring them down with you?"

"I thought you might like to pick one to wear today. I can make it into a rosette for you to pin to the shoulder of your dress." He took that opportunity to scan her from head to boots. "Ye look nice."

Her cheeks heated up at his perusal and his words. "Um, thank you. Wearing one of the tartans is a good idea. While you get your breakfast, I'll look through them." And she would get a brief break to pull herself together! She was as bad as the other women in the dining room who were staring longingly after Conor.

Abby had to get out of her chair to reach the samples and saw a pretty young woman heading toward Conor in the buffet line. Abby scanned her hand, and sure enough, the pretty woman was wearing an engagement ring. Abby considered leaving the samples where they were so she could stop the young woman from talking to Conor. Instead, Abby stood her ground. What was going to happen between the bride and Conor was none of her business. He would have to save himself.

As a distraction, she rifled through the tartans and wouldn't allow herself to watch what was going on. She chose the Black Watch plaid which would look nice with her cream-colored winter dress. She wouldn't let herself glance at Conor again until he took his place beside her.

"So, what did *she* want?" Abby asked, not able to stop herself. Her tone was a cross between snide and jealous and gave away the emotions she tried to keep hidden. None of it was a good look on her.

He gave her a quizzical, one-eyebrow-up expression. "She asked if I was going to be at the bridal show today. I gave her our booth number."

Abby stood, trying to give herself some space. "I need more coffee." She went to the carafes without saying anything more. She seriously wondered how she was going to get through today and tomorrow. But after they got back to Whussendale, she was going to call Deydie to see if she could come and stay in Gandiegow until Rory and Diana's wedding. That should work out for both her and the Gandiegowans.

She walked back to the table. Conor held up the newly made rosette sash from the Black Watch tartan. "Pin it to yere right shoulder. Do ye have any safety pins with ye?"

The rosette was beautiful and she kept her gaze glued to it, instead of ogling the beautiful Scot. "Thank you." She felt awkward and anxious and needed an escape. "Yes, I have pins in my room." Which gave her a good excuse to leave him. "I'll head up and get this pinned on. I'll meet you in the booth before the show opens."

He frowned at her. "What about the rest of yere breakfast?

Where's the coffee ye went to get?"

She shook her head. "I don't really have an appetite right now." She felt silly for not filling up her cup. But this was what she got for letting Conor discombobulate her. Without meeting his eyes first, she rushed for the elevators, trying—unsuccessfully—to slow her pulse.

Thirty minutes later, she found Conor in the booth with the iPad booted up and ready.

"Thanks," she said, pointing to the device.

"Come here," he said.

She stayed rooted to the spot, making him come to her.

"Let me adjust yere sash for ye." He unpinned the only visible safety pin and readjusted the rosette. "I'll hold it in place while ye pin it from the inside." At least that was a consolation. If he'd tried to slip his hand inside her dress to take care of the pin himself, she wouldn't have been able to stop him; that was how mesmerized she was by the color of his eyes.

Five minutes later, the announcement came over the PA that the bridal show had begun. A flock of women came to their booth. Abby tried to steer them to the iPad to enter their information for the giveaway, but they only wanted Conor's attention.

Conor saved the day by taking the iPad from Abby. "Come this way, ladies. Ye don't wanna miss out on a chance to win a free wedding shawl, do ye? The shawl is 100% Scotland made. Whussendale is a sheep-to-shawl operation."

The women sighed in unison. Yes, Conor had a nice burr.

He patiently spoke with each woman as Abby passed brochures to him one at a time to give to the bride. Abby wasn't surprised that several brides were from America. After the first rush, where he'd gathered the women's information, he glanced over at Abby. "Do you need to take a break? I've got this, if ye need to grab something. I expect ye're hungry."

"No. You go. Get something to drink or you'll be hoarse be-fore the day is half over. I'll hold down the fort for a while." With Conor gone, Abby would get the chance to actually do her job.

"All right, then." But as Conor walked away, a crowd of women followed him. She hoped they wouldn't go so far as traipsing after him into the men's restroom. Her other concern was that no one else would stop by their booth without her kilt-wearing partner in attendance. But that wasn't the case. Soon a new group showed up and she was able to educate them on the benefits of having a wedding in Whussendale.

The rest of the day stayed busy. After Abby took a short break in the late afternoon, she sent Conor to buy bottled water for them both, but really she was trying to give him a rest from all the prospective brides, their friends, and their mothers. He was only gone a moment when a woman appeared who was not as young as the average bride they'd seen that day. She also seemed very unhappy for a bride as she picked up one of the brochures and perused it.

"When's the big day?" Abby asked the black-haired woman.

"Oh, ah, there's no big day." She glanced around as if searching for someone.

"Are you here with your fiancé?" Abby asked.

"Um, no. I was told there was a man in this booth?" The woman looked as if she'd been crying.

"Uh, yes, he's taking a break." Abby picked up her bag to dig out a tissue, when the woman pulled one out for herself. "Um, he'll be back momentarily. I'd be happy to answer any questions you might have about Whussendale and the Hitched in Scotland wedding venture." Though Abby felt pretty sure she knew the answer to her query.

"No, thank you."

Abby moved the iPad toward her. "Would you like to enter the giveaway, while you wait?"

The woman didn't even glance at her or the iPad. "No. I'm fine."

Abby picked up her phone and typed a short text to Conor. YOU ARE NEEDED BACK AT THE BOOTH.

A few moments later, Conor came around the corner with a pleasant smile on his face. He had probably been mobbed by beautiful brides during his break. She couldn't blame the brides and she couldn't blame Conor for enjoying the attention he was getting.

To her surprise, he stopped short when he saw the woman leaning against their table. His happy demeanor disappeared and was replaced by an irritated frown. He walked straight to the woman, as if he knew her, and said brusquely, "What are ye doing here?"

Conor pressed his hand against his forehead, wishing this was only a bad dream. But it wasn't. The woman he'd known for a good chunk of his life, the woman who betrayed him, stood two feet away. He'd often wondered what he would do if she came crawling back to him. Would he take her back or would he revel in telling her to hit the road? But lately, he hadn't thought about her at all.

What in the devil was she doing here now?

When Morag's eyes met his, he knew something was wrong. Automatically, his irritation fell away; he'd seen her with that sad expression before. He turned to Abby, who apparently was trying to piece together what was going on as she faded into the background of the booth. "Abby, this is Morag. Can you give me a minute with her? I'll be right back."

He didn't wait for Abby to answer but guided Morag from the booth and out to the lobby, which was a long hallway with several different entrances to the vendors' enormous room.

He pointed to a long bench that stretched against the wall. "Take a seat and tell me what's wrong."

Morag burst into tears. "Da passed away." She collapsed onto the bench.

"What? How? Was he sick?" Conor had no hard feelings toward Clyde. *Aye*, the man had been surly, but he'd given Conor a job in the butcher shop and a living wage when Conor had neither.

"He passed in his sleep," Morag said around sobs.

Conor sat beside her and slipped an arm around her shoulders as she cried. He felt as if this was the least he could do. "And yere mum? How's she doing? The rest of the family?"

"I don't know. I left as soon as I found out. We had no idea it was coming," Morag said tearfully.

Conor's mobile dinged. He glanced at the notifications. "It's from Hugh."

"Did he tell you that I stopped by Whussendale first?" Morag said.

"No." Conor frowned at his phone.

"Don't be upset with him. I made him tell me where ye were," Morag said.

Conor read the text. Your ex-wife came by the mill looking for you. She said it was a family emergency. I meant to text you earlier. Sorry.

Better late than never, Conor thought.

Morag looked at him longingly. "Can ye come back with me to Glasgow?"

Her grief was sincere; Conor didn't doubt that. But …

"What about Steven?" Conor asked evenly.

Morag shook her head. "It's over between us. It didn't work out."

Conor felt a lot of different emotions at that moment. One of them was vindication, though it wasn't a very Christian thought to have. It wasn't even that he was glad that Morag and Steven didn't work out because he certainly didn't want his marriage back any more than he wanted a kick in the head. How many months had he wasted, hoping to hear that Morag and Steven had split up? What had happened to make them break up? But the biggest surprise was that the anger he'd wallowed in was gone. The truth was that he wasn't at all invested in Morag's comings and goings. The tears streaming down her face didn't affect him as they once had. He definitely didn't have the strong feelings of betrayal that he'd felt when he came back to Whussendale. Those feelings had waned since he'd met Abby. It was because of her that Conor looked at things differently now.

Morag reached out and touched his arm. "I thought you might let us have another chance."

It must be the grief talking. Conor knew people processed grief in different ways. Bizarre ways. For her to come here and ask for another chance, it was as if she believed he was the one who had abandoned her. Cheated on her. Was she for real?

He was glad Abby hadn't heard Morag. She might get the wrong idea and think he wanted to get back together with her.

He shook his head. "Sorry, Morag. The answer's no." He said it as gently as he could because she looked spent, fragile. "I'm truly sorry for your loss, though. Clyde was a good man." Her father, the only male in the family full of females, had seemed so glad when Conor joined their ranks.

"But will ye come back to Glasgow with me?"

"Of course I will." Conor didn't think she was in any condition to travel alone. And for some reason he felt dutybound to return her to her family. As though he'd seen a baby bird fall from the nest. "How did you get here?"

"The train."

Good. With the state she was in, he was glad she hadn't been behind the wheel.

Morag gave him a sad smile. "The last train to Glasgow leaves in forty-five minutes. I wish I'd had your new number so I wouldn't have had to spend time tracking you down."

"Yeah. Sorry." He was kicking himself for that, too. At the time, he'd been beyond angry and hadn't wanted to hear from Morag under any circumstance. Except through his family law solicitor, of course. But Conor couldn't have imagined that her father would die so young. For a moment, Conor wondered why Hugh hadn't given Morag his number, when she'd been there ... but Conor was to blame for that. He'd made it very clear to everyone in Whussendale not to share his information with his ex and her family. His motto was: New phone, new number, new life.

Whether Conor liked it or not, he'd get Morag home safely. He'd do this for Clyde. He squeezed her hand. "Wait here for a minute, while I tell Abby where I'm going. Then I'll take ye home."

Morag gave him another sad smile while he stood. His mind was reeling as he walked away. He pulled out his phone again and called the first person who popped into his head.

When Declan picked up, Conor dispensed with the pleasantries and got straight to the point. "Are ye free to do me a favor?"

"That depends," Declan said cautiously. He was probably remembering their last, unpleasant encounter.

"I need ye to come to Inverness to help Abby at the bridal show. I have to go to Glasgow. My father-in-law passed away." Conor didn't feel the need to call Clyde his *ex*-father-in-law; everyone in Whussendale knew his story.

"Sure, mate," Declan said.

"How soon can ye get here?" Conor asked. They discussed the particulars. Tavon would drive Declan to Inverness straightaway. Declan would be here to work the booth with Abby tomorrow and then would help her break down the booth and pack up before driving her home. "One more favor?"

"Anything," Declan said.

"I'll need someone to help with Dublin."

"Aye. No problem. Magnus has been doing a good job of taking care of her. I'll get Tavon to walk her for ye."

Conor wrapped up the call. "I guess that covers it. I've gotta go. I'm taking Morag back to Glasgow on the train."

"Don't worry about yere uncles. Especially Magnus. When Tavon gets back to Whussendale, he can help him in the weaver's building until I return. Whenever that is."

"I really appreciate you dropping everything at a moment's notice," Conor said feeling grateful.

"No problem. I know ye'd do the same for me, or anyone else here, for that matter."

Conor hurried back to their booth. Abby was showing a group of women how to sign up for the giveaway on the iPad. "I hate to interrupt, but I need to speak with you. It's urgent." That train to Glasgow wouldn't wait on them.

"Where's Morag?" Abby asked expectantly. "Is she all right?"

"Her father died. I'm taking her home to Glasgow."

Abby visibly blanched. Perhaps it was the mention of *home* and *Glasgow* in the same sentence. She pulled it together, though. "Please tell your, um, wife for me that I'm sorry for her loss." She didn't give him time to correct *wife* to *ex-wife* as she continued. "But I do need to know what to do. Can I legally drive your vehicle back to Whussendale?" She was wringing her hands. "I hadn't expected to be driving, at least not right away. And I haven't even thought about how to get a driver's license here."

"Don't worry," Conor said. "Declan is on his way to take my place." But Conor didn't like how that sounded. He definitely didn't want to be replaced, when it came to Abby. He didn't want Declan kissing her. Or taking his place in her bed! "I mean, Declan's coming to help you out. With the bridal show," Conor clarified. He'd have to text Declan to bring his best kilt to wear tomorrow. Damn! He didn't like the thought of Declan wearing his kilt and showing off his legs to Abby!

Abby frowned. "What about the plan to visit bridal shops on the way home?"

"Declan can do that with you." But Conor wasn't happy about that either.

"When will I see you again?" Abby said in a near whisper.

He reached out and squeezed her hand. "I'm not sure. But I'll be in touch."

"Okay." She didn't look okay. She looked sad and uneasy, or that could just be his ego imagining that she was going to miss him. "Is there anything I can do for you?"

Conor wanted to tell her not to fall for Declan. Or for any other man, for that matter. "Aye, there is something you can do. Dublin is spending time with both Magnus and Tavon. Do you mind, when you get back to Whussendale—"

"Of course, I'll check in on your uncles. Plus, Dublin can stay with me." She gave him a cheeky smile, which made him feel better. Maybe they were going to be okay. "That girl likes me better than you anyway."

Conor smiled back because Abby never disappointed. "Aye, Dublin really loves you." Abby got a funny look on her face ... as if he'd been the one making the declaration to her. He had to say something to get her off that track. "Remember, Dublin belongs to Kieran. Uncle Magnus might fight ye about which one of ye will keep Dublin. I'll let you two work that out. Okay?"

"Okay," she said.

He laid a hand on her arm. "I really have to run, lass." A list was forming in his head. He'd have to tell Declan to pick up his room key at the hotel's front desk. Then he needed to let Magnus and Tavon know that Abby would take over with Dublin when she returned. He also couldn't forget to get a hold of Kieran to let him know that he would be staying in his flat in Glasgow. It was one thing to take Morag back to her mother, but it was quite another to stay in the same house with her.

He couldn't help but notice that Abby seemed a little lost. But he had no choice. No time to fix it. He had to help Morag and the rest of her family while they got through these next few days. "I really am sorry that I have to bail." He wished he could give her a kiss so she wouldn't look so sad.

"Yeah. Me, too." Then she straightened her shoulders. "But I understand."

As he walked away, Conor made a silent vow to make it up to Abby. He just didn't know how, yet.

Chapter 16

ABBY WALKED BACK to the bridal group she'd been helping before Conor dropped his bombshell ... the *I'm leaving with Morag* bombshell. She couldn't help but be disappointed. Disappointed on every level! Disappointed that Conor wouldn't be here with her to the end of the bridal show. Disappointed that Conor was leaving with Morag. But mostly, that Deydie had been right. Conor really did want his wife back. All this time, Abby hadn't fully believed it. She'd felt down to her toes that she and Conor had a connection. A real connection! That they were soulmates. Otherwise, she wouldn't have gone to bed with him. Or maybe she would have. She kind of had it bad for him. But now, she would have to accept that Deydie had been right all along.

Another disappointment was that she wouldn't be able to take Conor to the wool mill or at least see his excitement when she told him that she'd specifically set up the tour for him. What a bummer!

"Will you excuse me?" she said to the group. "I need to run

to the restroom." She handed them the iPad to put in their information. "I'll be right back." Normally, she wouldn't leave an iPad with strangers and step away. But desperate times called for desperate measures. Besides, this was an emergency.

She hurried off after Conor. When she stepped into the long hallway, she had to jerk back because Conor was sitting right there with his wife.

Abby saw Morag reach out and touch his arm before saying tearfully, "I thought you might let us have another chance."

There it was. The truth. Which was the death knell to Abby's hopes and dreams. She swiped away a tear and rushed back to her booth. The iPad was resting safely on the table. A short time later, the announcer came over the loudspeaker to say that the event was closing for the day. "Come back and see us tomorrow!" Abby wasn't feeling his enthusiasm. Only devastation.

On autopilot, she pulled out colorful bed sheets and covered the tables so everything would stay as it was for tomorrow's show. She set the trashcan in the aisle for the janitor to empty overnight and then retrieved the iPad and slipped it into her bag.

She left the event space, feeling numb. It wasn't just Conor who wanted Morag back. Morag wanted him back, too. Abby wanted nothing more than to go back to her room and cry. But there was too much to do. First, she needed to download all the emails she'd collected today. Several people had made appointments to visit Whussendale and she needed to send them thank you notes with a detailed reminder of their appointed time. To be truthful, this evening she didn't even have a free moment to wallow in her misery as she so desperately wanted to do.

When Abby got back to her room, she made herself get right to work. Two hours later, she received a text from Declan. I'M

HERE IN CONOR'S ROOM. ARE YOU HUNGRY? DO YOU WANT TO MEET DOWNSTAIRS FOR A SANDWICH?

As she was typing *no*, her phone rang, sending her blood racing. Her silly heart thought it was Conor who was calling, but when she looked at the screen, it was only Declan.

"Hey," he said, when she picked up.

"I was just texting you back. I'm not hungry." She really wasn't in the mood for company, either, especially if Declan was going to be his bright, sunny, teasing self.

"Come on, Abby. I came all the way here to help you. The least you can do is watch me eat."

She couldn't even produce a chuckle. At that moment, her stomach growled. Her therapist would tell her that she would have to keep on living. "On second thought, I'll get a little something. A sandwich or a burger."

After she washed her face, she met Declan downstairs at the pub. It was packed but they found a table near the entrance.

Sitting with Declan, she once again recognized that she didn't get that giddy feeling around him like she did when she was near Conor. They were companionable, yes, but she wasn't attracted to Declan, who cheerfully filled in all the quiet spaces with talk about his tourism business and how anxious he was for the business to take off. "It will be late spring before things really get rolling."

"What are you going to do in the meantime?" Abby asked.

"Odd jobs." He motioned to the room. "Like this. Filling in for Conor or for anyone else who needs me."

"I really appreciate you coming all this way." But Abby missed Conor. She was kicking herself for not spending time with him the last couple of nights when he'd asked her. She'd squandered her chance to have him all to herself. She wondered what he was up to right now. But she had to stop that train of thought. He was getting back together with his ex-wife.

Again she thought about Deydie, the person who'd given Abby the heads-up about Morag. She wished the old quilter and her quilting ladies were here right now to help her get through this. But they probably had better things to do than babysit Abby and her broken heart.

"Are ye all right?" Declan had concern written all over his face. "Are ye feeling peaked?"

"I'm fine. Maybe I overdid it today." If not physically, well, a broken heart was exhausting.

"Ye better get some rest. Tomorrow, let me do the heavy lifting, okay?"

There was no real heavy lifting but she would definitely let him take up the slack. Abby certainly wasn't feeling chatty, which was a requirement when running a booth. "Did you bring a kilt with you?"

"Aye. Conor told me to." Declan gave her a questioning look. "The reason being?"

"Eye candy for the attendees. You're going to use your good looks to reel 'em into the booth. Do you think you can do that?" But Abby already knew he was a born charmer.

Declan expanded and gave his chest a one-handed pound. "I'm happy to be of service. Ye know I don't mind a job where I can show meself off to a flock of birds."

"I knew you'd enjoy this aspect of the job. But there's more than just brides at these shows. There are bridesmaids with weddings on their mind. You should be careful with how you flirt with them or next thing you know, you'll be coming to me to plan the wedding for you and one of those birds."

Declan shook his head, laughing. "Nay. I'm not the marrying kind. I like women too much to settle down with just one."

Abby smiled at his declaration. "Those are famous last

words. I've heard more than my share of best man stories about the groom who'd said the same thing. Just so you know, the universe has a way of turning *never getting married* into happily-ever-afters." She stood and Declan stood, too. "I'll see you in the morning."

But there were a lot of hours between now and then. Too much time alone for her to think. Her brain was already spinning out of control. Plenty of hours and minutes to pine over Conor.

It was going to be a long night.

Conor glanced over at Morag, who was dozing in the seat across from him. The train's clickety-clack had lulled his ex-wife to sleep within minutes of leaving the station. Which gave Conor time to sort through things.

It was strange for him to be here with Morag, though it wasn't that long ago that being with her was normal. Now that he'd gotten some time, space, and perspective, he wondered why he'd ever grieved his less-than-satisfactory marriage. He'd only been going through the motions—work at the butcher shop and then home to Morag, who never seemed satisfied with him, their house, or their life in general. Why hadn't he realized that they'd both been living only half a life?

And had he really done the right thing by accompanying Morag to Glasgow this evening? He was like a man standing at the center point of a seesaw. On one end was Morag, who was grieving her father's death, and at the opposite end was Abby, who needed help to get her wedding planning business off the ground. He stood in the middle of the seesaw, leaning this way and that, as both women needed him.

But he had to admit that things with Abby were more complicated. So many emotions about her swirled around him. In many ways, he had to admit that he needed Abby more than she needed him. There was something bright and wonderful about the American lass that brought him into the light, too, whenever she was around. A man could get used to being with a woman like that.

What really worried him was whether he'd let Abby down by leaving with Morag. At least he hadn't abandoned Abby to her own devices. Declan would be there to help so Abby wouldn't be all alone. It wasn't the perfect solution and it made him wish that he could be in two places at once. He still worried about Declan getting his hooks into Abby, but there was nothing he could do about it now. Except …

Conor pulled out his phone and called Abby, but it went directly to voicemail. He left her a message. "Hey, Abs. I was just calling to see if Declan made it there." But that wasn't why he'd called. If he wanted to know whether Declan was there or not, he should've just called Declan himself. Conor tried again. "Did things end up well today? Just wondering. Well, um, talk to you soon." He hung up, wishing he hadn't called at all.

When he glanced over at Morag, he saw that she'd woken up and was watching him.

"Who were you talking to? The woman from the bridal show?" She made it sound as if she were asking after a dirty washcloth.

Conor had nothing to hide. "Aye. I was leaving her a message."

"Who is she? What did you say her name was?"

"Abby Potter. She's come to Scotland to be Whussendale's wedding planner." He tried to sound nonchalant, but his feelings were anything *but*.

Morag eyed him closely. "If you have yere sights set on her, you have to know that she's not right for you."

He wouldn't ask his ex-wife to elaborate. Morag may think she had the inside scoop, but she'd done a lot of damage to Conor. He wasn't going to discuss Abby with Morag at all. What could he say anyway? He was still trying to figure out what was going on between them. They'd become good friends. He liked being around her. They'd had incredible sex together. All things that were none of Morag's business.

"What is Steven up to these days?" Conor volleyed back. He probably shouldn't have done it, but he had to redirect Morag. "Any word from him?"

Morag gazed out the window. "He calls every day."

"Did ye tell him about yere da?" Conor sincerely wanted to know. He hoped his old friend had been kind and gracious about Morag's loss.

"Aye. He wants to come to the funeral."

"Oh." Well, that was something. "What did you tell him?"

"I haven't decided yet."

Surprisingly, Conor felt bad for his old friend. Apparently, Morag had grown weary of Steven, too, just like she had of him.

"Steven always liked yere da," Conor reminded her. "Or so he told me. I think you should welcome him to the funeral. Let him say goodbye, too."

"We'll see," was the only thing she said. She closed her eyes, as if to let Conor know that she was done talking.

Two hours later, the cab pulled down the street where he and Morag used to live, only houses away from her parents. The butcher shop and Steven's pub were on the next street over. At one time, Conor's whole life had been on these two streets, and he was flooded with all sorts of memories. Mostly unhappy ones. He reminded himself that he had gotten out and built a new life in Whussendale. A much better life.

"Who's been watching the butcher shop since yere da passed?" Conor asked. He wondered if one of Clyde's friends had taken over. Or maybe they'd closed the shop until after the funeral.

He was surprised when Morag answered, "Steven has been watching the counter."

For a second, Conor was confused. "But you said that you and Steven were over."

Morag pulled him to a stop in front of her mother's house. "I guess you might as well know; I'm pregnant, only two months along."

Conor went from confused to shocked and then to infuriated. This had been a huge source of contention between him and Morag. She never wanted to have children, and he did. Which was something they should've talked about before getting married. But they hadn't. Conor guessed that she and Steven hadn't either.

"So, this is why you're calling it quits with Steven?" Conor asked.

"Mostly." She turned away from him. "I don't know."

Morag had never been good at understanding what she was feeling and why, which had her taking her feelings out on others around her. When they were married, his solution had been to give her space to figure it out on her own. Maybe he should've tried to help. "What is your reason for not wanting children, Morag? I never asked but I should have."

She shrugged and he waited. Finally, she said, "I guess I didn't want to be tied down. I saw what happened when women had babies. Their children were attached to them at the hip. They let themselves go because all their energy goes to the raising of the bairns. Mothers can't go and do things whenever they want."

"I hear what ye're saying. But it doesn't have to be that way. Ye've got an advantage over most people," he said.

She looked at him. "How's that?"

"You have ye're mother and aunts close by to help. They love children and would be happy to be there for you when you need a break."

She nodded. "That's exactly what my mum said when I told her and Da that I was pregnant. Da was so excited. You should've seen him grinning from ear to ear. He said I was lucky because he believed Steven would make a good father." She looked at Conor questioningly. "Maybe I should give Steven another chance?" She started crying again.

"I know I don't get a vote, but if I did, I'd say that yere da is right. Steven will be an attentive father. Ye should give yere family—you and Steven and the babe—a chance." Apparently, Morag's tears had taken away any ire he'd had over their past. He'd let it go. It felt like ancient history.

The front door opened and Morag's mother, Edin, and her four aunts ran out to greet her.

"We were so worried. Where were you?" Edin asked. Only then did she seem to notice Conor. Her initial shock turned to coolness immediately.

He braced himself for whatever resentment her family felt toward him. He'd had no contact with Edin or Clyde since Morag banished him. Told him to pack his things. Conor wasn't even to reach out to her father to tell him that he wouldn't be returning to the butcher shop in the morning ... or any mornings after that. She'd said that she'd handle it. Even though Conor hadn't liked being ordered about, he'd done what Morag had asked; it was, after all, her family. But now he wondered if he shouldn't have said something, because they were acting as if he was the one who'd left the marriage, not her.

He stepped forward, having enough experience with death to

know how to behave appropriately around the bereaved: be courteous and sensitive. "Hello, Edin. I'm deeply sorry for yere loss." Some might think that this was an empty, overused statement, but he meant it and her family surely knew that his words were coming from a good place. He assured himself that just being here, especially since he was no longer part of the family, was showing Morag's family how much he respected Clyde.

It must've been the right thing to say because Edin's frown softened. She gave him a sad smile and briefly patted his arm. "Thank you for the condolences." She turned her attention back to Morag and her sisters. "Everyone, get inside. We don't want to catch our death of cold." Saying the word *death* apparently stopped her in her tracks and she looked shaken up, but only momentarily. Edin had always been stoic and firm. Morag slipped her hand around her mother's waist, and they walked into the house with the aunts following, making for a solemn procession.

Conor picked up his duffel and followed them inside, too. It was strange to be back here in this house. Everything was as it had been when he was part of the family. The same bench near the front door, hooks for hanging their coats, and the mud tray to hold their boots. Except the mirrors were covered to keep Clyde's ghost from being confused and not leaving the house. Conor noticed while he slipped off his Wellies that the clock in the foyer had been stopped. He assumed all the clocks in the house had been stopped, as was done when his own da died.

Reluctantly, he went to the parlor and peered in. Strange to think about Clyde's ghost. Conor felt like a ghost himself; he, too, no longer belonged here. He didn't fit in with Morag's family anymore and he had no idea how to proceed.

But Kieran's words came back to him. Conor didn't want their house filled with people when their da died. But Kieran set him straight. "Death is a community event. Being together forges stronger bonds through shared grief." Conor's duty was to be here whether it was uncomfortable or not.

Morag's aunts openly assessed him, which was damned uncomfortable, too.

"Edin, is there anything I can do?" Conor asked.

"Aye," answered the oldest aunt, who was also the bossiest. "Ye can bring the folding chairs down from the attic and set them up in here."

He nodded and gladly left the room. He took his time bringing down the chairs, wanting to give the women plenty of opportunity to talk amongst themselves without him in the way. After all the chairs were set up, he helped himself to a glass of water in the kitchen. When he returned to the parlor, Morag excused herself, claiming a headache, and off she went to bed. Conor stood there, feeling awkward. He was certainly glad he'd texted Kieran about staying at his flat. It would give Conor some solitude, while remaining close enough to help Morag's family with anything they needed.

"If there's nothing else you need at the moment, I thought I'd head out," Conor said to the room filled with his ex-wife's relations.

"That's fine. Ye may go," Edin said.

No one else said a word as he left the house. He wished more than anything to be with Abby right now. Something about her made him feel warm, comfortable, and wanted.

When Conor got back to Kieran's flat, he pulled out his phone to call Abby. But he stopped himself. She'd had a long day at the bridal show and he didn't want to wake her if she'd made it an early night.

He was tired, too. Too tired to even watch the telly for a bit. The only thing he did was text Keiran that he'd made it to the flat. Tomorrow, he'd check in with Magnus and Tavon. And Declan. Of course, he'd love to have a long conversation with Abby, but he knew she'd be busy with the show.

Conor climbed into bed and fell asleep, but somehow his brain remained in overdrive, giving him vivid dreams. Once again, he was back on the teetertotter, trying to remain balanced but falling off every time a buzzer sounded.

He woke up in a panic to the pounding on the front door. His first thought was *Who died this time?*

He pulled on his jeans, then hurried to the door. Kieran's voice could be heard before Conor actually saw him. "Can ye undo this bluidy chain so I can get in?"

Conor slipped off the chain and opened the door wide. "What are ye doing here? What happened to yere deployment?"

Kieran dropped his duffel. "Got back early. I've been calling yere phone but ye didn't pick up. Did ye turn it off?"

That explained the buzzing noise in his dream. "Sorry. I slept through it, I guess."

Kieran gave him a quick bro hug. "Did ye take my bed or the guest bed? I'm beat."

"Guest bed," Conor said.

"Good. I'll talk to ye in the morn before I head out to get Dublin in Whussendale."

"Hold up for a second." Conor was just now coming fully awake. "Could you possibly stay in Whussendale until I get back? I know Declan said Tavon would help Magnus, but I think ye would do a better job of it. And the uncles would certainly like to spend time with you, too."

"Aye. I have some annual leave to use. How long do you think you'll be gone?"

"I dunno. The funeral's next Saturday. It'll give everyone enough time to get here."

"How're Morag and her family holding up?"

"As well as you can imagine. No one expected Clyde to go first." But Conor had seen his mother's or his father's deaths coming either.

Kieran ran a hand through his short hair. "Aye. It's never easy." Even though he was eight years older than Conor, the two of them were often on the same page, especially when it came to family matters. "Just keep me in the loop so I can plan accordingly."

"Will do."

"It's good to see you, brother. Now, I'm off to bed."

Chapter 17

THE NEXT DAY, Declan did a great job of playing the part of the flirty Scot with no need for coaching from Abby. He must've been giving off extra pheromones because there was a lot of giggling and sighing over her friend from Whussendale. The only real difference between Declan and Conor being in the booth was that Declan was collecting phone numbers for himself from the bridesmaids ... and a couple of brides!

One twenty-something came to Abby. "Where is the guy who was here yesterday morning? I wanted to give him my phone number, too."

"Oh, right, yeah, he had to leave," Abby said, admiring how brave this woman was to ask for what she wanted.

The woman wrote down her number and held it out to Abby. "Do you mind giving this to him when you see him?"

Abby didn't accept the paper. "Yeah, about him—he's taken."

Declan must've overheard the exchange because he spun around and gave Abby an *Oh-really* smile.

Clearly, Conor hadn't told Declan that he had gone away with Morag and that the two of them were getting back together.

Right before noon, there was a bit of a ruckus as a crowd of women, mostly older ones, made their way to the booth. Leading the pack was Deydie, with Diana in tow.

"There's our wedding planner!" Deydie's voice boomed. That woman certainly didn't need the loudspeaker to be heard! "We had some last-minute shopping to do in Inverness and thought we'd come to see what was here, didn't we, Diana?" She elbowed poor Diana in the ribs.

"Yes, yes. Hi, Abby." She glanced over at Declan. "Where's Conor? Deydie said he was going to be here with you."

"Oh, well, I guess you didn't hear." Wasn't Deydie always up on the latest gossip? "His ex-wife stopped by yesterday with news. Her father passed away suddenly."

With a fierce glower on her face, Deydie stepped forward in front of Diana to be in Abby's line of sight. "Damn that boy! Did he leave with her then?"

"Yes. He accompanied Morag back to Glasgow." Abby looked away, afraid Deydie might see the depth of her devastation.

Bethia moved forward and put her arm around Abby. "Are ye all right, sweeting?"

"Oh, yes. Fine. I'm fine." But her words weren't as convincing as she hoped they would be. She pointed to Declan. "Declan came to help me today. He's doing a great job."

Deydie dug her phone out of her dress pocket. "I'm going to call Coira to see what she knows."

Abby put her hand on Deydie's phone. "Don't." He made his choice, she stopped herself from saying. Besides, too many people were standing there, and they might see her mist up or something more horrific might happen ... like she might sob. "Everything's fine." She glanced around desperately, not sure what to say. "Uh, Diana, was there something specific you wanted to see while you're here? Perhaps flower arrangements? Or ideas for bridesmaids' gifts?"

But Declan sauntered over then and saved Abby by directing his entourage over to greet the Gandiegow group, introducing them as the quilters who would be making the keepsake quilt for their wedding, if they chose that option. Next, he regaled them with a story about the magic of Whussendale and Gandiegow, which made Deydie beam. Abby took that opportunity to slip away in hopes of pulling herself together in the restroom.

But she wasn't lucky enough to make a clean getaway. Deydie and Bethia followed.

The second Deydie got in the restroom, she hit Abby where it hurt. "I told ye the lad still had a torch burning for that wife of his. Lassie, ye shouldn't have staked any hopes on him."

"That's enough," Bethia said in a kind tone. "Can't ye see that Abby is broke up about his leaving?"

Deydie put her arm around Abby. "The truth hurts. Ye know that I'm not one to sugarcoat things. But I will make ye this promise. Ye'll be okay. Mark my words: two years from now, this will have worked itself out."

"You're right. I'm okay." Which was a bald-faced lie. Even though Abby had tried hard not to, she had pinned her hopes and dreams on being with Conor. Just possibly she'd even visualized them getting married in Whussendale. But that would never happen now. "You're right, Deydie. I was dumb to think that Conor and I had made a connection."

Deydie dropped her arm. "Damn straight I'm right."

Bethia pulled Abby in for a hug. The emotion that hit Abby was shocking. She wasn't used to motherly love and wasn't prepared when the first sob escaped her. And she couldn't stop the sobs that followed. She cried for all the love she'd missed out on throughout her life, and she cried for the love she would never have from Conor.

To her surprise, Deydie patted her back. After a few minutes, Deydie went to the sink and wet a handful of paper towels, then held them against Abby's cheeks and forehead. Abby felt like it was her cue to nix the tears.

"Ye're going to be all right, lassie," Deydie said determinedly. "Ye've had yere tears. Now pull yereself together and get on with life. Ye don't need a man to make ye happy." Deydie belted out one of her signature harrumphs. "I'm as happy as happy can be. And I ain't got no man to speak of." But Abby had heard the other quilters talk about old Abraham Clacher, who had a crush on Deydie, and suspected that Deydie hadn't deterred him in any way.

Yeah, the realization hit Abby hard; even Deydie could get a man, when Abby couldn't.

Well, Deydie shouldn't be the yardstick by which Abby measured her own happiness. If she was being truthful with herself, there was only one man who would fit the bill for her. A good-looking Scot who wove beautiful tartans and kissed like a son-of-a-gun. The one who made her smile. The one who made her smoldering hot. The one she had fallen in love with. But he was the one she could never have. Conor had gone off with his ex-wife, who wanted another chance with him. Abby had heard it with her own ears!

"Can you give me a minute to pull myself together? I'll be back to the booth shortly."

"Aye," Bethia said. She took Deydie's arm and guided her toward the door. "We'll see ye back at the booth." But as they left, Bethia was whispering in Deydie's ear.

Abby splashed water on her face and adjusted her makeup and lipstick. When she got back to the booth, Declan was entertaining a new group of attendees.

Deydie hustled over to her. "Let me do ye a favor."

"Sure?" Abby said uncertainly. Deydie wasn't known for being benevolent. It was too late to ask what favor Deydie was going to do for her as Deydie waddled away and over to where Declan was standing.

Declan was busy handing out brochures and bragging about the charms of Whussendale while charming the pants off the women around him.

Deydie grabbed his arm and spun him to face her. "Lad, ye need to bring the wedding planner straight to us in Gandiegow when ye're done here." Deydie glanced at Abby just in time to see Abby's mouth fall open.

Abby rushed over to the old quilter. "No. No!" She'd told Conor that she'd watch Dublin for him. Or at the very least, help his uncle by sharing the dog. Dublin was sweet but she was a bit of a handful.

Deydie shook her head at Abby and then turned her gaze back on Declan. "Lad, do ye hear me? Gandiegow. Bring Abby to Gandiegow as soon as heavenly possible."

This time Declan looked at Abby. Surely, he could see her hesitation. "Um, yeah, Abby and I are planning to stop at several shops on our way back to *Whussendale*." Good man. Apparently, he read Abby's expression correctly and emphasized Whussendale as he should, which Abby appreciated.

"Nay!" Deydie bellowed. "Abby's needed in Gandiegow for Rory and Diana's wedding. Last minute things to handle. It's all-hands-on-deck, don't ye know!"

Yes, Abby had agreed to help out with the Gandiegow wedding and she wasn't sure how she was going to be in two places at once. Declan looked back at her, imploring her with a shrug. She opened her mouth, but this time, Deydie grabbed her arm and dragged her to a secluded corner before she spoke.

"Ye're coming to Gandiegow. There's no two ways about it. Bethia and I believe ye need time away from Conor to put ye on an even keel," Deydie said.

"But Hugh expects me back in Whussendale." Abby's statement was true. "He's the one who hired me."

"Don't worry about Laird Hugh. I'll square it with him," Deydie promised.

Deydie and Bethia were probably right that she needed distance from Conor to heal. She'd talk to Declan about helping out with Dublin until she returned.

"Okay. If it's all right with Hugh and Sophie, then I'll gladly come to Gandiegow."

Diana reached out and pulled Abby in for a quick hug. "Oh, thank you! I really appreciate it. I really do need help figuring out what to do for the bridesmaids. And it will be wonderful to have you there beforehand to make sure everything goes smoothly."

"Yes, I'll help wherever I'm needed. We'll chat about bridesmaids' gifts soon, too."

Deydie rubbed her chin. "Ye know, ye coming to Scotland might just be a blessing for some of the older quilting ladies in Gandiegow. Extra hands would certainly lessen the load that we carry. Some of those ladies are getting up there in years."

Abby smiled at her. It was funny that Deydie didn't consider herself one of the older ladies, though her wrinkled face told the true story. Abby put her arm around Deydie, just like the old quilter had embraced her earlier. "I'm happy to help."

She looked at the women around her and realized that for perhaps the first time in her life she wasn't truly alone. She had a community of women to help her get over Conor, and getting over him would be the most difficult thing she'd ever do. That was saying something, considering how her mother had raised her—no hugs, no kisses, no lullabies, no kind words or validation. But her mother had been only the first part of Abby's story. Abby was determined to move beyond her upbringing. At the end of the day, her mother was who she was. There was no changing her. Abby could only change herself.

Conor spent the whole morning running errands for Edin and her sisters. But he'd been around enough to learn that Clyde had put the butcher shop up for sale last month. Edin said he'd wanted to retire and caravan around Scotland with her. There were already two prospective buyers, which was a blessing, according to Edin's eldest sister. Conor left the room when Edin started to cry.

Conor didn't mind being busy, as it kept him out of the house and away from the sadness there. It also kept him from worrying about how Abby was getting along at the bridal show with Declan. Conor wanted to call her, but he didn't want to interrupt when she was busy speaking with potential clients. In fact, he really shouldn't call her until he was certain that she was done taking down the booth.

"Conor?" Edin broke into his thoughts.

"What can I do for you?" he asked.

She handed him a list. "I need ye to run to the butcher shop and pick these things up."

The request halted him. Didn't Edin know that Steven was tending the counter? Or maybe that was only yesterday. Conor scanned the room for Morag to see if she could tell him. But she'd gone with one of the aunts to check on the flowers.

Edin frowned at him. "Why aren't ye gone already?"

"I'm going now." Conor walked out the back door. He needed

to pull his shite together before he made it to the butcher shop. If Steven was there, Conor wasn't sure what he was going to say to him.

When he reached the butcher shop, he hesitated for a moment before opening the door and going inside. Once again, he had the sensation of a place being familiar and at the same time, feeling foreign. It had been a long time since he'd been here.

"I heard ye'd come to town," said a familiar voice.

Conor looked up and nodded. "Steven." His former friend was wearing a white butcher's apron and a white cap. "I came to town to show my respect for Clyde."

"I figured Morag would run to you," Steven said evenly without a tinge of anger or reproach.

Conor had no reply to give. He could've said that Morag had known him for a long time, but that wouldn't have done any good. Instead, he walked closer to the meat case and peered inside.

Steven shifted so he was directly across from Conor. "She said ye're more understanding than me."

Conor snorted. "Hardly." As an afterthought, he held out the list for Steven. "Edin needs these things for tonight."

Steven took the list and scanned it. then looked at Conor again. "Did she tell ye why she left me?"

Apparently, Steven thought Conor was his therapist.

"She told me she's with child, if that's what ye're getting at."

Steven stared out the window, looking devastated.

Conor decided to throw him a bone. "This isn't really about ye. She's never wanted kids. I think she's scared to be a mum."

"It feels personal."

"If it's any consolation, I told her to get back with you. Raise the baby together. Be a real family." All the things Conor wanted but couldn't have.

Steven turned to Conor, having more life in him than he did a moment ago. "Really? Ye did that? Told her that we should stay together? Do ye mean it?"

"Surprisingly, I do." Conor couldn't believe it, but it was true. He didn't want Morag back. And if she made Steven happy, of course he wanted them to be together. Any animosity or feelings of betrayal that he'd held on to were gone. Wiped away. The slate clean. Just like that. Or maybe he'd been growing past his anger for some time now. Having Abby in his life had changed his perspective. "Did Morag tell ye that Clyde basically told her the same thing that I told her?"

"I'm not surprised at Clyde. He's been wanting to be a grandda," Steven said. "I'm glad he got to at least know that his line would carry on."

"Will ye be coming to the house tonight? There's been a constant stream of people." Conor was feeling lighter and, apparently, magnanimous.

"I wasn't sure if I was welcome or not," Steven said, as he wrapped up two roasts.

Conor nodded. "I understand, but ye should be there. Ye're family." Conor wasn't family anymore. "I'll let Morag know it was me that told ye to come."

Steven nodded. "Did ye know that Clyde was selling the shop?" It was feeling like old times with Steven. *Male gossiping,* his uncles called it.

"Aye, I overheard the women talking about it. Edin wonders if he was having a premonition about dying."

"Sounds like her," Steven said.

"Sounds like grief. People do and say strange things when someone dies," Conor said.

"I guess that could explain why Morag brought you home," Steven said thoughtfully.

But Glasgow wasn't home anymore. Whussendale was.

"Hey, listen," Steven started but then paused for a second before carrying on. "I want to thank you for bringing her home safely."

"No problem."

"She didn't take the news about Clyde very well. She was pretty broke up about it. They all are."

"Morag is going to need you to lean on." Which meant Conor would have to be gone. Morag was probably going to be a little messed up for a while from her da and all. Baby hormones wouldn't help the situation either. At least that's what he'd learned from watching the telly.

"I hope Morag will take to heart what you and Clyde told her."

"You should tell her, too," Conor said.

"I did. I told her I want the babe. She knows I'm excited about us having our own family," Steven said. "It's all I ever wanted for us."

"Tell her again," Conor advised. He never thought he'd be in this position, and the Almighty knew that he never expected to want Steven and Morag back together. But here Conor was. He had to do something to help. When everything was settled, he could make his exit. He just needed to find the right time.

Chapter 18

ABBY KEPT REMINDING herself to look on the bright side of things. As soon as the booth was loaded up and they were on the road, she and Declan made all the stops that she and Conor had planned—a florist, a bridal shop, a bakery known for their wedding cakes, and even a quilt shop—because Deydie insisted a quilt shop had to be added to the list. Abby offered stacks of brochures to the owners and managers of each shop to hand out to their customers. The stops were quick as Abby didn't want to take up too much of their time. Soon they were done and headed toward Gandiegow.

As consistent as ever, Declan helped Abby by monopolizing the conversation during the long drive and she was grateful. Her thoughts were too jumbled; she needed time to sort out how she felt about Conor, but more importantly, she had to figure out how to get over him and put her heart back together.

When Declan steered the van down the steep hill to Gandiegow's parking lot, he glanced over at her. "Did ye let Conor know where ye were going to be?"

She was taken aback, because for the whole trip, he hadn't mentioned Conor, and he hadn't gotten personal. "Uh, no. I haven't spoken to him." She didn't plan to. She had to remain strong. Resolved.

He gave her a disapproving frown. "I think ye should talk to him."

"Don't worry about it," Abby said with mock lightness. "He'll be fine."

Declan grumbled sarcastically. "I must worry. Ye know the man is going to want answers, and we both know who he's going to ask. And ye've told me nothing."

"True. I haven't told you anything on purpose. That way you'll have plausible deniability." She nodded, proud of herself for coming up with that. "That's just me looking out for you."

"Nay. That's just *you* getting *me* into a whole lot of trouble … again."

She sat with that thought for a moment, then said quietly, "Sorry."

"It's okay," Declan said. "I'll give ye cover, but ye know he'll be able to find out rather quickly. I don't know if ye noticed, but word travels fast in Scotland, especially between our two villages."

"Yes, I've noticed."

Declan parked the van, got out, and went to the back to pull out her luggage. "How about I take this to Quilting Central for ye?"

Abby took the bag from him. "No, that's okay. I've got it."

"Will I see ye soon in Whussendale?" Declan asked.

"I'll be gone a while. At least through Rory and Diana's wedding. They need my help."

"Sure. Whatever you say." He went to the driver's side of the vehicle. "Well, take it easy."

"You, too." Abby watched as the SUV went back up the hill. She glanced out at the ocean and suddenly felt like she could breathe. She'd made it to Gandiegow. The quilting ladies would be there for her. Ever since Conor had left the bridal show, Abby had done one thing right; she'd successfully ignored his calls and messages, not letting herself listen to his voicemail or read his texts. She knew she was prolonging the inevitable by ignoring what he had to say. But she already knew what was in those messages. Conor and Morag were back together.

Well, Abby was too busy, anyway, to waste time thinking about him, worrying over her broken heart... and kicking herself for giving herself to him without knowing whether he cared for her as much as she did for him. A stupid mistake, one she would never make again.

She picked up her bag and walked into the village, to Quilting Central. She needed to ask Deydie where she was supposed to stay.

As she made her way along the walkway, she noticed the changes to the village. The new railing along the pier had been installed and painted white. Just that small addition made the village even more idyllic and charming. The church had a new coat of paint as well, making it look as crisp and new as a wedding gown.

No one seemed to be out and about, but when she opened the door to Quilting Central, she found the majority of the women inside.

Deydie was on the stage, barking out orders. It looked like stations had been set up on the tables that usually held sewing machines. There was a floral arrangement station covered by silk flowers and bouquets. One group of women were hemming Diana's wedding dress. Finally, there was a group making centerpieces for each table. Abby was amazed at how industrious these women were. It looked like she wasn't needed in Gandiegow after all.

Deydie and Bethia joined her.

Bethia spoke first. "Deydie and I have come up with a solution for ye."

Deydie bobbed her head. "Damned straight we did."

"What kind of solution?" Abby asked warily.

"A traditional Scottish solution," Deydie answered.

Abby looked to Bethia. "And that would be?"

But it was Deydie who answered. "I told ye that you could be happy without a man. But Bethia thinks ye're still young enough to want one."

That answered nothing.

"There's an old Scottish tradition," Bethia said, "that if a young woman prays on November 29th to be married, a sign will appear on the next day—St. Andrew's Day."

Deydie gave her a serious look. "We all know that ye had yere heart set on Conor Masterson, but that door's been closed. By the end of this week, the Almighty will reveal to ye the man ye're supposed to marry." She nodded definitively, as if that were the gospel truth and the end of the discussion.

"Take heart, sweeting," Bethia said, as she patted Abby's shoulder. "Yere prayers will be answered."

Abby wasn't sure what to say to this irrational old wives' tale. "Um, thank you, I guess."

Deydie handed her a clipboard. "Now that that's cleared up, I'm turning this over to ye. Bethia said ye should take over and I listened to her."

"Are you sure? It looks like you have things well in hand." Abby glanced at the clipboard. "But you're right. If you and Hugh want me to work on weddings here in Gandiegow, too, it's best if I become accustomed to your system." She smiled at

Deydie. "I'm happy to do whatever needs to be done."

Deydie and Bethia escorted Abby to each table so she could speak with the person in charge of that project. At one point, Abby tried to hide a yawn, but Bethia saw it.

"You better head to Duncan's Den and get settled in. We have a big day tomorrow. Actually, the whole week is booked from dawn to dusk."

"Aye," Deydie said. "Ye need to be on top of yere game if ye're going to throw weddings here in Gandiegow."

"Thanks. It's been a long weekend at the bridal show. You're right. I need to get a good night's rest if I'm going to be any good for Rory and Diana this week."

The next day, Abby worked with Diana on the final seating chart and the zipper bags they'd decided on for the brides-maids. Abby was looking forward to meeting Diana's sister, Liz, and her mother, Victoria, when they arrived later in the week. Diana and her family would be staying at Thistle Glen Lodge, along with other members of Diana's family and her former co-workers at Three Seals Publishing. When Abby was settled into her room at Duncan's Den, she assumed she was too tired to barely give a thought about Conor. But she was wrong. She wanted to hear his voice. But Deydie had cautioned her not to call him, though he'd left her another two voice messages today and three texts. She turned off her phone and stowed it in the drawer in the bedside table.

On Wednesday, Abby met with Dominic and Claire at Pastas & Pastries about the catering, working out the exact timing of the food. The best part was sampling the menu. Just like at the impromptu wedding she'd attended here earlier, the food was amazing.

On Thursday, Abby and the quilting ladies decorated the church and the Grand Dining Room. Abby kept glancing at the door, expecting Conor to magically appear, but she was only setting herself up for disappointment. She was still hoping, though all hope had been lost. Conor had chosen Morag and that was the end of it. Unfortunately, her heart wasn't very accepting or hadn't gotten the memo.

Friday held a flurry of activity as out-of-town guests poured into the village. The American tradition of a rehearsal dinner was not done in Gandiegow and Abby was relieved that she didn't have to spearhead that particular activity. Diana's sister, Liz, and her best friend, Parker, took the lead and held a hen party at Quilting Central, while Rory and his groomsmen gathered for a steak dinner and cigar stag party at the restaurant.

All evening, more people arrived, filling up Thistle Glen Lodge, Duncan's Den, and Partridge House, Gandiegow's B&B. Colin's farm, a few miles outside of town, had taken on boarders, as well. With Deydie and Bethia's help, Abby had secured a few more farms in the area to take on any guests who needed last minute accommodations. Always have a back-up plan, was Abby's motto. She had moved her things from Duncan's Den to the room over the pub to give herself some privacy.

While the other women enjoyed the hen party, Abby was checking and doublechecking every item on her list. Finally she closed her notebook, ready to call it a night. But Deydie and Bethia stopped her before she got to the door and pulled her to the side.

"Do ye remember what we told ye?" Deydie asked.

"You've told me a lot of things this week," Abby said. "Deydie, I think you're wonderful but you do know that you've bossed me around from morning until night, every day since I arrived in town."

Deydie laughed. "Damned straight! It's my job to keep everyone in line. You included." She patted Abby's arm. "We think ye've done a fine job of making sure Rory and Diana have a great day."

"Thank you. Now, what is it that I'm supposed to remember?"

"About saying your prayers tonight so ye can figure out who ye're going to marry," Bethia reminded her.

"Oh, yes. Sure." But Abby didn't put much stock in that particular Scottish tradition.

"Mind me," Deydie said. "Say yere prayers tonight and ask the Almighty to show ye a sign."

"Okay, I will," Abby promised. She'd do it for these two, because they'd been so good to her.

Both the old women hugged her tightly, which once again reminded Abby of what she'd been missing all these years. She walked to the pub and found the place filled with noise and merriment. She waved and nodded to everyone who called out to her as she went to the steps behind the bar that led to her room upstairs. Even though the pub was hopping, she knew she had to get some rest. She readied for bed, turned out the lights, and climbed under the pile of quilts. It was this time of the night that she dreaded most because her thoughts always turned to Conor and what he might be up to. But the other thing was on her mind, too.

"Dang it!" She slung off the quilts and went to her knees just like she'd seen children do on TV shows and in movies. "Hey, God. Abby here. I'm not sure if I'm doing this right or not, but here goes. Deydie and Bethia said I should reach out to you and ask for a sign of who it is that I will marry." Truth be told, she was destined to be a spinster. She knew it and surely God knew it, too, since he was supposed to be all-knowing. This whole tradition was ridiculous. And she was ridiculous in joining in their superstitious ways. But at least when she was questioned tomorrow, for surely she would be, she could honestly tell the old quilters that she'd done what they asked. "I don't know what else I'm supposed to say, God. I guess that's all for now. Bye. Over-and-out. Um, amen."

Abby climbed back into bed, and because there was still one more matter to attend to, she said a silent prayer for Conor's happiness ... even though his happiness wasn't going to include her. With that done, she rolled over and fell asleep.

The next morning, Abby felt a little hungover, even though she hadn't imbibed yesterday. Two breakfasts were scheduled, one for early risers and one for those who wanted to sleep in. Abby went to the first breakfast, where Rory introduced her to his brother, Kin, a police officer like him. She felt like she was filling out the grid of Gandiegow's loved ones whom she'd heard about. Keeping her mind busy, thinking about these new acquaintances, was helping to keep her from worrying over Conor. All she wanted was that he would be happy with Morag this time around.

Abby planned to head to the church after breakfast to make sure everything was set for the 1:30 p.m. ceremony. But when she left Pastas & Pastries, she glanced back at the walkway that led to the parking lot—and stopped short, stunned to see two familiar faces, two people who *hadn't* been invited to the wedding—Aaron and her mother! At first thought, she wondered if her eyes were playing tricks on her. A Scottish mirage. But when Aaron raised his hand in greeting, Abby knew it must be them and her heart sank. Frustrated, she rolled her eyes heavenward. "Are you kidding me? I don't need this right now." God had certainly thrown a monkey wrench into her day by having these two show up unannounced in Gandiegow. Abby had no choice but to change her plans and direction, from going to the church to greeting her mother and Aaron.

When she got near enough that they could hear her over the waves crashing against the walkway, Abby hollered, "What are you doing here?"

But the question she really wanted to ask, and not to these two either, but to God himself ... was this supposed to be the answer to her prayer, the *sign* she'd asked for? Was it possible that she was supposed to marry the man whom she'd recently left at the altar?

Abby looked heavenward and scoffed. "Really? You can't be serious!"

God must have a pretty dark sense of humor.

Chapter 19

STILL IN SHOCK, Abby closed the distance between herself and the uninvited visitors. Her mother glowered at her, and Aaron's expression was full of scrutiny. It was surreal that they were here in Scotland. She wished she'd never said that prayer last night in hopes of finding her future husband. It made her feel so damned uncomfortable to think Aaron might be the sign Deydie and Bethia had promised.

"What are *we* doing here? It should be obvious," her mother said, half-mocking and half-accusing as she propped her hands on her hips. Abby knew all too well about her mother's Superwoman pose—a power play—and chose to ignore it. "We're here to bring you home!"

Abby couldn't believe it. She was a grown woman! What made her mother think she could come and get her like she was some naughty child at a sleepover. "No, Mother. I'm staying." *Sign* or no, Abby wasn't going to bend to her mother's will this time.

Aaron gave her his wounded-puppy-dog look, which

appeared ridiculous on a thirty-nine year-old man. She'd swear he'd perfected it by practicing in front of a mirror. "Abby, darling, you've been dodging my calls."

She'd done more than that. She'd blocked his number!

Her mother huffed. "What do you have to say for yourself, Abigail?"

Joann knew Abby wasn't a fan of her given name—probably the reason she'd used it. Frustrated, Abby sighed. "Listen, you caught me at a bad time." Which was the truth. "The wedding ceremony is in an hour."

"What?" Aaron sounded outraged. "You're getting married? Does your fiancé know that we just broke up?"

Married? Hardly, Abby thought. And she wanted to correct Aaron. *They* hadn't broken up. *She'd* seen the light and called it quits. "I'm the *wedding planner.*" She didn't want to explain the whole story, how Rory and Diana were outsiders, too, who had been brought together when Rory came to town to solve a series of crimes. "I'll find you and Mother later." But where could Aaron and her mother go right now? Abby thought quickly and pointed to the three-story building. "Over there. That's Pastas & Pastries, the restaurant. I'll meet you there in a bit. Get something to eat and then I'll be by to take you to the wedding—a real Scottish wedding." There were other practical concerns with them showing up unannounced. Like where could she put them for the night? Maybe one of the outlying farms with a couple of rooms available? Abby would have to worry about that later.

"You're going to abandon us ... again?" Aaron simpered, making Abby recoil. How had she ever been engaged to this man?

"Are you sure we won't get food poisoning there?" Joann said. This wasn't the first time she'd criticized a restaurant before actually tasting the food. "I'll just order some bottled water."

"The food is good. But do what you want. Tell Dominic and Claire, the owners, to put your meal on my tab," Abby said. "Now, I really have to go."

Joann slipped her hand into the crook of Aaron's arm. "Come on. I know when we're not wanted."

If you knew that, why did you come? Abby mentally screamed—it was best to not speak it aloud. Instead, she said, "I'll be back as soon as I can."

Half an hour later, Abby found the church in perfect order. The Gandiegow decorating committee had done a beautiful job, which left Abby nothing to fuss over except to leave the wedding book for the guests to sign. "I suppose I better check on my mother," she grumbled as she closed the church door behind her and set her sights on the restaurant.

As soon as Abby joined Joann and Aaron at Pastas & Pastries, she peppered her mom with questions. "How long do you plan to be here? When are you heading home? Did you arrange a place for you both to stay tonight?" She tried not to sound impatient for them to leave Scotland. But she was.

"*We* have a flight out tomorrow," Joann said.

Well, that answered the question about whether Aaron would be staying longer or not.

"I have to be back at the clinic on Monday. Besides, Romeo needs his mummy so I can't be gone too long."

Which begged the question. "If you're here, and I'm here, who's watching Romeo?"

Her mother glared. "Yet another reason why you have to leave this place and come home. I had to abandon Romeo with my new assistant. A stranger! My poor little man seemed very unhappy about it, too. Romeo needs family looking after him."

Abby shook her head. Yeah, her *poor little man* was a devil in cat's clothing. She had to keep that sentiment to herself, too. "I'm sure your cat will survive."

Her mother frowned, not at what she'd said but at Abby herself. "What in the world are you wearing?"

"My wedding planner clothes."

"Pants? And in all black, too?" her mother groused.

"In the summer, I usually wear a black dress. But yes, this is appropriate."

"Black! It's not a funeral you're going to."

"Mother, I know what I'm doing. I wear black because I need to blend into the background, in case I'm caught in photos or videos."

"Well, black washes you out."

Abby didn't think so. Over the years she'd gained a lot of confidence in her wardrobe. A stylish high-necked blouse, black slacks, and cute, comfortable, boots was one of her *go-tos*, and she thought she looked great.

"I think you should give up on all this wedding planner nonsense," her mother said matter-of-factly. "Don't you think so, Aaron?"

He looked as if he wished that Joann hadn't put him in the middle. "Maybe this was something she needed to do to get it out of her system. But when we're married, Abby, you won't have to work at all."

Abby didn't acknowledge either of their statements or the fact that they were tag-teaming her. "People will start arriving at the church. I need to be there in case anyone has questions. Do you want to come with me to the church now or come on your own later? There's only one church in town. You can't miss it with its steeple and all."

"We'll come now." Joann stood and smoothed out the lines of her blood red dress.

Aaron stood, too. He wasn't as tall as Conor or as manly as Conor. But what man could compare to the Scot she couldn't get off her mind?

"I have a place for us at the back of the church," she explained as they walked. "I'll get you two seated and then I'll be in the narthex with the bridal party until after the bride processes down the aisle. I'll slip in beside you then." She'd have to make sure that her mother was seated closest to the aisle so Abby wouldn't be stuck sitting next to Aaron. She just didn't want to give him the wrong idea or feed his delusion that they could ever be together again.

Abby checked on the groomsmen and the bridesmaids who had gathered in the narthex. Rory was with Father Andrew, waiting at a side door that led to the sanctuary. When everyone was ready, Abby was to cue the bagpiper, Reid McCartney, who worked alongside Rory solving major crimes in Scotland. Another of his coworkers, Corey MacTaggart, was ushering people to their seats. Both of them, Abby found out, were big flirts.

Abby checked with Diana, "Are you ready?"

"Yes, I'm ready." She was beaming like the sun. Abby signaled McCartney to start playing Caledonia. MacTaggart did his job by slowly escorting Diana's mother down the aisle. After that, Father Andrew and Rory entered the sanctuary. When they were in place, Abby sent Diana's sister Liz and Rory's brother Kin to process down the aisle, as matron of honor and best man. The rest of the bridesmaids and groomsmen followed.

After everyone was in their place, Abby was free to find her seat next to her mother and her ex. She frowned when she saw that Aaron had switched places with Joann, which forced Abby to sit next to him. As soon as she sat, he reached for her hand, but she pulled away. "No," she hissed. Couldn't Aaron and her mother take the hint that they were done and over?

For the first time, Abby was glad Conor wasn't here. She didn't want him to see her with Aaron ... sitting next to him! Conor would get the wrong idea. But the truth was—and she better start facing it now—Conor wouldn't care who she sat next to. He was back with his ex like he wanted. Besides, seeing Conor now, with her emotions so shredded, would be a bridge too far. With the duties of the wedding and the complication of her mother and Aaron's impromptu visit, she felt fragile. If Conor had come to the wedding, surely he'd have Morag in tow. Which would be too much for Abby to handle. Yes, a bridge too far.

She actually wondered if she was ever going to see Conor again. Or—*oh lord!*—would Conor bring Morag to Whussendale to live? Probably. Her heart sank even more at that thought.

If Conor did move Morag to Whussendale, what then? Abby couldn't bear to see him being all lovey-dovey with another woman. She wouldn't be able to stay in Whussendale. Especially if Morag shared the cottage with Conor next door to hers!

Abby's mind wandered this way and that and was surprised when the ceremony concluded. She'd missed the whole thing! She quietly slipped from her seat and went to the narthex as Rory and Diana signed the register. Apparently, Aaron and her mother were going to be her shadows, as they followed her to the narthex, too.

"What can we do to help?" Aaron must be trying a new tack with Abby; he'd never offered to help her with anything before.

"Thank you. I have it under control. Photos are next. You and Mother can explore the town now. The sunset will be around 3:30 today. Right after that, we'll have the speeches in the Grand Dining Room on the second floor of the restaurant. I'll meet you there. The wedding meal starts at 5:30." This was going to be an extra-long day. The wedding itself wasn't the problem. It was these two hanging around, expecting her to entertain them and then to move back to St. Louis with them. She hoped they would give her a break from both. She needed a little peace in her life, not upheaval.

Aaron put out the crook of his arm to her mother. "Let's go see what this little Scottish village has to offer."

Joann laughed sardonically. "I'm not optimistic there will be enough to occupy our time since this place is microscopic and we have a couple of hours to kill."

Abby thought of something else for them to do. "Don't forget to check out Quilting Central. Think of it as a museum. There are some amazing quilts hanging on the walls." Joann didn't sew, but she thought Abby had real talent when it came to quilting. In this one area she hadn't completely let her mother down.

Neither one of them acknowledged her suggestion but walked away companionably. Abby wondered something, and not for the first time either. Aaron was ten years older than Abby and fifteen years younger than Joann. Yes, it was a hefty age gap between Aaron and her mother, but Abby thought they actually made the perfect couple. The whole time Abby and Aaron dated, he spent a lot of time on the phone with her mother. They enjoyed each other's company more than she'd enjoyed spending time with either one of them. Plus, they had a lot in common professionally. Joann ran the fertility clinic and Aaron was a fertility lawyer. Abby wondered if she should subtly let them know that she wouldn't be opposed if they decided to get together.

Abby pulled herself back into wedding planner mode as people exited the sanctuary. A lot of the day still stretched before her and there was a long list of tasks to manage between now and bedtime. One of those things was to find a place for her mother and Aaron to sleep. But first, she needed the photographer to jump into action.

The portraits of the bridal party and the families went smoothly. The final shot was of the happy couple with the sunset photo-bombing the background in glorious pink, orange, and blue. Abby couldn't believe their luck. It was perfect picture moments like these that made it easy to believe in a higher power.

Abby thought again about the prayer she'd said last night, the one Deydie and Bethia had talked her into doing. She must not have said it right to have gotten the wrong *sign*. At that moment, Aaron waved to her as the two intruders—she really should stop thinking of them like that—stepped off the pier. She didn't wave back. Instead, she looked heavenward. "*Sign*, my foot! Now, please, cut it out."

Conor had been a good soldier all week, helping Morag's family with everything they asked of him. And he did things that weren't asked of him, too. Like making himself scarce when Steven would come by after closing the butcher shop for the day. As each day came and went, Conor could see that Morag was softening more and more toward her new husband.

There had also been a constant flow of people stopping by with food plus to give their condolences to Edin and Morag. Conor did his best to stay out of the way then, too, so he wouldn't have to explain why he was here, being the *ex* and all. This week was not supposed to be about him, but Clyde, and he did his best to make it that way.

However, the activity at Morag's house didn't stop Conor from thinking about Abby. A few days ago, when he'd texted Kieran about her, his brother apologized. He'd been called back to headquarters and hadn't yet made it back to Whussendale.

When the funeral finally rolled around, Conor was relieved … and on so many levels, too. He donned his kilt and sat in the back of the church by himself. Morag's family was ushered into the pews off to the right and were essentially blocked from prying eyes during the ceremony. But he did see Steven follow Morag into the family pews. It made Conor happy that Morag had support during this difficult time.

When the funeral was done, the family was signaled to process out behind the casket to the cars waiting to take them to the cemetery. Conor slipped from the kirk and headed back to Edin's house instead. The family should be allowed to grieve over the gravesite without him there.

Later, the house filled up once again, this time for the wake. When the stories began, Steven wrapped an arm around Morag and led her into the parlor. She gave him a sad smile and laid her head on his shoulder, looking comforted. Conor was glad. It seemed as if those two were going to make it. He still couldn't believe that he'd helped them out. But it was the right thing to do. Especially with a babe on the way.

He scanned the rest of the room. Edin was surrounded by her sisters, while Harold, one of Clyde's longtime friends, told a funny story about fishing with Clyde on the River Tay. At the conclusion, everyone smiled and laughed. The stories were a way to transition from sadness to getting back to normal.

Conor realized he'd done all he could do here. He was glad he'd come, but now it was time to leave. No one noticed when he laid the note on the table, the one he'd written last night for Morag's family. He slipped out the back door. This was the best exit for all of them. He was closing the door to this part of his life … the past.

He headed to Kieran's flat. The first thing on his list … to call Abby to tell her he was coming home. He rang her up as he put the last of his things into his duffel bag. Again, he was surprised and concerned when she didn't answer. Actually, his concern had turned into panic. Why wasn't Abby picking up? Why hadn't she answered any of his texts? He was worried he hadn't handled things correctly with her when he'd left with Morag and was anxious to fix it.

He grabbed his duffle, locked the door, and headed to Queen Street Station. He wished he had a car here in Glasgow as it would be the fastest way to get back home to Whussendale. While he waited for the train, he arranged for a shuttle, which meant he wouldn't get home until early evening. He checked his phone again. Still nothing from Abby.

Abby corralled the bridal party. "Let's head to the Grand Dining Room above Pastas & Pastries and start the speeches. Dominic and Claire said they have appetizers ready for us, too." She texted her mother. MEET ME AT THE RESTAURANT. IT'S TIME FOR THE SPEECHES.

As Abby walked past Quilting Central, Deydie and Bethia hustled out and pulled her to a stop.

"Wait up, lass," Deydie said. "We met yere mum." The old woman screwed up her face. "Ye're a nice lass. Handy, too. Ye must take after ye da." Bethia nodded in agreement.

Now wasn't the time to tell these two that she had no idea who her father was. She'd even done a couple of those genetic tests but hadn't found any relatives yet. Most people looked at her differently after they found out that she was a test-tube baby, which was the reason she was pretty closed-mouthed about it. But when she had a quiet moment with them, she'd shed some light on her past. She trusted them to treat her the same as always.

"We have good news," Bethia said. "Don't worry about finding yere mum and the young man a place to stay tonight. Rachel, who owns Partridge House, has spoken with her mother-in-law Robena. She's made room for them at their farmhouse just outside of town."

Deydie bobbed her head. "Rachel's husband, Brodie, said he could drive them there after tonight's festivities. Brodie always sings several songs at our céilidhs so it'll have to be after that."

"Aye, he has a beautiful voice," Bethia added.

Deydie laid a hand on Abby's arm. "Ye've done a right good job of managing the wedding today. We know we threw ye into the fire to test yere mettle and we're impressed with how well ye've done. We're grateful for yere help."

These women got to Abby, and she felt like she might mist up. The way everyone spoke about Deydie, Abby felt certain that the old woman wasn't prone to dishing out compliments or giving any grand show of affection. "I'm glad I could help."

"It's just the start of things to come." Deydie pounded her on the back. "Now get yereself off to the Grand Dining Room. Make sure the microphone is working. There's plenty here who want to make a speech or two about our Diana and Rory."

"Will do." Abby gave them both a smile before she hurried off to the restaurant. As she did, she came up with a solution to at least one of her problems: if Conor and Morag lived in Whussendale, Abby could make Gandiegow her home! She felt accepted here and she wouldn't have to see Conor every day with his wife. What would she do about the contract she'd signed with Hugh? Well, she'd just have to think about that tomorrow. Tonight, she was on a schedule.

At the Grand Dining Room, Abby made sure everyone was comfortable, with drinks and food, before the speeches for Rory and Diana began. The speeches were a mixture of funny stories and heartfelt sentiment. Abby could tell how much Gandiegow loved the newly married couple by their glowing words, even though neither one grew up in the village.

Immediately following the speeches was the three-course meal, starting with lentil soup, a main course of venison casserole, grilled salmon, and rosemary roasted potatoes and seasoned vegetables. The meal ended with two desserts: a dark chocolate tart and cranachan with handmade shortbread. The food was spectacular; the company Abby sat with ... not so much. Both Aaron and her mother harangued her again about moving home. But St. Louis didn't feel like home anymore.

"The Langston Biologics Company is still waiting for you to contact them about setting up an interview," Joann said. "I forwarded you all the emails. Did you see them?"

Aaron reached over and squeezed Abby's hand before she had a chance to stop him. "The job would be perfect for you and your excellent organizational skills."

"I've been too busy to check my emails." That was partially true. Actually, she'd avoided her inbox in case Conor had tried to contact her there. She suspected his voicemails and texts were about explaining how he owed it to Morag to give *them* another chance. But Abby didn't want to hear it or see it in writing either. She was the ostrich who planned to keep her head stuck in the sand until her heart could handle hearing the truth from him. It might be next week ... or possibly never.

Abby needed to try once more to get her mother and Aaron off her case. "I'm not sure what I can do to convince you that I'm not coming back to St. Louis." She could end up anywhere—Whussendale, if Conor and Morag decided to live in Glasgow or wherever they wanted to land. Gandiegow, if Hugh sanctioned it. Or maybe back in the States. But she didn't want to move back to St. Louis—ever. Having a hefty distance between herself and her mother had been good for Abby. She'd never felt more confident or comfortable with herself than she did here in Scotland.

She didn't give her mother or Aaron a chance to say another word but stood. "I have to speak with the band." They were setting up and gave her the perfect excuse to escape her mother's glare and Aaron's sad eyes.

After confirming with the band that they were going to play "Take My Hand" by Skerryvore for the first dance, Abby stopped by Rory and Diana's table. "Are you about ready for the céilidh to begin? You'll start things off with the first dance."

"Oh, aye," Rory said as he put his arm around his wife.

Abby noticed their plates were still full. "Oh, it looks like you haven't had a chance to eat. We can hold off the dance for a while, if you want."

Diana shook her head. "I'm too wound up to eat right now."

"Me, too," Rory agreed.

"I'll have Dominic put your plates in the refrigerator for when you're ready. Okay?"

They nodded. The newlyweds were radiant, and Abby couldn't help but be envious of them and their happy future.

Abby's watch alerted her that a text had just come in. She checked to see who sent it. Conor again. She sighed before clearing the notice and going back over to her mother and Aaron. "Can I get either of you anything?"

The leader of the band announced the first dance.

Joann stared at Abby. "You do realize that you'll have to dance with Aaron sometime tonight. It's the least you can do."

"Yes, Abby," Aaron agreed. "I did come all this way to see you."

"Not now. I'm still working." She nodded toward the table where the three-tiered wedding cake waited. "I have to make sure everything is ready for the cutting of the cake." But Abby knew she couldn't put off dancing with Aaron forever. Joann would never stand for it. Also, dancing together would give Abby a chance to tell Aaron once and for all that they were through. She'd be nice about it, but firm. She had to put an end to this chapter of her life. Whether he wanted to hear it or not. "I have an idea. Why don't you two dance while I work?" Abby was proud of herself for coming up with a short-term solution.

But something niggled at her. She was no better than Aaron, who hadn't accepted that they were through. Abby decided it was time for her to take a long look at herself in the virtual mirror. What happened with Conor was a fling. Basically, a one-night stand. She needed to take a page from her own book and accept that Conor would not be a part of her life, even though she desperately wanted him to be. Yes, she'd fallen hard for him. But she was tough and needed to move on. Whether she wanted to or not.

Chapter 20

WHEN CONOR LEFT for the train station, he suspected the day would drag on and it did. After what seemed like forever—the train trip and the shuttle ride to Whussendale—he was finally delivered to his village. Now he could find out why Abby had ghosted him. And whatever he'd done wrong, he'd make it right. But as he grabbed his bag from the boot of the shuttle, Coira called out to him.

"Conor, I'm so glad to see ye." Coira held a box in one hand, and with the other, she held on to Irene, her young grand-daughter.

Coira never seemed to have much need of him, even during the quilt retreats she ran in Whussendale, and he thought it strange that she needed him now. "What can I do for ye?" Though he really didn't have time to waste—he needed to see Abby and get to the bottom of what was going on!

Coira shoved the box at him; he took it automatically with no thought to what was inside. "Deydie called and told me to bring this Royal Stewart wedding shawl to Gandiegow."

He wanted to say, *Yeah, so, ye better get to that.* Instead, he waited for her to explain.

"I had Magnus find one in yere stash. Now that ye're here, ye can take it for me. Ye are, after all, in charge of the wedding shawls, right?"

"Aye, but—"

Coira cut him off. "As ye can see, I'm watching little Irene while John and Maggie are having a special night." She patted the box in his hands. "Thank ye."

"Fine. But first—"

She cut him off again. "Ye better leave now. Of course, Rory and Diana's wedding ceremony is over, but Deydie said the wedding shawl can be presented any time before midnight." She looked at her watch. "There's no time for ye to dawdle."

He exhaled his frustration. "Okay. I need to run by my cottage first and pick something up." He should be able to rope Abby into going along with him to Gandiegow. Being alone in the car together would work to his advantage. But then it hit him. Abby was most certainly already in Gandiegow, as Deydie had wanted her to help with the weddings there, too.

With a wave of her hand, Coira rushed away with little Irene in tow.

As he hurried to his cottage and rounded the corner, he saw that his lights were on. That was strange. He rushed to his door and opened it. Kieran was there, sitting in the rocking chair by the fire. Dublin was beside him, getting her ears rubbed.

"Hey," Conor said, dropping his duffle to the floor. "I thought you were at headquarters."

"I was. I just arrived back in Whussendale and picked up Dublin from Uncle Magnus," Kieran said. Dublin jumped up and ran to Conor, wagging her tail.

Conor reached down to give her some attention but stopped

when there was a knock at the door. "Come in."

Declan stepped inside. "Coira told me ye were back."

"Thanks for filling in for me at the bridal show." He wanted to ask about Abby but decided he'd better get the pleasantries out of the way first. "I really appreciate it. Did everything go all right?"

Declan looked worried. "Has Abby reached out to ye to tell you where she is?"

"Nay." Conor didn't like the look on Declan's face. "Is she okay?"

Kieran came over to stand beside him.

Declan shook his head. "I don't know, mate. She seemed, uh, upset, not quite herself. She had me drop her off in Gandiegow."

"For the wedding, I suppose?" Conor peered at Declan and was feeling impatient to get on the road so he could see Abby. "Is there something you want to tell me?"

"Aye. Deydie and some of the quilters from Gandiegow showed up at the bridal expo on Sunday. Abby hadn't been in that great of a mood before they arrived, but something Deydie said seemed to really bother her."

"Figures!" Conor muttered. Deydie had a way of souring things for a lot of people.

"I just stopped by to tell ye about Abby before ye heard it elsewhere. I gotta run."

When the door closed, Conor turned to Kieran. "Come with me to Gandiegow?"

"Sure. Dublin and I will ride along."

What Declan said about Abby's mood was sinking in and Conor felt a sense of dread. Having his brother come along to Gandiegow made Conor feel somewhat better. Though they'd never talked about their feelings before, maybe he could talk to his brother about Abby now. But Conor wasn't sure whether he was going to get more of the same. Most people saw Kieran as a happy-go-lucky guy, but Conor knew the real Kieran. The person he'd been before he'd bottled up his emotions after his girlfriend died.

Maybe it was time for their relationship to change. Conor could use his brother's counsel. First, though, he'd have to get Kieran to stop teasing him and treating him like the baby brother. As far as Conor was concerned, they were both on equal footing now.

Ten minutes later, they were in the car and on their way to Gandiegow. Conor glanced over at Kieran for a moment before putting his eyes back on the road. "I need some advice."

Kieran, usually quick with a response, remained quiet. He probably guessed it was something serious and he usually only engaged in light conversation. Which was strange, since his work with the military was serious ... serious enough that he couldn't talk about it.

Conor continued. "I need some advice about women." He paused for a moment. "Actually, it's about Abby."

"I figured as much," Kieran said.

Dublin popped up and hung her head over the front seat as if she needed to be part of the discussion.

"I don't have much to offer when it comes to advice about women." Kieran's tone indicated Conor should already know that.

Conor decided to push harder, something he'd never done before. "Ye never speak of Minnie."

"I suspect ye know why," Kieran said.

"All I know is she died in an accident," Conor said.

"Aye." Kieran was quiet for a full minute before continuing. "So Da never told ye the whole story?"

Conor was only nine at the time. "I overheard someone saying that ye were there when it happened," Conor said.

"I was." More silence. "Minnie and I had been arguing that evening."

"About what?" Conor asked.

Kieran shook his head. "Nothing important. Something trivial, I'm sure." He sounded so sad. "She made me stop the auto so she could get out, get away from me. She said she needed to think."

"That doesn't sound so bad," Conor said. Certainly not bad enough to never speak of it.

"I pulled off the road and she got out. But then I guess she decided to cross the street. She stepped out in front of a car … and was gone." Kieran looked out his window as if watching the scene replay on the deserted road to Gandiegow. "I couldn't believe it. I thought we were destined to be married and start a family. But she had no future—*we had no future*—because of a disagreement."

"Is that the reason you've never found anyone special again?" Conor knew his brother dated casually, but never anything serious.

"I guess. I try to never think on it." Kieran rubbed Dublin's head. "So what's going on with Abby that ye need my help?"

"Ever since I left the bridal show with Morag, Abby has ghosted me," Conor said succinctly.

"Then, you and Abby have been dating?" Kieran asked.

"Not exactly dating. More like spending time together. But more than that. All I know is that we have something special. A connection. Actually, it's unlike any connection I've ever had with a woman, including the time when I was married."

"What did ye do to *eff* it up?" Kieran asked.

"Nothing. Nothing that I know of, anyway. I just took Morag back to Glasgow. And then got roped into helping her family. I thought it was the least I could do to show my respect for Clyde.”

“He was a tough old bastard,” Kieran said fondly. “Nobody could wield a meat cleaver like that man.

Conor paused for a moment to pull his thoughts together. “Ye know, I saw Steven while I was there, too.” Conor frowned at what he was about to say. “I actually gave him some marriage advice. Which seems ridiculous, considering. By the way, Morag is pregnant.”

“Ye’re kidding! She said she never wanted children,” Kieran said.

“I know. I’m not sure what the Almighty was thinking in that corner. Morag and Steven get a kid, and I don’t.” Conor may have forgiven Morag and Steven on some level, but he still felt resentful about not having a family of his own.

“And Abby, what about her? What do you want me to say?” Kieran said. “The obvious reason she’s not talking to you is because you left with Morag.”

“But I gave her a full explanation by way of text. And when she didn’t answer that, I left her voicemails.”

“Then I guess it’s good that we’re going to Gandiegow. Ye can talk to her face to face.”

“But what if she won’t talk to me? Listen to my side of things?” His words reflected how desperate he felt.

“You have only two choices,” Kieran said.

“And they are?”

“Either you corner her and make her listen ...”

“Or?” Conor didn’t think Abby would take kindly to being detained.

“Or you become a reiver and steal her away to somewhere private and plead yere case.” Kieran kissed Dublin’s snout. “If this lass means as much to you as I think she does, you have to do everything in your power to win her back. Do ye ken?"

"Aye." Conor just wasn't sure what kind of mood Abby was going to be in when he saw her in Gandiegow. What if the Gandiegow quilters tried to keep her from him again? "Ye're right. I have to try."

"Going after the one ye love is worth the risk, when ye weigh it against a life alone," Kieran said. "Believe me, I should know."

Conor mulled over his brother's words for the rest of the trip. As soon as Conor parked and opened the car door, the music hit him, and he knew the céilidh was in full swing. The merrymaking could be heard all the way to the parking lot despite the wind howling, the waves crashing against the walkway, and the swirls of snow kicking up around them. Dublin, not fazed by either the noise or the storm coming in, lumbered out of the car and went to a tree across the lot to do her business.

"I'd say the festivities are going strong," Kieran said.

"Well, at least there's no doubt of where we'll find the happy couple." Conor pulled the box with the tartan in it from the boot.

"I suspect the whole village is there." Kieran whistled to Dublin, and she came running. He snapped on her leash. "We'll follow you. I haven't been to Gandiegow since I was a kid. The uncles brought me here once. I can't remember what for."

"The reception is being held above the restaurant in the Grand Dining Room," Conor said. "This way." He was anxious to see Abby and felt certain she would be there directing things for Rory and Diana's reception. Surprisingly, the closer he got to the restaurant, the easier he could breathe. He suddenly realized he hadn't drawn a full breath since leaving Abby all those days ago. He wondered how she was doing without him. He didn't want her to be miserable, but he did hope that he'd been missed.

Conor, Kieran, and Dublin made it to the restaurant and climbed the stairs. Unfortunately, Deydie was waiting at the entrance of the Grand Dining Room. "It's about damn time that ye made it here. Coira said ye'd left ages ago."

"Coo traffic jam," Kieran said, apparently still protecting his little brother.

"Who the hell are *ye*?" Deydie asked with a glower that would have most men cowering.

It was time for Conor to return the favor. "This is Kieran, my older brother."

"Brother? He looks old enough to be yere father."

Kieran laughed. "Not quite. I'm only eight years older."

Deydie turned to Conor. "Give me that box."

That's when Conor saw Abby. His heart pounded so hard, he was afraid everyone could hear it above the music. But then he realized what she was doing. Dancing with another man!

Conor nodded in Abby's direction as he squeezed the box tighter. "Who is that? With Abby?"

Deydie gave him a horrifying smile. "That's her fiancé from the States."

"Her ex-fiancé, don't ye mean?" Conor said, hoping he was right.

Deydie shrugged, giving him a satisfied look. She took the box away from him and walked to the front table where Rory and Diana sat.

"Let's get out of here," Conor said, starting to turn, but Kieran stopped him by clamping a hand on his shoulder.

"Go cut in. Say yere piece while ye can." Kieran nodded as if he didn't need to voice the obvious. But then he did. "I'll never have a chance to make things right with Minnie. But ye have this moment. Make the most of it. Say what ye have to say, because ye don't know what tomorrow will bring."

"Okay."

Kieran patted his shoulder twice before releasing him.

Conor took a deep breath before taking his first step. He didn't know exactly what he was going to say to Abby. But he had the long walk from here to there, through all the tables and then the dance floor, to figure it out.

On closer examination, Abby and her ex seemed to be having a serious conversation. Her eyebrows were pinched together and she was holding him at a distance. Maybe things weren't as hunky-dory with her ex as Deydie had implied.

Abby was so engrossed in what she was saying that she didn't seem to notice Conor until he was tapping on her ex's shoulder. "May I cut in?" He didn't give her ex a chance to answer, but took his place, pulling Abby close.

He breathed her in. Soaked her up. He was relieved when she relaxed in his arms. But then she pulled away.

"What are you doing here?" she said incredulously. Not the response he expected from her. "Where's your wife?"

He pulled her closer, but this time he kept enough distance so that he could see her face. "I'm not married."

"Where's Morag?" Abby's lips were formed into a hard line.

"I don't know. I suspect she's at her mother's house. With her husband, Steven."

"What?" she sputtered. "But Deydie said you wanted her back."

He'd have to have a serious talk with Deydie later about staying out of his business. But for now he had to get real with Abby. He shook his head. "I don't know where Deydie is getting her information. It's not possible to want Morag back—because I'm in love with you." He couldn't believe he'd just blurted that out. He hadn't even been conscious of being in love with her. But it made sense now. It all made sense. She'd been all he could think of ... night and day. He wanted to be with her now and forever.

With a puzzled look on her face, Abby shook her head. "But Morag asked for another chance?"

He smiled at her. "Did you not hear what I said?" Unfortunately, there was a song change, the music going from soft and slow to loud and fast. He took Abby's hand and walked her to the door. He didn't care that every eye in the place seemed to be on them as he pulled her into the hallway.

Instead of repeating what he'd said or giving her a chance to speak, he kissed the hell out of her. He'd let his lips do the talking. And she kissed him back. But suddenly, his fervent kiss turned tender. He pulled away but not too far. "I said, I love ye, Abby Potter. What do you have to say to me?"

She searched his eyes, looking at him with wonder. "But how?"

"Because I do."

"But you left with Morag. She said she wanted you two to get back together."

He shook his head again. "She didn't really want me. She never did. Not even when we were married. And I certainly don't want to get back together with her, which I made perfectly clear. To answer why I left with her, I was dutybound. For a long time, her family was my family. I owed it to her mother to pay my respects to Clyde, Morag's da. He was a good man."

"So, you definitely made sure Morag knows you don't want her and you're sure she doesn't want you?"

"Aye, on both counts. Steven, her husband, gets the credit for winning Morag over. Of course, the babe helped, too. They're going to have a little one."

"Oh."

"Now, can we get back to talking about *our* future?" he asked.

"*Our* future?" She looked as if that were unfathomable.

Oh, crud! He'd jumped the gun. "Well, maybe I'm being too hasty." She hadn't said she loved him, too. Maybe he was the only one who was feeling it. Just because she kissed him back didn't mean that she cared for him as he did for her. "Tell me that ye care for me, too. Even if it's only a little bit."

She shook her head, looking at the floor. "I can't."

He couldn't breathe again. He dropped his arms, the breath leaving his lungs. But she stepped closer, wrapping her arms around his neck, pulling him close.

"I don't care for you a *little bit*." She smiled as she gazed into his eyes. "I care for you a *lot*. I love you, too, Conor Masterson."

He picked her up and twirled her around. This time, the pounding in his chest felt good. "I'm a lucky man."

She laughed. "We're both lucky." She paused for a second. "Did I see Kieran as we were walking out the door?"

"He came with me as moral support."

The Grand Dining Room went quiet. Conor wondered for a second if the attendees were trying to listen in on the conversation they were having in the hallway. But then someone blew into the microphone.

"Let's see what's going on." Abby pulled Conor back to the doorway but didn't let him go. Which made him extremely happy. He kissed the top of her head and squeezed her.

There was a bit of commotion. From between the tables, Dublin appeared, running toward them with Kieran not far behind. Abby squatted down to greet her. "Hey, girl."

"Abby, keep it down back there!" Deydie hollered over the microphone. "It's time to present one more gift to the happy couple. Get up here, Rory and Diana."

They stood, then Rory helped Diana onto the stage so she didn't trip over her dress.

Deydie gave the crowd and the couple her terrifying smile. "Gandiegow and Whussendale are so pleased that ye two got hitched."

Love overcame Conor and he couldn't help himself from leaning down to kiss Abby firmly on the lips.

"Save it for later." Kieran smiled at them before he grabbed Dublin's dropped leash. He walked her to an open seat at one of the back tables.

Bethia took the microphone as Deydie handed the box over to Rory and Diana. "It's a wedding shawl to commemorate your big day."

Deydie leaned into the microphone. "It's also to be the first warm blanket to cover your future bairn."

Diana turned red. Rory laughed and said, "Do ye know something I don't know?" He turned to his bride. "Wife? Is there something ye need to tell me?"

She smiled and shook her head. "No. Sometimes those two put the cart ahead of the horse."

Deydie opened her mouth to defend herself, but Bethia pulled the microphone away from her. "Congratulations, you two!"

The whole room applauded.

Conor leaned down and whispered into Abby's ear, "Do ye want to get out of here?"

With a disappointed smile, Abby tilted her head to the side. "I can't. Gandiegow put me in charge of this shindig."

"Speak of the devil." Conor wrapped his arm around Abby's shoulder as Deydie and Bethia made their way to them.

When they got there, Deydie grabbed her arm. "We want to speak with ye." And pulled her away from Conor.

He felt her loss instantly. Didn't these women understand that he'd only just secured Abby as *his*. He went to Kieran and sat beside him, feeling deflated.

"So?" Kieran said. "Is everything good?"

"Aye. I guess. But apparently, Deydie and Bethia have something they need to speak with Abby about, in private."

Kieran gave him a look that said he understood how it was when it came to respecting their elders.

Conor sighed. Abby was her own person and a strong lass. She could stand up to the quilters of Gandiegow. He was sure of it.

"What is it?" Abby wanted to get back to Conor. Be in his arms. Kiss him again.

Bethia glanced at Deydie with a worried expression. "Deydie has something she needs to say? I guess I do, too."

Deydie shifted from one foot to the other. "I might have been wrong about Conor wanting his wife back." She screwed up her face as if admitting she was wrong had caused her physical pain. "When his wife left him and he moved back to Whussendale, he was in a state."

"Everyone in Whussendale was worried about him," said Bethia. "We all wanted him to be happy again. We knew him as a boy, when he worked at the mill during the holidays. He was such a sweet lad."

"We're sorry," Deydie said with a huff, as if that was all she was going to say on the subject.

"All's well that ends well," Bethia said.

"You're forgiven. Both of you." Abby wrapped her arms around them for a group hug. "But there's just one more thing."

"What's that?" Deydie said, stepping back.

"That tradition, about praying for a sign on the eve of St. Andrew's Day?" Abby frowned at them. "I don't think it works. In fact, I know it doesn't. The first man I saw today was Aaron, my ex-fiancé. It was quite upsetting to think he was the *sign* that God sent for me."

Bethia smiled and patted Abby on the back. "We should've told ye that it wasn't an exact science."

"Besides," Deydie said, "who said it was the *first* man ye see? I think Conor showing up here to claim ye is a perfectly good sign that you two should be together. The Almighty knows what He's doing."

"It's all in God's timing, ye see," Bethia said in her comforting tone.

Deydie harrumphed. "Ye just didn't interpret His will correctly."

Abby laughed. "I suppose you're right. Now, if it's okay with you two, can I get back to my man?" Her Scot. The one who loved her!

"Aye," Bethia said.

Deydie gave her one of her famous scary smiles. "In fact, we'll let ye off duty for the rest of the night, if ye like. But heed my warning. We don't approve of ye lying with Conor before ye're married."

Abby wouldn't tell them it was too late for that.

"There's a certain order to things around here," Deydie added. But then she frowned. "Some of the lasses don't always think so. If ye're one of them, stop by the general store and pick up protection to keep yereself from getting in the family way."

"We just want ye to be careful," Bethia said.

These two! Abby gave them a hug. "I love you both. And appreciate you so much!" She meant it. "But Conor and I can't leave just yet. There's one more thing I need to do. I need to introduce him to my mother."

"We understand," Bethia said. "Do ye want us to go with ye?"

"No. I'll be all right." She really would, as long as Conor was by her side.

"Good luck," Deydie said. "It ain't going to be easy. Remember, we met yere mother."

"I know." Abby returned to sit next to Conor. She had to break the news that there was some unpleasantness they'd have to hurdle before they could leave. It wasn't ideal that she'd be introducing Conor to her ex, as well, since Joann and Aaron were a package deal. Which would certainly be uncomfortable for all parties involved. But if she didn't introduce her mother now, when would she get the chance? Joann would not take it well that Abby was staying in Scotland and going against her wishes. Her mother held grudges like no other. Maybe Abby was getting ahead of herself, but she doubted if she and Conor got married that her mother would attend the ceremony. But then Abby got an idea of what to get her mother for Christmas.

Conor put his arm around her. She leaned into him and whispered, "I need to introduce you to my mother. That means you'll be meeting Aaron, also."

"I'm fine with that." Conor nuzzled her and kissed her.

She stood and took his hand. "Let's get this over with."

Together, they walked hand in hand to her mother's table.

"Conor, this is my mother, Joann, and this is Aaron. Mother, Aaron, I want to introduce you to Conor Masterson. He lives in Whussendale, too, a journeyman weaver at the mill. He's making the wedding shawls for Hitched in Scotland. You saw Deydie give the couple one of those shawls tonight."

Conor put his hand out to Joann. For a second, Abby wondered if her mother would take it. Finally, she did.

"Nice to me ye," Conor said. He turned to Aaron next and

stuck out his hand. "Sorry for cutting in earlier. I hope there's no hard feelings. There was something urgent I needed to tell Abby."

"Sure. No hard feelings." To Abby's surprise, Aaron shook Conor's hand graciously. Maybe she'd gotten through to him before Conor whisked her away.

"So, you're a weaver?" Joann asked.

"Aye. My first career was as a butcher."

"And why aren't you doing that now?"

"My ex-father-in-law owned the butcher shop."

"So, you were married?"

"Divorced now."

"What are your intentions with my daughter?"

"That's enough, Mother," Abby cut in. "This isn't the Inquisition."

"All right. I just want to make sure that you're not throwing your life away on a nobody."

"Let's go." Abby took Conor's hand.

"Just let me say one more thing." He didn't wait for Abby's reply but sat next to her mother. "I think your daughter is a remarkable person. She makes me happy and I believe I make her happy, too." He glanced up and gave her a brief smile before continuing. "I don't want to say more as things are new between us. I don't want to scare her away, Joann. But I believe we will have a future together. I hope that is enough to ease your mind."

Her mother nodded and looked away. "Goodnight, Abigail."

"Goodnight, Mom. Aaron, take care." There was nothing more for Abby to say.

But as she walked away, she knew it was past time to accept she would never have the mother she'd wanted or deserved all these years. But now she could get the love she wanted from her *found family*, which included the new friends she'd made here in Scotland, and Conor ... the love of her life.

Epilogue

A LOT HAD CHANGED in the last year. To start, Conor had made sure that the first Hitched in Scotland wedding was their own ... at sunrise on Easter. Abby moved into Conor's cottage and they had plans to add two more bedrooms at the back of the house.

Declan often came over for dinner. He'd become a tried-and-true friend to both of them. The only problem was that he turned down every blind date that she and Conor set up. Apparently, Declan liked playing the field.

Abby had become a regular at the quilting groups in both Whussendale and Gandiegow. After she finished the Touch of Celtic quilt that she'd designed, she made Hugh and Sophie's new baby a quilt with thistles on the front and minky on the back to make it soft and cuddly. Spending time with her quilting friends brought Abby so much joy. She couldn't believe her luck. Deydie and Bethia told her it wasn't luck at all, just the Almighty's will coming to pass.

Another nice change was that Kieran had retired from the

military and settled in Whussendale, working with Magnus in the old weaver's building. The new weaver's building had been finished two months ago and was already up and running. This was Conor's domain. When Hugh, Magnus, and Conor had finally had a productive conversation about the future, it was decided that the new modern weaving machines would help fulfill orders more quickly and keep customers happy. Conor had hired two experienced weavers from Scots Woollens to help with the state-of-the-art machinery. Surprisingly, Uncle Magnus would often come to the new weaver's building during his lunch break to watch the machines put out massive tartans in a short period of time. He said he could accept a little modernization as long as it didn't interfere with his beloved Victorian-era looms.

Another shocking change was that Abby and her mother's relationship had improved. Abby believed it was the Christmas present she'd arranged to be delivered from the shelter in St. Louis to Romeo on Christmas Eve—the marmalade kitten, she'd picked out online—whom her mother had named Juliet. According to her mother, Romeo was a changed man. He loved his kitten and nurtured her like she was his very own pet. Mother said Aaron had taken over babysitting for the cats when she was out of town, a perfect solution for both felines and humans. Abby knew her mother and Aaron were still thick as thieves—going out to dinner several nights a week, seeing movies, and vacationing in Bermuda together. They'd actually attended Abby and Conor's wedding together; Joann exclaimed she and Aaron had a *marvelous time*—her own mother's words!

Abby and Conor were getting ready to celebrate their second Christmas together. Their first had been celebrated at a nice hotel in Inverness, away from their friends and family in Whussendale. This Christmas came early for them on St. Andrew's Day, when Kieran presented them with a puppy from Dublin's first litter. Conor named their puppy Limerick, in keeping with their family tradition of Irish first names. Magnus picked out the runt of the litter, saying that Darling Girl needed to come live with him. Abby, Conor, and Kieran promised to help with Darling Girl, making sure Magnus wasn't over-burdened with caring for a rambunctious puppy.

Abby was pleased with how Kieran had opened up to Conor about their parents, filling in the blank spaces in Conor's memories of their family. Both she and Conor had made great strides on the family front, which now seemed fortuitous. Abby and Conor were in the family way, expecting a baby in March ... on their second anniversary. Joann was surprisingly thrilled about the news. Deydie and Bethia said they weren't surprised in the least.

And as for her and Conor? They were both excited to be raising their child in the village of Whussendale. No big city for their family. Deydie declared their bairn would be a citizen of Gandiegow as they had adopted Abby to be one of them as well. Also, since Deydie couldn't help but to be in the middle of everyone's business, she'd announced that Abby was having a girl. Apparently, the old quilter was never wrong on that count.

This morning, Abby sat down at their small kitchen table and pulled the new quilt design she'd made with her child in mind—three coos and a sheep with a row of stone cottages at the top and at the bottom of the quilt. She couldn't wait to get started. Tonight, when they gathered, she'd ask the quilting ladies to help her pick out fabric. She had plenty of time to get it completed before their baby arrived.

Conor took the seat next to her. He picked up her hand and squeezed it. "How are ye today, Mrs. Masterson? Is there anything I can get for ye?"

"I always feel wonderful, when we're together like this," Abby said, smiling at the Scot who'd changed her life. "I don't need anything but you."

He brought her hand to his lips and kissed it. "My love for ye grows bigger every day, ye know."

She laid her free hand on her expanding belly and grinned. "My love for you grows bigger every day, too."

"Aye, I can see that," he laughed but then turned serious. "I'm so glad the Almighty brought ye to Scotland." He gazed at her, his eyes confirming his heart felt words. "I'm especially glad ye agreed to get hitched to me."

She smiled at him. "Hitched together forever."

Conor pulled her onto his lap. "Aye, hitched ... to the love of my life."

Abby gazed at him for a long moment, feeling so grateful for everything that had brought her to this place in her life—the good and the not so good—but it made up a life that she wouldn't trade for the world.

"I love you, Conor."

"I love ye, too, Abby."

Then she kissed him and everything dropped away, the both of them getting lost in the magic of their love.

Welcome to the charming Scottish seaside village of Gandiegow...

To Scotland with Love
Book 1, Kilts and Quilts

★ Amazon #1 Best Seller

★ Publishers Weekly starred review*

★ New England Readers' Choice Best 1st Book

★ Golden Quill Best 1st Book

CAITRIONA MACLEOD once chased hard-hitting stories as an investigative reporter—until she traded ambition for love. But when her husband is found dead in his mistress's bed, she flees to her childhood home in Scotland, seeking solace in a grandmother and birthplace she barely remembers.

Healing is Cait's only goal—until she stumbles upon the Sexiest Man Alive, Graham Buchanan, a movie star with secrets of his own. A Gandiegow native, Graham hides out in the little village between films, protecting his son and his privacy. The last thing he needs is a journalist looking for a story, especially one as irresistible as Cait.

Quilting with her gran and the other women of the village brings Cait a peace she hasn't known in years. But if she turns in the story about Graham, the people of Gandiegow will never forgive her for betraying him. Should she suffer the consequences to resurrect her career? Or listen to her battered and bruised heart and give love another chance?

"Griffin's lyrical and moving debut marks her as a most talented newcomer to the romance genre."

-Publishers Weekly starred review

Patience Griffin grew up in a small town along the Mississippi River. She has a master's degree in nuclear engineering but spends her days writing stories about hearth and home in the fictional small towns in Scotland and Alaska.

Connect online at
www.PatienceGriffin.com

If you enjoyed reading Hitched in Scotland, *recommend* it to your friends or your book club. And please *write a review*. If you write a review, please let me know. I would like to **thank you** personally. Email: patience@patiencegriffin.com

For signed copies, visit: **www.PatienceGriffin.com**
While you're there JOIN Patience's Newsletter! To find out about events, contests, and more!

Don't miss Patience Griffin's delightful new series

Penguin Random House, Berkley imprint presents:
THE SWEET HOME, ALASKA NOVELS

Heartwarming
Romantic Women's Fiction
set in the wilds of Alaska.

BOOKS by PATIENCE GRIFFIN

———————⊰⊱———————

Kilts and Quilts series:
Romantic Women's Fiction

#1   *To Scotland with Love*

#2   *Meet Me in Scotland*

#3   *Some Like It Scottish*

#4   *The Accidental Scot*

#5   *The Trouble with Scotland*

#6   *It Happened in Scotland*

#7   *The Laird and I*

#8   *Blame It on Scotland*

#9   *Kilt in Scotland*

#10 *Hitched in Scotland*

———————⊰⊱———————

Sweet Home, Alaska series:
Romantic Women's Fiction

#1   *One Snowy Night*

#2   *Once Upon A Cabin*

#3   *Happily Ever Alaska*

———————⊰⊱———————

The Wishing Quilt